A WINTER'S WISH FOR THE CORNISH MIDWIFE

JO BARTLETT

Boldwood

First published in Great Britain in 2021 by Boldwood Books Ltd.

Copyright © Jo Bartlett, 2021

Cover Design by Debbie Clement Design

Cover photography: Shutterstock

A CIP catalogue record for this book is available from the British Library.

Paperback ISBN 978-1-80048-961-5

Large Print ISBN 978-1-80048-960-8

Hardback ISBN 978-1-80048-959-2

Ebook ISBN 978-1-80048-963-9

Kindle ISBN 978-1-80048-962-2

Audio CD ISBN 978-1-80048-954-7

MP3 CD ISBN 978-1-80048-955-4

Digital audio download ISBN 978-1-80048-957-8

Boldwood Books Ltd
23 Bowerdean Street
London SW6 3TN
www.boldwoodbooks.com

For my favourite midwife, Beverley Hills. Thank you for your friendship and support, from those early days with our newborn boys, to the victorious games' nights, when of course we never cheat! Your advice for the Cornish Midwives' series has been invaluable and you are an inspiration as a midwife and a friend xx

PROLOGUE

'Mum needs to know if she should tell people we're having the list at Debenhams or John Lewis?' Aaron's tone was every bit as urgent as his text message had suggested when Toni had opened it:

RING ME NOW.

All in caps. It had sounded important, and maybe it was to Aaron, but Toni was already drumming her fingers impatiently on the desk. They were childhood sweethearts and he'd known her her whole life, yet somehow he still didn't seem to know her well enough to realise that this definitely wasn't something she'd consider to be a priority.

'You asked me to ring you urgently in the middle of my shift, to decide which shop we want our gift list at?' They hadn't even had their engagement party yet and they were already being rail-roaded into choosing what pattern they wanted to stare at over breakfast and dinner every day for the rest of their lives. Just the thought was like a band tightening around Toni's chest, and the fact it was obvious Aaron's mother was pushing her agenda again made her jaw ache. Twice, in the last week alone, Aaron had woken Toni up and told her she was grinding her teeth. She'd wanted to tell him that it was her body's way of letting go of a bit of the tension, after seven years of his mother calling all the shots. Except, if she said what she wanted to, there'd be no going back.

Sometimes she wasn't even sure that would be a bad thing, but if she turned around and told someone with MS that she wasn't going to dance to their tune any more, Toni would instantly earn the title of the worst person in the world. For most of the last seven years, she'd have agreed with anyone who said that. When Judy, Aaron's mum, had first been diagnosed – just before the two of them had been about to head off and see the world, after two years of saving every penny they'd earned – he hadn't even needed to ask her to put their plans on hold. It had been Toni who'd said they absolutely couldn't go, not when Aaron's whole world her been turned upside down and his mother was still reeling from the news. They'd decided not to take a gap year to travel before uni, so this had always been the plan, working like crazy in the two years that followed graduation to save enough money to spend six months seeing the world, before they found themselves in the stranglehold of a mortgage. She'd been happy to put the plan on hold, but one year had turned into five and then they'd just stopped talking about it at all.

She'd been about to broach it again and had come up with a plan to make sure it would happen this time. They had a mort-gage now, so things would have to be different, but they had a bit of a nest egg recouped to start the trip off and the rental income from the flat would help a lot too. Port Agnes was popular with tourists all year round and she was sure they'd have no trouble renting it out. When she'd ended up delivering the grandson of the man who owned Kerensa Holidays and who rented out properties all over Port Agnes to holidaymakers, she hadn't been able to resist asking the proud grandfather about the likelihood of getting a decent income from the flat as a holiday let. She rushed home from work that night, desperate to talk to Aaron about it and already buzzing at the thought of when they could start their trip.

Letting herself into the flat, the last thing she'd expected to see was Aaron kneeling in the hallway, a red velvet box in his outstretched hand like a cliché of every wedding proposal she'd even seen. For a moment she'd been convinced he was joking, but then he'd started to speak.

'I've been thinking about doing this for a while.' Aaron's hand had been shaking and she still wasn't sure, looking back, if it was because he was nervous, or because he'd been waiting for her to get home from work, kneeling in the hallway, for God knows how long.

'We don't need to do this. We're fine as we are.' It probably wasn't the sentence that anyone offering up a proposal wanted to hear, but she hadn't been able to stop herself. She didn't want to get married to Aaron, or anyone – not yet.

'Maybe we don't need to do it, but I *want* to do it and I don't want to wait any more. It's not like we've only been together for a few months.'

'Exactly, so what's the rush?' Even as she asked the question, the look on his face had been answer enough. It wasn't Aaron that desperately wanted to arrange a wedding, he was doing this for Judy.

'When Mum had her latest relapse, she told me she couldn't bear the thought of dying and not seeing me married or meeting her grandkids.'

'So you're proposing to me because your mum told you to?' She hadn't been able to stop the laughter, but it had sounded hollow even to her own ears. 'I think this might rank as the least romantic proposal of all time.'

'It's not like that sweetheart and you know it.' Aaron had got up at that point and wrapped his arms around her. Even as she'd tried to stay mad at him, she'd known she couldn't. All he ever wanted to do was make everyone else happy. He spent half his life juggling his mother's needs with trying to have a life of his own and those were just the demands Toni knew about. It was impossible to stay angry at Aaron and he was the best friend she'd ever had; the best friend she was ever going to have. It was just that sometimes she had a horrible feeling it was all they were now and that whatever else it was they'd had before had been lost along the way.

'I'm just not sure now's the right time for all of this...'

'Please don't turn me down.' His eyes had searched her face and she'd found herself giving in. After all, agreeing to marry him didn't mean they had to run down the aisle the next day, did it? Or even the next year come to that. But she hadn't reckoned on Judy having a hand in every decision about the wedding, right from the very start.

When Toni had opened the little red velvet box the ring had been in, it was exactly as she'd pictured it, because she'd seen it hundreds of times, on the third finger of Aaron's grandmother's left hand. When she'd died, Judy had given the ring to Aaron with the instruction to use it when he proposed. It wasn't a suggestion, but then it never really was with Judy. Even before she'd got ill, she'd been domineering, not wanting to loosen the apron strings she had firmly tied to her only son. But the illness had almost given her free rein and, as crazy as it was to even think it, sometimes Toni wondered if Judy actually enjoyed being able to play that card.

Even before Aaron had taken to doing everything his mother asked, the proposal had always been a question of when, not if, as far as both of their families were concerned. Toni's mother had met Aaron's mother at a parent and toddler group in the village hall and, by the time their babies were a year old, the two women were best friends and Aaron's parents had moved into the house next door. Neither Mandy or Judy went on to have other children, so Toni and Aaron were always destined to be close.

The joking about them getting married had apparently started before either of them could walk, but, when they'd finally shared their first kiss at thirteen, it had been much more of a dilemma than it should have been as to whether they took it any further. There was no chance of them having a normal, casual romance, like almost every other teenage couple embarking on their first relationship. If it all went wrong, they'd still have to see each other at every family get together, not to mention the annual holidays the two families had twice a year.

It was why Toni had been trying to push down the feelings she'd had lately too, the sense of not being able to get enough air into her lungs when she thought about the wedding. It wasn't because she didn't love Aaron, she did, but she just wasn't always sure if it was the sort of love that was supposed to sustain forever, and what then? What if they split two families apart one day, because they couldn't make happily-ever-after work out? Or worse still, what if they settled for bearable-ever-after because they'd never known anything else and never given themselves the chance to find out? It was why she'd been so desperate to go travelling and reinstate the plans they'd had in their early twenties. Seeing the world would be great, but the truth was it was only a tiny part of the reason she'd so desperately wanted to go. They needed to test whether the route they'd had mapped out for them their whole lives was the one they really wanted to take and whether they really wanted to do it together. Except now, travelling was off the table again and they were hurtling towards a lifelong commitment, but all she wanted was to put on the brakes, just for a little while. Aaron's voice broke into her thoughts and the struggle to breathe seemed to get all the harder.

'I think Mum just wants to be able to tell people where we're having the wedding list in case anyone asks at the party tonight.' Aaron's tone was gentle and patient, as it unfailingly was, but right now it made her want to scream. Toni could have counted on the fingers of one hand how often he'd raised his voice in conflict with her over the seventeen years they'd been together. He was always capable of seeing someone else's point of view, which was probably why he'd decided to extend his studies with a part-time master's degree in psychology. He wanted to understand what made people tick, so he'd really be able to help them work through their problems. He just wanted to make everything right all the time and it must have been killing him knowing he could never really make Toni and Judy happy at the same time. But he was the ultimate good guy, and he was always going to prioritise his mother's happiness, now that she'd been diagnosed with MS. The trouble was, his unfailing goodness just ended up making Toni feel even more awful, as she didn't have it in her to be anywhere near as selfless as he was. Seven years felt like long enough to hold off on their dreams, but apparently it wasn't and insisting otherwise would have made her the villain. That still didn't stop her having a seven-year itch that she just couldn't seem to soothe.

With the hours Aaron was already doing as a youth worker, life was pretty full on. There were times when, despite sharing a sunny third floor flat in Port Agnes, they barely saw each other at all. For at least two weeks, Toni had been looking for the perfect opportunity to talk to Aaron about the wedding, about slowing down the juggernaut they'd released the handbrake on. She had the germ of an idea for a solution, something that would give them both a bit of space to make sure this was what they really wanted and that they weren't just doing what was expected. She needed to find a way of putting it to Aaron, but the right moment just hadn't presented itself yet. This definitely wasn't the right moment, but suddenly that didn't seem to matter any more.

'I think we should put the wedding back by six months.' The words just came out of her mouth, bubbling over like lava and every bit as unstoppable.

'What? Are you telling me you don't want to get married?'

'I'm not saying never, I'm just saying not now, not until we're sure.'

'We've been together seventeen bloody years; how much longer do you need to be sure?' It was so unusual for Aaron to raise his voice that for a second Toni lost the power to speak. He was right, it sounded ridiculous when you said it like that, but it was time apart they needed – time away from everyone's expectations and each other's – to be really sure this was right for them, and they weren't just marching like lemmings towards their fate.

'I just need a bit of space, I think we both do, so we can be sure this is what we want.' All the pre-prepared speech she'd practised, about why this could be so good for them, had fallen out of her head. Even though she knew she wasn't conveying what she'd meant to say, she didn't seem to be able to put it right.

'I don't need space, Toni. I know I love you; I always have.' Aaron gave a shuddering sigh. 'So you want to postpone the engagement party too? This is going to kill Mum.'

'No it isn't!' She almost screamed the words this time. None of the things they were doing at his mother's bidding would kill her if they didn't do them, but it was as if Aaron had been brain-washed. This was going to be their whole life if she didn't make a stand. Judy would dictate where they lived, when they had a baby, what they called it, where they went on holiday. Every last part of their lives would be controlled by Aaron's mother, and it was almost like she was sitting on Toni's chest, controlling the amount of air she could get into her lungs. It wasn't enough.

'Don't do this, Toni, please, not tonight. Mum's put so much effort into organising the party and she's so excited. We can talk about this afterwards. Please just give her tonight.'

'Do you love me, Aaron?'

'Yes, of course, I—'

'No!' She cut him off, she needed to know. 'I mean *really* love me, more than you love anyone else?'

'You know I do, but things with Mum make it complicated.' Aaron sighed again. 'Are you saying you don't love me? Is that why you don't want to get married?'

'I do love you.' She had to bite her lip to stop herself from adding the rest. The truth was, she wasn't even sure what the rest would be: *I do love you… but not like that*, or *I do love you… but not enough to spend my whole life in your mother's shadow*. Any of the ways of finishing the sentence would break Aaron's heart and that was the last thing she wanted. She really did love him and the one thing she was certain of was that she'd always want him in her life. No matter what.

'I'd marry you tomorrow; you know that, don't you?'

'Uh-huh.' The problem was she didn't know *why*.

'So we can go ahead with the party tonight and talk about the rest of it later?' He sounded almost desperate now, but all it was doing was convincing her she was right. He should have been desperate to find some sort of resolution with Toni, some way of reassuring her that everything would work out the way they wanted. But all of Aaron's desperation was targeted towards his mother getting the party she'd been planning and nothing else really mattered, at least not as much. Toni was always going to come second, but worse than that, Aaron would always put himself last.

'If that's what you really want.' Toni stared at one of the ambulances pulling into the hospital as she blinked back the tears that were threatening to spill out for no good reason. Nothing had changed in the last five minutes, except that she was certain now that something had to change, no matter how much it might hurt.

'What about this wedding list, then, where shall I tell Mum we want it?'

'Wherever you want.' Her words sounded as empty as she felt, but they couldn't keep having this conversation and going round and round in circles. He wanted to put off talking about every-thing that mattered until after the party and she could go along with that too, if she had to. Looking at her watch, Toni let out a long breath. She needed to be back on the ward in five minutes, babies didn't wait for anyone, and she was more grateful than ever for the job that had never once made her question if she'd picked the right career.

'I'm really worried about you; you've been so different lately and I just want you to be happy.' Aaron's voice was strained, as if the tension of trying to please two such different women was literally pulling him in opposite directions. The only person Aaron should have been worrying about was himself, except he never would.

'It's nothing. I'm just a bit stressed with work and the wedding plans; we both are. We seem to be getting through paracetamol like we're running our own pharmacy lately.' She wasn't going to tell Aaron the solution she'd come up with, not now. They needed to be face-to-face, to talk things through calmly, without the spectre of the engagement party looming over them. Two hundred people, most of whom she barely knew, with the catering and entertainment all decided by her mother-in-law to be. She had to get that out of the way first, before she even had a chance of persuading Aaron that her plan really could be the perfect solution for everyone.

'I think you're right. Aren't weddings supposed to be the most stressful things you can go through?'

'I think that's divorce.' They both laughed and for a second she could almost picture the old Aaron, the one she'd fallen in love with.

'Either way, I can't seem to shift this headache. But, if you really want me to, I'll talk to Mum before the party and see if I can get her to calm down a bit about everything when she's chatting to everyone tonight about the wedding plans, as if all the arrangements are already a done deal.'

'No, don't worry. We can sort it all out after the party and let your mum have her night, I know how much she wants it.' Toni held in the sigh that would have taken the final traces of air out of her lungs. She just needed to hold on for a little bit longer. 'Have a break this afternoon if you can and maybe even see if you can get half an hour's sleep before the party; you've been half-killing yourself, working and studying like you have, never mind the wedding. I've got to get back to work, but there's a box of the stronger painkillers in the bathroom cabinet, take a couple more of those and hopefully you'll feel better soon. Although you might find it goes by itself once this party is out of the way. I'll be back by six, so make sure you're not in the shower, because I'll need to jump in if I'm going to have time to get ready.'

'I could always wait in there for you. That would be bound to make me feel better.' Aaron was teasing her, but part of her was pulling away from him physically too. When you were suffocating, it turned out all your basic survival instincts kicked in and you'd do whatever it took to come up for air – even if that meant leaving someone else behind.

'I love you Aaron Cunningham, you do know that don't you?' Loving him had always been the easy bit and that would never change, no matter what.

'Of course I do and I love you too.' Aaron breathed out slowly. 'That's why I count to ten every time Mum gets a bit too carried away with the wedding plans, because, when it comes down to it, just like I said, I'd marry you tomorrow.'

'I know you would.' She couldn't bring herself to echo his words, even if leaving them hanging in the air felt cruel – like someone telling you they loved you and getting no response. As far as she knew, they'd never lied to each other and she didn't want to start now. They just had to get through the party and there'd be plenty of time to put the brakes on the wedding plans. She wanted six months, that was all, for both of them to be sure – and once she told him her plan, she was certain he'd see how perfect it was. If they were meant to be together, they'd know after that and what was six months after all? They had all the time in the world.

* * *

Toni's throat was burning. She was late and there were no spaces in the car park outside the flats. Aaron's car was in the only bay reserved exclusively for them and she'd missed the chance to nab one of the other communal ones. She had to leave her car in the community car park, almost half a mile away from the flat, because there were no spaces in the side roads nearby either. Having their engagement party on the weekend of the Silver of

the Sea festival in August wouldn't have been Toni's choice – Port
Agnes was rammed with visitors – but then Toni wouldn't have
chosen to have a party at all.

Despite that, the first thing she was going to do when she saw
Aaron was to apologise to him. He didn't want a party either, he
was just being his usual self and going along with it to make other
people happy. For once in her life, she was going to try to be as
good-hearted as Aaron and do the same thing. The best chance
he had of enjoying the night was to believe she was even half as
excited as his mother was, so she was going to channel her inner
Judi Dench and give the performance of a lifetime, because if
anyone deserved a night off from all the tension there'd been
lately, it was Aaron. The rest could wait.

Except now she was running late for her own big night. She'd
been held up with the delivery of a baby at the end of her shift,
when one of the midwives on the night shift had called in sick
and she'd had to cover until the other on-call midwife arrived. It
would be a case of jumping straight into the shower, doing the
best she could with her hair and make-up in the time she had,
and ending up feeling even more uncomfortable as the centre of
attention at the party than she already would have done.

The words she wanted to say to Aaron after the party was over
were all set out now, though. She'd run through them in her head
at least a hundred times over and it all made perfect sense. For six
months, they'd do their own thing, and if they still wanted to be
together at the end of that, then they were obviously made for
each other. It wasn't about dating other people, at least not from
her point of view, it was about truly knowing their own minds.
Toni would use the six months to go travelling and Aaron could
focus on finishing his master's. It would also mean he could
spend every spare moment he wanted to with his mum before he
settled down to family life. As far as Toni could see, it was the

perfect solution for everyone. If she missed Aaron even half as much as she expected to, then she'd know he was the one for her. She was taking a big risk that he might realise he preferred life without her, but it was a price she was willing to pay for his happiness, as well as her own. Aaron was never going to put himself first, so just this once she was going to do it for him. All they had to do was to get the party neither of them had asked for out of the way first.

'For God's sake!' Toni was tempted to use a much stronger expletive as she shut the door of the flat behind her. All her good intentions about being Miss Sweetness and Light were going out of the window already. The sound of the shower running in the bathroom was immediately obvious. If he thought there was any chance of them spending some time in there together now, then he was sadly mistaken. Even if he still had shampoo to rinse out, he was going to have to get his butt out of the shower and do it under the kitchen tap. Her apology would have to wait until she didn't have the scent of disinfectant clinging to her skin, the way she always seemed to when she came back from work.

'Aaron, come on, you know I haven't got long!' she called out as she pushed open the bathroom door. It was too steamy at first to see anything much at all; he must have had the shower almost too hot to stand under. 'Bloody hell, it's like a sauna in here.'

Even as she moved towards the shower, she still couldn't see him; it was shrouded in such a thick mist the glass was almost opaque.

'What on earth are you doing in there?' Pulling back the door the words caught in her throat. Aaron was slumped down in the bottom of the shower, in such an odd position that it left no doubt in her mind that he wasn't just pulling some sort of prank. 'Aaron! What's wrong? Get up!'

Reaching out to grab his shoulder, Toni's hand was shaking.

Despite the hot water cascading onto him, when she touched his skin, she knew it was already too late. The steamy air was instantly filled with the sound of screams. At first, she didn't even register that they were coming from her, until her legs gave out from under her. Aaron was gone.

1

There was an air of melancholy about September, even somewhere as beautiful as Port Agnes. The autumn sunsets arrived earlier than they had just weeks before, but the sea, which stretched out from the Cornish Atlantic coastline to beyond the horizon, was still relatively calm. Part of the sense of melancholy was down to the shortening days, and the leaves on the trees beginning to die in a blaze of rust and gold, but there was more to it than that – at least for Toni.

Five years after losing Aaron, September still marked the weeks following his death and the aftermath when Toni had finally started to accept he really wasn't coming back. At such a young age, there'd had to be an autopsy following Aaron's death. The result revealed he'd suffered a massive brain haemorrhage that they'd said would have been incredibly difficult to do anything about, even if the weakness in the blood vessels had been discovered in time, and which, mercifully, he wouldn't have known anything about either. Toni had lost her fiancé and her best friend in one devastating blow, and Judy and Simon

Cunningham had lost their only child. All of them had lost the future they'd mapped out so carefully, if only in their own heads.

The funeral had eventually taken place in mid-September, and Aaron's mother had been so distraught that she'd had to be restrained from throwing herself onto his coffin as it was lowered into the ground in the churchyard at St Jude's. The cakes that Judy had baked in the hope of convincing Reverend Sampson to squeeze in a Saturday wedding the following summer, had instead been exchanged for a burial plot in the churchyard, where space was almost non-existent. Despite the fact that Aaron's parents lived in Port Tremellien, they wanted the funeral to be held in nearby Port Agnes, at the church where Toni and Aaron's wedding had been planned.

It had given them all some comfort that Aaron's plot was on the side of the church that looked down into the town, where the flat he'd shared so briefly with Toni was just a few streets back from the harbour below it. Not that Toni really believed Aaron could see any of that with his own eyes, but it always gave her something to talk about when she went to see him. Nobody knew just how often that was, partly because she rarely talked about Aaron to anyone who hadn't known him in life.

As close as she'd become to the other midwives in the four years she'd worked at the Port Agnes midwifery unit, most of them didn't know she'd lost her fiancé the year before she'd started there. To them she was just no-nonsense Toni, with sharp edges and just the hint of a soft side that only occasionally appeared – usually in support of a troubled expectant mother, or a woman in labour. Even when she'd accompanied her friends from the unit to the Silver of the Sea festival, which took place around the anniversary of Aaron's death each year, depending on when the bank holiday fell, she hadn't mentioned his name. There'd always be a get-together on the anniversary itself, with her parents and his, and that was painful enough, without having to talk her friends through what had happened – reliving it all over again.

If the world thought she was cold, better that than constant enquiries about whether she was okay; she couldn't afford to peel back the layer of armour she'd built up after Aaron's death to check. She'd had to be the strong one, holding it together for Judy and Simon, and her own parents. She didn't know how long she had stayed slumped by the shower tray before she found the strength to call 999, or to phone Aaron's parents and tell them that their beloved only son was gone. His mother had got to the flat only moments after the ambulance. The paramedics confirmed what Toni had known the moment she'd reached out to touch him. It didn't stop a hysterical Judy begging them to keep trying to bring her boy back, beating her fists against the chest of one of the poor paramedics when she realised there was nothing he could do except take Aaron away.

Toni had wanted – with all her heart – to undo the words she'd said to Aaron that afternoon on the phone, words that might have left him in any doubt about how much she loved him. Seeing him lying there, with all life extinguished, she'd have done anything to bring him back. There was no way of easing Judy's pain, pain that Toni felt acutely responsible for causing. Maybe if she hadn't added to his stress in the run up to the engagement party, he'd have had a chance to get to the doctor... but thinking like that was the road to hell. All she could do was promise Aaron that she'd do whatever it took to make things as bearable as they could be without him for his mum and dad. He'd spent the last seven years of his life focussed on making his mum's every wish come true and it was Toni's turn to take on that mantle.

The next time Toni had seen Aaron was the night before the

funeral, in the chapel of rest at the undertakers. Part of her hadn't wanted to go, but Judy had desperately needed her and it had been the start of Toni trying her best to fill Aaron's shoes – putting herself at the bottom of the pile to make everyone else's feelings her priority, just the way he'd always done.

'He looks so peaceful, doesn't he?' Judy had given Toni a watery smile that definitely didn't reach her eyes. Forcing herself to nod in response, she'd stared down at Aaron. He'd looked as though he was wearing a mask and peaceful wasn't the term she'd have used to describe him. But Judy had needed to hear the words.

'He does.'

'I'm so glad the two of you got engaged before this happened, but it breaks my heart – almost as much as losing Aaron – that you've already lost the love of your life, so young.' Judy had reached out, her tears plopping down to the place where their hands were joined. 'Promise me that we won't lose you too, Toni, we couldn't bear it.'

'Of course you won't.' Mandy, Toni's mother, had taken the words out of her mouth before she'd even had a chance to reply. 'She's never going to find someone like Aaron again and we're all going to miss him so much, but we've got to stick together.'

'I can't stand the thought of anything changing and Aaron not being around to see it.' Judy's body was wracked by a heaving sob. 'Seeing you with someone else would have broken his heart, but I—'

'Don't even think like that.' Whatever Judy had been about to say, Toni had cut it off. Talking about moving on after Aaron's death wasn't something she'd even wanted to think about back then, any more than Judy had. She hadn't realised just how big a promise she was making, though, because at that point she could never have envisaged meeting someone who would make her want to break that promise. What she'd agreed to, in that chapel of rest, was effectively to freeze time. She was Aaron's fiancée and that's what she'd always be.

The last time she'd seen Judy had been at Aaron's anniversary dinner, marking the five years without him. As usual, she'd joined her father, Steve, and her mother, at Judy and Simon's house in Port Tremellien, just along the coast from Port Agnes, right next door to her parents' own house.

As always, Judy had made a buffet with all of Aaron's favourite things, and Toni had been tasked with carrying the platters from the kitchen to the dining room. She'd been on her way back to collect the last platter, when she'd heard her mother and Judy talking, and she'd paused outside the kitchen door.

'It's so sad that Toni hasn't been able to move on after losing Aaron, but then she was never going to find someone like him again.' Her mother's tone conveyed an odd mixture of sadness and conciliation.

'I know it's selfish, but part of me has always been very glad that Toni's never found someone else. The thought of her having other in-laws is almost unbearable, it's—'

'Hello sweetheart, what are you doing loitering here?' Her father had come up behind her, almost making her jump out of her skin and drowning out the conversation Judy had been having with her mother. He'd shuttled her into the kitchen and put an end to her eavesdropping. Not that it would have revealed anything she didn't already know. She belonged to Judy and Simon Cunningham for life; she'd made that promise when she'd got engaged to their son and when she'd reassured Aaron's mother, after he'd died, that nothing would ever change that. The fact that there was someone else in her life now was a secret she hugged close. She hadn't meant to fall in love with Bobby, but the harder she'd fought against it, the less she'd been able to resist.

What amazed her most was that someone like him wanted to be with someone like her in the first place, even if she hadn't had enough baggage to overload a luggage carousel in an airport terminal. He was young and effortlessly attractive, with honey-coloured skin and the mix of kindness and tenacity any man would need to get through midwifery training and the sort of judgements that came with that. She might barely recognise the person she'd become since Aaron had died, but she still had the same mid-length, mid-brown bob she'd had for almost her whole life. And it was only really when she was with Bobby that she saw any sparkle in the eyes that matched her hair, a nondescript shade of brown, so unlike Bobby's dark brown eyes which shone with warmth. He was way out of her league and she knew it. The oddest thing was that he seemed to think it was the other way round, but he must have been just about the only person in the world who'd agree.

It couldn't be what she'd had with Aaron anyway, because she'd never be able to tell the four people she considered to be her parents about his existence. Bobby wasn't going to be content with staying a secret forever, though, and in truth they were already on the brink. But she could never choose him, knowing it would break Judy and Simon's hearts all over again. She'd just have to take the blows when the time came. After all, she was the strong one and putting her needs behind theirs had become second nature. Until Bobby had come along.

'Where are you?' The voice on the other end of the line sounded breathy and panicked, even though Toni had answered her phone on the second ring, using the hands-free function in her car.

'Just parking outside the unit, what's up?' Toni pulled the car to a halt and waited for an answer from Anna, one of her closest friends, who also happened to be her boss and who had recently discovered she was pregnant.

'I'm spotting and I wondered if you could check me over, if you've got time before your first clinic?' Anna had told Toni on their last shift together that she was only a few days away from her twelve-week scan. They both knew it was the milestone all pregnant women wanted to get to, in order to start believing that everything was going to be okay. At thirty-nine, and with this being her first pregnancy, Anna was higher risk than most and categorised as a geriatric mother.

Not that Toni would have used that term, especially given that the most fitting description would have been *miraculous*. Not long before her wedding, Anna had been told she had the fertility of a woman in her mid-forties and had been prescribed a fertility drug as a last-ditch attempt to fall pregnant. She'd been warned that she was facing very long odds, but had decided to give it one last shot before embarking on an adoption journey with her husband, Brae.

The couple's discovery – the day after their wedding – that Anna was pregnant, had been a thrill for all the midwives at the unit, who were in unanimous agreement that they had the best boss in the world. All of which meant that the prospect of Anna losing her miracle pregnancy was making the skin on the back of Toni's neck prickle. Facing up to the prospect that she might have to be the one to confirm Anna's worst fears, she swallowed hard. The least she could do was be there for her friend.

'Of course, where are you?' Toni had an hour before her first clinic, but she wouldn't have hesitated either way. For once, the other patients would just have to wait.

'I'm already in consulting room three. I'm terrified of trying the Doppler out on my own.' Anna's voice caught on the words. 'What if I can't hear anything?'

'I'll be two minutes. It's going to be okay.' Toni disconnected the call and grabbed her bag, offering up a quick prayer to whatever deity might be listening that she was right. There was a team of midwives at the unit, but she was particularly close to Anna, Ella and Jess, the four of them forming a really close bond over the past two years, since Ella had joined the team. So it was no surprise that Anna wanted Toni to be there to support her, especially as Ella was out on home visits and Jess had the day off. It was always nerve-wracking examining a woman who was fearful that they might be losing their baby, but when it was one of your best friends, the prospect was absolutely terrifying.

'How are you doing?' Toni forced herself into the no-nonsense mode that she was so well-known for, acting as if she had no doubt that everything was going to be okay, despite the fact that nausea was swirling in her stomach. 'Does Brae know you're here?'

'He's on his way up.' Anna bit her lip. 'I didn't want to worry him at first as I thought the spotting might stop straight away, but there's still a bit.'

'How much?' Toni was already rolling paper out onto the examination table, speaking deliberately so Anna wouldn't hear any wobble in her voice. The last thing she needed was for Toni to add to her panic. Normally she wouldn't use a Doppler to listen to a baby's heartbeat until the mother-to-be was in the second trimester, when there was almost a guarantee of hearing it. The heartbeat could be picked up as early as eight weeks, though, and with Anna just shy of twelve, Toni was pretty confident that she'd be able to hear something. Assuming everything was okay.

'The bleeding was nothing major, but enough to scare the hell out of me.' Anna shivered and Toni briefly touched her arm. She wasn't one for hugs or any overt displays of affection as a rule, but sometimes she let her armour slip just enough to break the habit she'd developed over the years, in a desperate attempt to keep a lid on her feelings.

'Any cramps?' Her voice was falsely breezy, but all she could do was hope that staying as professional as possible was helping. She had to get as much information as possible from Anna either way.

'Nothing new, but I've had what feels like period pains on and off ever since I found out I was pregnant, which I put down to the pregnancy starting to stretch out my prehistoric uterus.' Anna tried to laugh, but it sounded slightly maniacal and then she bit her lip again. 'I just hope it hasn't let me down.'

'Try not to worry, let's get you checked out first and see what this baby is up to.' Toni felt a bit of a hypocrite when she could sense her own pulse quickening. Telling Anna not to worry was like trying to hold back the sea in circumstances like this and, just as Toni was helping her onto the examination table, Anna's phone started to ring.

'It's Brae.' She looked at Toni before answering the call. 'Hello, yes, we're inside. Toni's just going to check me over. If you come to the delivery doors, one of us will let you in. No, don't worry, I'm fine, I'm sure it's going to be okay. Yes, I know, uh-huh, okay, I love you too.'

Listening to the one-sided conversation, Toni's shoulders relaxed just a little. Whatever her examination of Anna uncovered, Brae would be there to support his wife. Everyone knew Anna and Brae were a couple; you couldn't say one of their names without thinking about their other half. It was the same with Ella and her fiancé, Dan. And once upon a time it had been the same with Toni and Aaron. It had been so deeply rooted in her identity, and such a part of who she was, that the first year after he'd died she'd found it hard to sign Christmas or birthday cards without automatically adding his name.

'I'll go and let Brae in, you get yourself as comfortable as you can and try to relax.' Toni gave Anna a half-smile, knowing she was asking the impossible. Anna just needed an answer, her hands visibly shaking despite the warmth of the consultation room. The fact that she'd asked Brae to use the delivery entrance, obviously meant she didn't want Vivienne, their new receptionist, to know there might be an issue with the baby. If the worst case scenario was true and the baby was already gone, Anna and Brae were going to have to find a way to process it themselves before they shared the news with everyone else. The last thing Anna would want was everyone jumping to conclusions or second-guessing what was going on. Toni knew from bitter experience that it was possible to hold it all together in the toughest of times, up until the point when someone asked if you were okay and that's when it all fell apart. It was part of why she'd grown a hard shell over the years, so no one ever felt the need to ask her that question. But Anna wore her emotions on her sleeve at the best of times and the fact that everyone at the unit loved her would make their well-intentioned enquiries inevitable. All of which meant that Toni was almost as happy to see Brae as Anna would be.

'Oh Toni, thank God you were around to see her.' Brae gave her one of his trademark hugs. He was a big bear of a man, but so kind and gentle that not even Toni could protest. Not that he'd have given her a chance anyway. 'Is she okay?'

'She's fine, apart from being a bit worried, but the spotting is probably nothing. It happens to a lot of women and Anna's pregnancy was always likely to be a bit more demanding, at her grand old age!' Toni winked, guessing that the best thing for Brae was to stay upbeat and that he'd recognise it as a joke. If she was honest, she needed to keep things light-hearted every bit as much as he did. She couldn't even bear to think about how she'd handle things if the news wasn't good.

'Don't let her hear you say that, or she'll put you on call for nights for the next six months!' Brae managed a brief smile, before they hurried back down the corridor to his wife. Whatever the outcome, they needed to know.

'Sorry if I made you panic.' Anna's voice was muffled as Brae wrapped his arms around her. 'I wanted you to be here to hear the heartbeat for the first time if everything's okay. But I also wanted you to be here if it isn't...'

'It's going to be okay, we've got Toni here and everyone knows she's unflappable. And the other bit of good news is that you got me out of peeling about half a tonne of potatoes in preparation for tonight.' Brae ran Penrose Plaice, an award-winning fish and chip shop down by the harbour, which was famous for miles around, and he was following Toni's lead and keeping things light.

'Right, let's see where this little one is hiding shall we?' Toni silently willed the sound of her own heartbeat pulsating in her ears to quieten down, as she squirted some gel onto Anna's stomach, moving the Doppler across the bump that was already putting in an appearance. First pregnancies usually took longer to show, but this was another likely side effect of being an older expectant mother, everything was a bit less elastic than it was in younger women. Toni just hoped it was a good sign that the baby was still in there and growing as it should be, too.

'Can you hear that!' Brae had a grin that could have lit up the whole of Port Agnes, as the reassuring rhythm of the baby's heart came through loud and clear, and Toni would have happily high-fived him if she hadn't been holding the Doppler. Now it was her turn to bite her lip to stop herself from crying, even as her whole body seemed to slump with relief that the baby's heartbeat was not only loud and clear but had also been incredibly easy to find.

'Oh thank God, Toni you're a star!' Anna was grinning too and Brae kissed the top of her head, the relief in the room tangible. 'I was so glad it was you here to check me over, I don't think I could have coped with Ella and Jess bursting into tears on me before we even knew what was going on!'

'You know me, cool as a cucumber.' No one would ever know that Toni's heart had been racing as hard as it had, and Brae nearly knocked the Doppler out of her hands to give her another hug, his face wreathed in smiles as he pulled away again.

'So everything's definitely okay?'

'It sounds perfect, but if you're still worried and you don't want to wait until next week, there's always the Early Pregnancy Unit.' Toni was smiling too. It had been much easier to find the baby's heartbeat than she'd expected, especially as Anna was still in the first trimester, and the fact that it was so clear really was the best of signs. 'Shall we have another listen?'

'Yes please! It's already my favourite sound in the world.' Anna laughed, as Toni immediately located the heartbeat in exactly the same place as she'd found it first time around. Sliding the Doppler back towards her, though, she suddenly stopped, her eyes widening as she heard the heartbeat again. Moving it two inches in the other direction, the sound disappeared, but when she pushed it another two inches further in that direction, she picked up the heartbeat again.

'What's wrong?' Brae had spotted the expression that had crossed Toni's face before she'd been able to stop it. Even someone as practised as she was couldn't always hide their emotions, and right now they were bubbling really close to the surface.

'I know your uterus is still only the size of a large orange right now, but either this baby is a proper little athlete, bouncing from one side to the other...'

'Or?' Anna looked at her, her eyes widening exactly as Toni's had.

'Or what? What's going on?' Brae looked from Toni to Anna and back again.

'Or the two of you are expecting double trouble.' For once Toni couldn't stop her emotions bubbling over, laughing at the expressions that crossed Brae's face in rapid succession as he turned to his wife who was nodding and half-laughing, half-crying.

'They did say there was always a slight risk of this with the fertility drugs I was taking.' Anna was shaking her head, a big smile on her face, even as the tears started rolling down her cheeks. 'I thought I was just getting really fat, really quickly.'

'You'd better go down to the Early Pregnancy Unit and get a scan to be sure, but if I was a betting woman, I'd say it was twins.' Toni looked at Brae again, trying to guess whether he could take one more joke. 'Although I suppose there's always a chance there could be three in there!'

'Budge over Anna, I think I need to lie down.' Brae was grinning, despite his words and when he folded Toni into yet another of his bear hugs, she didn't even try to resist. Sometimes it was hard watching other people get all the things she'd have had by now, if Aaron had lived, whether it was with him or someone else, but not today. Today all she felt was pure joy for two of the nicest people she knew. Twins might be double trouble, but if anyone had enough love to handle that kind of instant family, it was Anna and Brae.

2

Bobby was getting used to the fact that he was now a fully quali-fied midwife, but it was some of the patients who had the most difficulty with it. No one seemed to have any issue with male doctors, but a male midwife still left quite a few of them open-mouthed. He was due to start going out on rounds, but he'd asked Anna to pair him with another of the team for the first visits to any patients he hadn't seen before in case they refused to be examined by him. The last thing he wanted was anything impor-tant to be missed at one of the check-ups, just because he didn't have the same anatomical make-up as his patients.

For most of his twenty-seven years, Bobby had lived with his parents, Joyce and Scott, but in the last year or so of his training, still juggling everything on a maternity care assistant's salary, he'd finally been able to move into a tiny studio flat in one of the narrow lanes that snaked uphill from the harbour at Port Agnes. Not that he hadn't loved living with his parents and never having to worry about having enough money to pay the rent and still be able to afford a pint of milk, but there came a time when you had to strike out even if he hadn't really been able to stretch to it at the time. His mates had enough fun taking the mickey out of his career choice, without the opportunity to call him a mumma's boy too. Now that he was finally qualified, he might even be able to pay the rent *and* afford to fully stock his fridge.

If things had been different, he'd have liked to suggest getting a place with Toni, now that he could pay his way, but he had more chance of his mates not ripping a strip off him for being a midwife than he did of that happening. Looking across the staffroom at her now, she had her bob-length hair tied back into a short ponytail like she'd had when they'd last had the chance to spend some time together. She been cooking for them at her flat and he'd walked up behind her, putting his arms around her and kissing the back of her neck. Just ordinary stuff that other couples did on a daily basis, but he could never do that where anyone else might see. Not that he ever would while they were at work, but it would be nice to be able to reach out and touch her arm in public, without her jumping like she'd been stung by a wasp.

The other midwives in the team must have known there was something going on between him and Toni, and, for a little while, he thought she might finally stop trying to hide it. But then there'd been the run-up to Aaron's anniversary and she closed right down again. He hadn't even seen her since she'd been to the annual get-together that Aaron's parents always hosted, but he could feel her pulling away, and now she wasn't even making eye contact with him. She'd been ignoring his messages since the last time they'd seen each other too, the guilt that always seemed to accompany time spent with Aaron's parents making her shut him out.

'Has Brae got over the shock of finding out you're having twins, yet?' Ella, who was the deputy manager of the unit and who would be taking over Anna's job when she started her maternity leave, smiled at her best friend.

'I'm not sure! On the way to the hospital for the scan, he kept saying, "It can't really be true, can it?"' Anna laughed. 'And I couldn't work out if he wanted it to be or not, but then he burst into tears when the sonographer confirmed what Toni had suspected.'

'Happy tears, I take it?' Toni looked up from her desk and Anna nodded.

'He still can't believe how lucky we've got, but then he's not the one already needing to get up for a wee three times a night!' Anna grinned, despite her words, and it would have been obvious that she was every bit as thrilled as Brae, even if Bobby hadn't known how worried she'd been that she might never have children. As one of three children himself, it was something Bobby had always assumed would be a given for him one day. The trouble was, there was only one person he could imagine wanting to have children with now. But he could hardly be a secret father the same way he was a secret boyfriend and, if he was honest with himself, he wasn't sure how much longer he could go on being that either.

'I thought poor old Brae's eyes were going to pop out of his head when I heard the second heartbeat.' Toni smiled, but she still didn't glance in his direction. She didn't seem to realise that her deliberate avoidance of him made things all the more obvious to everyone else, not to mention how bad it made him feel. He couldn't take his eyes off her when she was in the room, but she seemed to find it all too easy not to even acknowledge his existence.

'You just wait until Brae sees the babies being born.' Gwen, who was the oldest midwife on the team, and who had a reputation for near-the-knuckle comments, tapped the side of her nose. 'He'll never be the same again.'

'They do say it's the most amazing thing a man can witness,

watching his child being born.' Bobby deliberately looked straight at Gwen, who gave a raucous laugh in response.

'That they do, Bobby, but we know the reality, don't we? My Barry said seeing our second son born was enough to make his bits and pieces suck back inside him. He reckons it's nature's contraception, stopping you from wanting any more!'

'Just don't tell any of your patients that.' Jess smiled and shook her head. Bobby was secretly hoping he was going to be paired on home visits with Jess; at least she wouldn't want to talk about how fantastic her relationship with her other half was. He liked all of the other midwives, but he wasn't sure he could cope with having to ask Ella about the plans for her upcoming wedding, and Gwen was terminally nosey, so she'd keep chipping away all day, trying to get to the bottom of exactly what was going on between him and Toni. Jess had her own issues to worry about. She'd split from her husband almost a year before, in the wake of discovering she'd never be able to have a baby of her own naturally. Instead of wallowing in the unfairness of it all, she'd started the process of becoming a foster carer. She was an inspiration, taking life by the short and curlies to make things happen, and maybe it was about time Bobby did the same.

'I've put Ella and Toni on deliveries this morning, with the MCAs for support, so hopefully you'll be safe from scaring off any of the dads-to-be who turn up in clinic, Gwen!' Anna laughed again. 'Jess and Bobby will be out on home visits. I'm interviewing all morning to replace Bobby's MCA post and for the new midwifery role, but after that I'll be around to assist if we get more deliveries in than expected.'

Bobby breathed out, at least something was going his way. He needed to talk to Toni soon, but doing it out on their rounds, when their patients needed to be at the forefront of their minds, was not the place. Knowing that his old role was going to be replaced was odd too, and he couldn't help feeling that it was an end of an era in more ways than one. He'd been a maternity care assistant at the unit alongside his university course and now someone else would be starting that journey. Toni had been given the task of mentoring Bobby and it was how they'd first started to grow closer, having the opportunity to spend so much time together at work. He couldn't help thinking that with those opportunities gone, and Toni's unwillingness to risk anyone finding out about them, they were just going to drift further apart.

'Have you got some good candidates for both roles?' Ella asked and Anna nodded.

'It's looking like the most difficult part will be narrowing down who to choose, but I'm going to have to start thinking about maternity cover soon too. Ella will be covering the manager's post, but we'll still need more midwifery hours for patient contact. And with it being twins, I'm probably going to need to go on maternity leave earlier than I would do otherwise, or at least cut my hours down the further on I get.'

'Not to mention the fact that you're ancient.' Gwen looked completely deadpan as she delivered the killer line, but Anna just laughed.

'Yes, there's that too!' Anna stopped laughing, as the phone in the staff room started to ring, picking up the call. 'Hello, okay right and Jess is your midwife? Every three minutes? If you come in straight away we can check you over, but it definitely sounds like labour to me, so you'll need to make sure you bring your bag with you, too.' Anna replaced the receiver and looked across at Jess.

'That was Kirsty Barron; it looks like she's in established labour and she's really hoping you'll be able to be involved in her delivery as you've been looking after her the whole time. She seems quite nervous about how's she's going to cope. Are you happy to swap with Toni, so you can be there?'

'That would be great, as long as Toni doesn't mind?' Jess and Anna both turned to Toni, who gave an impressively casual shrug, but Bobby didn't miss the look that flitted across her eyes. She wasn't happy.

'Of course, no problem.' Bobby had heard that tone often enough to see through it, too. Toni didn't want to go out on rounds with him any more than he did, but sooner or later they were going to need to talk and maybe side by side in the car they'd finally get the opportunity. They still wouldn't be alone, though, they never really were. Somehow Aaron was always there, and after almost three years of being with Toni – whenever she could fit him in – Bobby was finally starting to accept that was never going to change.

* * *

Toni turned up the radio as soon as she started the car. Three Ports Radio wouldn't have been her usual choice, with its string of inane adverts, overly enthusiastic chatter and upbeat pop music, but it was perfect for a journey where the awkward silence needed filling whatever the cost. The last text Bobby had sent her had spelled out that their next conversation wasn't going to be an easy one.

✉ from Betty

I would say we need to talk but seeing as you aren't even responding to my texts that's pretty difficult. I think that says it all really.

His name was saved in her phone as Betty, after Aaron's dad had passed her mobile to her once and had asked why she had so many WhatsApp notifications from someone called Bobby. She'd explained about mentoring him and that he needed some help with an upcoming assignment. When Judy had asked if he was good-looking, Toni had laughed it off and called Bobby just a kid; he was almost nine years younger after all. But it hadn't stopped the tidal wave of guilt washing over her. Not just because she was lying to Judy, and it felt like a betrayal of Aaron, but because it was a betrayal of Bobby too. He had more maturity than she could have expected from anyone and had understood why she didn't feel she could tell the world about their relationship, at least at first. Almost three years down the line, he was finally running out of patience and the reason she hadn't replied to his messages was because she couldn't promise things were ever going to change – and that wasn't fair.

She had to let him go; he deserved so much more than this, but the thought of things ending between them made her chest ache. It didn't matter that it was the right thing to do, it still hurt like hell and she was already wavering. Maybe they could find a way to make it work, if he could just hold on for a little bit longer...

For a split second, when Judy and Simon had asked her how work was going at Aaron's latest anniversary dinner, she'd been tempted to finally admit that Bobby was more than just a work colleague. But Judy had launched into a monologue about what Aaron would be doing with his career by now, if he'd ever had the chance, and Toni's opportunity to mention Bobby was gone. She couldn't do that to Aaron's parents, or to Bobby come to that. He'd never be able to live up to her own parents' memories of Aaron either, and he'd be on the back foot from day one. Not to mention what it would do to Judy and Simon. It was something she couldn't bear even thinking about, because every time she did, she pictured Aaron's face and the silent promise she'd made when she'd seen him for the final time at the chapel of rest. She couldn't make Judy and Simon's pain any worse.

Putting Bobby through all of that seemed pointless, anyway. He was twenty-seven and he could have anyone he wanted, but for some reason he didn't seem able to see it. If she'd answered Judy's question honestly, she'd have been forced to admit that Bobby was *very* good-looking, with his dark brown eyes that always seemed to be laughing, just one part of the legacy of his Jamaican heritage on his mother's side. He was undeniably gorgeous, and Toni was definitely punching above her weight, whatever he might try and tell her. It was yet another reason why she wasn't expecting it to last; she saw how other women looked at him. So what was the point of hurting anyone by introducing him to Aaron's parents, or even her own?

'You don't have to turn the radio up quite so loud; I get the message that you don't want to talk.' Bobby didn't look at her as he spoke. The road out of Port Agnes towards Port Kara, where they were seeing their first patient, was still wet after a heavy downpour of rain first thing. The leaves were starting to come off some of the trees, but those still clinging on were damp, making the branches look like they were drooping down – the whole world seeming to mirror Toni's mood.

'I don't think now is the best time, that's all.' Toni sighed, knowing exactly what Bobby was going to say next.

'There's never a good time, though, is there, Toni?' He was still half turned away from her, looking out of the passenger window.

'We've been through it so many times, I'm not even sure what else there is to say.'

'Maybe you're right.' Bobby sounded defeated. It was the first time he hadn't tried to persuade her that they could find a way of making it work and her stomach felt as if it had dropped through the bottom of the car. If this was really it, she couldn't blame him, but she still had no idea how she would cope with the reality. All he was asking for was a normal relationship – out in the open – but she couldn't even give him that. 'I can't be your dirty little secret any more.'

'It isn't like that; you know it isn't.'

'That's how it feels, though. Like we're having an affair and that the worst possible thing that could happen would be anyone finding out about us. It's like you're ashamed of me.'

'Now you're being ridiculous! It isn't about you, it's about Aaron.'

'Exactly.' Bobby shook his head. 'And it's always going to be about Aaron.'

'Judy and Simon lost their only child, I'm all they've got and they've always said they couldn't bear the thought of losing me.'

'I understand that, I really do. The problem is, I'm starting to realise that you'd happily lose me as a trade-off. It's been nearly three years, Toni, and I thought if I just kept hanging in there, maybe you'd realise I was worth taking a risk on. You've met my mum and dad, it's not like they'd want to do anything to take you away from Aaron's parents and neither would I, because I know they've been through hell. But Aaron's been gone five years and, from everything you've told me about them, and about him, I can't believe they wouldn't all want you to grab some happiness with someone who loves you... as much as I do.' Bobby finally turned towards her, but Toni fixed her gaze on the road ahead, glad of the excuse not to have to look into his eyes.

'I can't do this now; I need to concentrate on the road. All these wet leaves are making it really slippery.' Her voice caught on the words and the fact she was gripping the steering wheel so tightly had nothing to do with the road conditions. She couldn't let him see her cry, even though her eyes were stinging with the effort of trying not to, because then he'd try and comfort her and all her resolve to do the right thing by him would be in danger of melting away. The truth was she didn't *want* to have the conversation at all, because there was only one conclusion. If Bobby looked her in the eyes, he'd be able to see it and know for sure that he was right – this was always going to be about Aaron. It had to be. Because the way he'd died, doubting if she loved him every bit as much as he'd loved her, was all her fault.

She'd told him she didn't want to rush into marrying him and he'd handled it with his usual calm, but that didn't stop it being the last conversation she'd ever had with him. And it was still imprinted in her mind. He'd told her he'd marry her the next day if he could and she'd left his words hanging. It had probably played on his mind for the rest of the day, with him waiting for some reassurance the next time he saw her. There was no way of knowing if it was the last thing he thought about as he stepped into the shower. Had he doubted her love for him, even as he lay dying?

He'd mentioned having a headache and she'd brushed it off when he'd admitted the stress was getting to him. She'd simply told him to take a couple of painkillers. She couldn't take back their conversation that day, or undo her part in making that stress even worse, but she could make sure she kept her final promise to him, whatever that cost her. Losing Bobby would be the ultimate price, but maybe it would be a relief in a weird sort of way – as if the debt she owed for hurting Aaron might finally start to balance up.

'How about meeting tonight to talk then, about seven? I've got some stuff at your place I think I should pick up.' Bobby's tone was tight. 'I wouldn't want your parents popping round and seeing my stuff and putting two and two together.'

'I thought tonight was your brother's birthday?' Toni didn't want to admit to Bobby that there was no chance of her parents discovering his stuff in her flat. Every time he left there she always went round, looking for any trace of his presence and making sure it was hidden away. When she and Aaron had chosen the flat, they'd deliberately picked Port Agnes, because being two towns away from their parents was just about far enough to ensure they couldn't keep popping in on the basis that they were just 'passing'. Now, with Bobby in her life, it had seemed even more important than ever.

'We're doing Jackson's birthday at the weekend. You know what Mum's like. She likes to make a big thing of everyone's birthdays and the fact that he's forty gives her even more of an excuse to go big with it this time.'

'I can just imagine.' Toni could picture Joyce bustling around the kitchen at their family home, like a modern-day Ma Larkin. She always seemed to have a banquet on the go and insisted on feeding all her visitors as if it was their last meal on earth. She and Scott had welcomed Toni with open arms and the thought that she might not see them any more made her eyes sting all over again. She swallowed down the emotion, just like she always did. It was time to focus on work, the thing that had been her saviour more times than she could count over the past five years. 'You're going to be taking on Sara Wright's care, aren't you?'

'Yes, if she's okay with it.' Bobby seemed more than happy to accept the change of subject, but then he was probably every bit as exhausted from having the same conversation over and over again, and getting nowhere, as she was. 'Her notes seem to suggest she's having a fairly straightforward pregnancy so far.'

'It seems so, but she's struggled with her weight a bit over the years, although she isn't the only one and I've hardly got room to criticise.'

'I wish you wouldn't talk about yourself like that.' Bobby wasn't saying anything he hadn't said before, but the fact he was still saying anything like that at all gave her a tiny slither of hope that he wasn't just going to disappear from her life altogether. It was selfish to want things to continue, but as much as she might try to hide it from the world, she had wants and needs too. Bobby was right at the top of that list, despite the fact she could never admit it, not even to him. So she defaulted to what she always did, brushing off his comments and pushing him away.

'I'm under no illusion that most people look at me completely differently to the way they look at women like Ella and Jess. I'm too tall and too broad to ever be described as feminine.'

'Is that how you'd describe Anna too, then?' Bobby furrowed his brow. 'She's tall.'

'Anna's willowy, like a model, and she's beautiful. The kindest description you could give of me is solid.'

'You're beautiful, too, and there's so much of you that people don't see, because you never let them.' Bobby's hand slid halfway across the gap towards her and her body had already started to respond as she forced herself to push his hand away, making him frown. 'I'm sorry, I know you probably don't want to hear things like that from me any more, but whatever you think, Toni, you'll always be beautiful to me.'

'Ah, but we both know you need new contact lenses, in fact the whole team do!' This time she finally managed a genuine smile. They'd relied on the excuse of a missing contact more than once when one of the other midwives had caught them getting much closer than colleagues usually did, even on a night out with the rest of the team, in the midst of a kiss. Those days were probably gone for good now, though. But if Toni thought about that for too long, she might find she'd forgotten how to smile altogether.

* * *

Sara Wright opened the door and Toni couldn't work out whether the look of surprise on her face was down to Bobby being there, or just the fact that there were two midwives standing on her doorstep.

'Oh God, I forgot you were coming!' Sara ushered them both inside the house. 'I'm sorry, I'd have whipped around and tidied up, if I'd remembered it was this morning. Although the good news is, I have got cake.'

'Don't worry about tidying up for us and cake's always good news! How are you recovering from your injury?' Toni had met Sara before, just after she'd broken her foot, and had ended up in the boot cast that was now making a resounding thwack against the laminate floor with every step she took. It also meant that Sara couldn't drive and that was why she'd been allocated home visits for the foreseeable future.

'It's a bit of a pain, but it's nice being able to work from home and not having to feel guilty for not keeping up with the exercises my personal trainer gave me.' Sara shrugged. 'It's his fault I dropped the weight on my foot in the first place! God knows what he's going to want me to try when I get the cast off, he's been totally fixated with me putting on as little weight as possible during this pregnancy.'

'You need to make sure you don't start any drastic new workout routines at this stage, but a bit of exercise will be good for you and baby once you feel up to it, and it might even make your labour more straightforward.' Toni followed Sara into the living room, with Bobby coming in behind them. 'Have you met Bobby before? He's going to take over from Jess as your assigned midwife.'

'Ooh lucky me, I thought my eye candy days were over now I'm not seeing my personal trainer and, unlike him, you're going to see bits of me that even my husband wouldn't recognise in the daylight. Sorry, I think my hormones might have started getting to me!' Despite her words, Sara didn't look remotely embarrassed by what she'd said and Bobby seemed to be taking it all with the spirit it was intended.

'Your sense of humour's holding up well, which is good news for this stage of pregnancy.' Bobby smiled at Sara, who at thirty-four weeks along was no doubt relieved that the end was in sight. 'When will you be able to stop using the cast?'

'Two more weeks they tell me, so just in time hopefully.' Sara lowered herself down onto the sofa. 'Let's get this bit over and done with then and I can rustle you both up a bit of cake; it'll give me the perfect excuse.'

'Sounds good to me. I'll measure your uterus just to check the baby's growth is on track, then I'll need to do your blood pressure and test your urine, if that's all right with you?' Bobby sounded like he'd been doing this for years and Sara nodded.

'Perfect. I'm guessing all the tests last time came back normal?'

'Absolutely. There was no sign of any protein in your urine and your blood pressure was good.'

'Especially considering I'm such a lard-arse!' Sara laughed. Toni had no idea how Bobby was going to react; she wasn't even sure how she'd have dealt with a comment like that.

'You've been exercising all through your pregnancy, up until the accident, you don't smoke, and you've done really well to keep your weight gain down as low as you have so far. You're doing all the right things and that's why your blood pressure is looking so good.' Bobby smiled and Toni's heart sank a little bit further. Letting go of him might be the only fair thing to do, but it was going to be incredibly hard to force herself to do it when she was around him so much, witnessing just how lovely he could be.

'You make me sound like a health fanatic! I haven't touched a drop of alcohol since I found out I was pregnant, but I still keep waking up with the sort of headache I only ever used to get when I'd had a very good night out the evening before, if you know what I mean!'

'That doesn't sound good—' Toni had gone hot as soon as Sara had mentioned the headaches. After Aaron's death, just the word became like a trigger point for her. Before, she'd have written a headache off as almost certainly nothing, which the vast majority of time it was. But she never did that now, and for pregnant women it could be especially dangerous: an early sign of pre-eclampsia. She exchanged a look with Bobby and he nodded, knowing exactly what would be going through her mind without her even having to speak.

'Have you had any nausea or changes in vision?' Bobby's tone was calm as he asked the first of the questions that would help rule out pre-eclampsia, waiting as Sara shook her head. 'Any pain under your ribs or shortness of breath?'

'No, nothing like that. Why, should I be worried?' Sara's face had lost its carefree look and Bobby gave her a reassuring smile.

'No, I don't think so. It's just that, sometimes, headaches can be a sign of pre-eclampsia, but you don't sound as if you have any of the other symptoms and checking your blood pressure and urine will be able to tell us for sure.' Bobby smiled again. 'I was going to ask you whether you've been needing to pass urine any more often than normal, but that's quite common for women in late pregnancy anyway, so it might be hard for you to tell.'

'Too right and that was another side effect my personal trainer discovered when he put me on the running machine for a jog. I think the dam bursting took us both by surprise. I'm starting to think he rigged that weight so it dropped on my foot!' Sara's happy-go-lucky demeanour was back, thanks to Bobby, and within ten minutes he was able to rule out pre-eclampsia too; the headaches were most likely a result of Sara not sleeping well this late in her pregnancy. The measurement of Sara's uterus put the baby's growth on track too and Bobby had proved himself more than capable of leading home visits. There was only one person who needed help with the prospect of Bobby going solo, and it wasn't him.

3

Jess plumped up the cushions for what was possibly the fifteenth time. It usually took about an hour to clean Puffin's Rest – her little two-bedroom apartment, overlooking the harbour – hoovering through, scrubbing the loo and flicking a duster around the surfaces. But somehow she'd made it last a good three hours this time. She'd even used a butter knife to run down the gaps between the wooden floorboards in the open-plan living area. She'd found the back of an earring, the wheel of a toy car – presumably from one of the holidaymakers who'd stayed before she moved in, when Puffin's Rest had been a holiday let – and some unidentified green stuff near the cooker, which she could only hope was pesto. She'd been so excited to find out she'd made it through to the assessment stage to prepare her to become a foster carer. It had been an added bonus to discover that Dexter, the social worker who'd led that training, would be responsible for carrying out her assessment. He'd seemed so empathetic and he'd gone out of his way to encourage her to proceed with the decision to become a respite foster carer, despite her misgivings about whether she was up to the challenge.

The rest of the team at the midwifery unit had been really supportive too, encouraging her to go for it, and Anna had made sure she organised Jess's shifts around the appointments for her pre-approval training and other meetings. She'd also had lots of encouragement from the women at the infertility group which she and Anna had set up earlier in the year. When Jess had discovered she could never have children of her own without fertility treatment, it had been devastating and made even more so by her husband, Dom, deciding it meant the end of their marriage too. At least that was his excuse. But the fact that he was having an affair with his boss's personal assistant might have been closer to the heart of things.

When that relationship had fizzled out, Dom had started to pressurise her into trying for kids again. If it hadn't been for Anna, Ella and Toni, she might have given up on the idea of fostering altogether, but they'd been there for her when she needed them most. Anna had set up the infertility support group after being told she'd probably never have children of her own, either, before the twins had come along and surprised them all. Running the group together had bonded the two of them even more. Becoming a respite carer meant that the fostering could be carefully planned around the times Jess booked off from work, with cover from agency staff if they needed it, and it also meant she didn't have to give up the career she loved to do it.

All of the fostering forums she'd subscribed to, and even a scary blog she'd found that had almost convinced her not to go through with the assessment, had said not to worry too much about the state of the house during the social worker's visits. One site, called Foster Chat, even had a forum set up especially for prospective foster carers and @funmum87 had written a paragraph that had made Jess's heart sing:

Don't get hung up on what your social worker's going to think about your house. My social worker always looks like she got dressed from an end of season sale in the Scope shop! And remember, being a foster carer is about being good enough, not being perfect.

None of the posts quite managed to stop Jess running through every worst-case scenario, though. If Dexter turned up and the sole of his shoe got stuck to the what-she-hoped-was-pesto, that big cross she was terrified of getting – which meant she'd never become a foster carer – might well appear next to her name. @funmum87 had obviously never had a social worker like Dexter either. Okay, so he had a slightly dishevelled look sometimes, but he definitely didn't look like he got dressed at a rummage sale in a charity shop. It would have made Jess's life much easier if he did. She probably wouldn't have spent quite so long staring into her open wardrobe, wondering what the hell a prospective foster carer was supposed to wear. She briefly considered her midwifery uniform. But then he might think she was exposing him to the risk of infection, lounging around the house in it, hours after she'd finished work. There was the dress she hadn't worn since the summer before last, at a wedding she'd been to with Dom, or the suit she'd bought for her interview at the midwifery unit three years ago. In the end, she'd settled for jeans and a white shirt, although only after trying on three other shirts first. God knew what she'd be like if she ever had to get ready to welcome a foster child into her home, but that was a problem for another day – if she ever got that far.

'It's like walking the plank!' Dexter smiled as she opened the door and for a minute she wondered if he was talking about the assessment. 'This platform at the top of your stairs, I half expected Captain Jack Sparrow to have a cutlass at my back.'

'It is a bit quirky.' The social worker who'd come out to do her initial visit, before she'd even been booked on to the pre-assessment Skills to Foster training, had warned her that the platform outside her flat might be a deal-breaker for the health and safety assessment. Before she'd moved in, visitors renting Puffin's Rest for a week or two didn't seem to mind the impracticality of an outside staircase. It hadn't been a concern to Jess at the time either. She'd just been grateful that Anna had been able to pull a few strings and that the landlord who owned the flat had been so grateful to Anna for delivering his children that he'd been willing to rent Jess the flat on a long-term lease.

Things were different now, though, and as much as Jess loved Puffin's Rest, she'd move to another flat if she had to. The six feet long platform outside the front door, at the top of the stairs that came up from outside the booking office, was never going to be considered child-friendly. The landlord had already put a flap in for Luna, the stray cat whose previous home had been amongst the lobster pots on the side of the harbour, until Jess had brought her home. Although she still wasn't quite sure whether she'd adopted Luna or the other way around. Either way, the landlord might be willing to help out again, although accommodating a cat was much easier than making Puffin's Rest child-friendly and she might have to resort to doing the one thing she said she'd never do.

'There is another way into the flat, through the booking office, and I can use that if I need to.'

'Don't worry, we can talk about all of that later.' Thankfully Dexter didn't seem to need any assurances just yet. Although the landlord had said she'd be welcome to go through the booking office for Port Agnes boat tours – which was directly below her flat and had an internal staircase to a door between the two bedrooms, which was bolted from the inside – she never had.

Despite being given a key, she just couldn't risk it. A legacy of being accused of stealing in her first ever foster placement as a child, meant she had an innate fear of being accused of doing something she hadn't. Overhearing her accuser saying it was all that could be expected from a child *like her* was a memory she couldn't bury, no matter how hard she tried. Ending up in the care of strangers after her mother had died and her father had abandoned her had been devastating enough, but knowing that some people viewed her as the lowest of the low as a result broke something inside of her that had never really been fixed. All of which meant she wouldn't risk going through the booking office and being accused of taking something that had been left lying on the side. Shaking herself to try and brush off the memory, she realised that Dexter was staring at her. 'So, can I come in?'

'Oh God, yes, sorry.' Jess stepped back to let him into the flat, heat flushing her face. He probably thought she was a hopeless case already, standing there like a statue until he had to ask to be let in.

'You don't have to be so nervous, I'm not here to try and catch you out. Honestly.' Dexter smiled again and a tiny bit of tension drained out of Jess's spine. 'Wow, what a view.'

'It's great, especially on an evening like this.' The Velux windows provided a floor to ceiling view of the sun as it set above the harbour, pinks, purples and a fading ball of bright orange that reflected a mirror image into the water. 'I know the windows probably look like a potential death trap too, but it's shatterproof glass –four times the normal thickness – and they can't be opened.'

'That's great, but like I said, we can worry about the health and safety stuff later. Is it okay to sit here?' Dexter pointed at one of the sofas that faced each other in front of the windows.

'Of course. Can I get you a drink?' Jess had bought everything she thought Dexter could possibly ask for, from orange juice to caramel latte pods for the coffee machine.

'Tea would be great, thanks. Milk, no sugar please.'

'Ooh that's the same as me.' Jess's voice sounded weirdly high, even to her own ears – as if Dexter's revelation that they liked their tea the same way was the most surprising thing in the world. God this was getting embarrassing already and they were less than five minutes in. 'Thanks for agreeing to see me so late, by the way. It's just that my shifts for the next couple of weeks all seem to be lates and I didn't want to delay starting the assessment.'

'No problem. A lot of foster carers have jobs, so I quite often do these twilight sessions.'

'Have you got a lot of assessments on the go at the moment?' Jess was trying to stop herself from worrying about the answer before Dexter even gave it. But it was easier said than done. If he had twenty assessments in progress, there had to be some that wouldn't make it through. The more competition she was up against, the harder it had to be.

'Only three.' Dexter smiled as she handed him the tea. 'So, is there anything you want to ask me about the assessment before we get started?'

'Do you want a biscuit?' Jess felt the colour rising in her cheeks again. 'I know that's not a question about the assessment, but—'

'Jess, you've got nothing to worry about and I'll let you know if I'm desperate for a biscuit at any point. But even if you're a rich tea kind of person instead of custard cream one, I promise I won't hold it against you.'

'Actually, I'm more of a chocolate chip cookie kind of girl. But it's good to know that my choice of biscuits isn't a deal-breaker.' She smiled and Dexter grinned in response; he really was a lovely man and once upon a time she might even have found herself attracted to him – if Dom hadn't put her off the thought of ever having another relationship. She was happy just with Luna for now and she couldn't see that changing. Plus, hopefully there'd be a revolving door of foster children visiting on respite whose lives she could make a difference to in some small way, even if they were only with her for the weekend. She just hoped that Dexter was a nice as he seemed and he wouldn't turn out to be like the Spanish Inquisition once they actually got started with the assessment.

'Good. Now we've got that cleared up, are there any other questions you want to ask me?'

'If I'm honest I just want to get started.' Jess sat opposite him, the muscles in her jaw clenching involuntarily as she waited for him to ask the inevitable first question: *So, tell me about your childhood...*

'What made you want to foster?'

'I, er...' Jess searched around for the right answer, the unexpected question making the words dry up in her mouth. Telling the truth was the easiest option, though. 'I was fostered myself from the age of ten and I suppose I just want to give something back.'

'So, it was a good experience?' Dexter had such a kind face. Meeting his gaze, she couldn't have lied if she'd wanted to.

'The first placement was only supposed to be short-term until my dad sorted himself out and I could go back home.' Jess swallowed hard. 'My mum had been killed in a car accident a few months before and he just fell apart without her. I think social services were hoping he'd get better, but he never did. So they had to find me a long-term placement instead, after about nine months.'

'And how was that?'

'Great.' She hesitated and, when he didn't respond, she had no choice but to fill the silence. He was far too good at this. 'At least it was great some of the time. They mostly treated me like a member of the family, but they'd have a holiday with their own kids every summer for two weeks and I had to go and stay with another foster family for respite. I get it, I suppose, but it proved I was never really one of the family, and then, when I turned eighteen, they decided they needed my room to take another placement. At least they were honest with me, but being told they'd get more income from another placement than they would from keeping me in supported lodgings stung a bit. I lived with friends after that, but I was on my own family-wise until I met Dom.'

'That's your ex-husband?'

'We're not divorced yet, just separated, but I've started the process.' Jess was really spilling her guts now. She didn't know how Dexter was doing it, but he already knew more about her than some of her friends did. 'I had to admit I was a bit surprised when the local authority said I'd be allowed to foster whilst I was still only separated.'

'Stability is the most important thing for children in care, you know that better than anyone. If you got back with Dom, or got into another relationship, you'd have to wait until you'd been together at least a year before you could be assessed as a couple, and we'd have to do the Form F assessment all over again. If you're just seeing someone and you're not living together, it will all be about managing the risk if they spend a lot of time here. So it's really important that you let us know if anything like that changes.'

'There's no chance of that. I'm not interested in finding anyone else and as for Dom...' She'd have to get this out in the open sooner or later, so she might as well tell Dexter whilst she was in the mood for blurting. 'He moved on straight away, with someone from his work, but I realised I wasn't nearly as upset about that as I should have been. Dom being part of a close-knit family was probably what attracted me to him in the first place. It was what I'd always wanted, and I realised I missed them more than I missed him.'

'That must have been tough to admit to yourself, but it's really positive you're able to understand why you acted the way you did. It's exactly what we want from foster carers, so they can reflect on their practice and on the behaviours of the young people they look after and find solutions to the issues that come up.'

'I've got to admit I never thought confessing to something like that would go in my favour!' At this rate she was going to able to relax enough to stop sitting with her back ramrod straight, as if she had a broom handle poked up the back of her shirt.

'You'd be surprised the experiences that help make someone a good foster carer. I've worked with loads of different people and they almost all have things in their pasts that were really difficult, but the ones who learn from those things make the best foster carers. The same goes for social workers.'

'Really? I thought you guys would know every pitfall going and have your lives all sorted.'

'Good job I didn't say yes to a biscuit or I might have choked on it! The hardest lesson I've learnt about myself over the years is that I can't "save" everybody and there are some things I just can't fix. It still doesn't stop me from trying, so I suppose you could say I haven't really learnt anything at all.' Dexter shrugged, but it was anything but casual. He'd been through some tough times too, that much was obvious, and for a moment Jess wished she was the one asking all the questions. But giving her social worker the third degree probably wasn't going to win her any brownie points.

'It really helps to know you're human too.'

'Last time I checked I was.' He grinned again and Jess's

stomach did an involuntary flip. She only liked him because he was being so nice. The last thing she wanted was for him to think she had some sort of crush on him; that was hardly likely to go down well and it wasn't true anyway. It was just that he was so different to Dom and she'd forgotten that her ex was the exception and not the rule when it came to how men treated women, especially when her father had been even worse. Folding her arms across her body, she deliberately kept her expression neutral. If it made her look defensive, it was a price she was willing to pay. She couldn't afford to let Dexter, or the other nice guys like him, chip away at her armour. She was a crazy cat lady now and that's the way it was going to stay.

* * *

Toni had only had a shower because she'd finished work – that was all. It had nothing to do with Bobby coming over in half an hour and neither did the fact that she'd shaved her legs and rubbed in the body lotion that matched her perfume. He was coming to collect his things, nothing more. She'd boxed them all up, instead of presenting them to him in the bag for life where they'd been shoved after the last time he'd come over, so there'd be no risk of any visitors spotting the tell-tale signs that she'd had a man staying in her flat.

The fact that it might really be over this time hadn't quite registered yet. After all, it was probably the sixth or seventh time they'd reached this point, but there'd been a different look in Bobby's eyes this time, something that seemed a lot like exhaustion. She'd known she was in the wrong and being horribly unfair by not replying to any of his messages, but she'd done it anyway, because it was easier than facing up to the combination of guilt and grief that always came with trying to balance what

Bobby deserved from her and the promises she'd made to Aaron's parents. What she wanted barely came into it. If it did, Bobby's stuff would be littered all over the flat. She liked coming home and seeing a pair of his trainers by the front door, or one of his hoodies hanging from the coat rack. It made the place feel more like home than it ever did when all his stuff was neatly packed away out of sight.

It wasn't like she'd dressed up for Bobby's arrival either, she was wearing an old shirt he'd given her, one of his in fact. He'd said he didn't wear it any more after losing the two top buttons, and just because he'd told her how amazing her legs looked when she had it on in bed one day, it didn't mean she was doing it for his benefit. It was comfortable, that was all, and she'd never been a silky nightdress or sexy underwear sort of girl. The shirt was hers now anyway, he'd said he didn't want it back, so she was quite within her rights not to pack it up in his box of stuff. He wouldn't miss the almost empty bottle of aftershave she'd kept either, which she already knew she'd be spraying on the pillow on the side of the bed where he usually slept, after he was gone. She liked the smell – that was all – and it was going to take time to get used to that not being around.

She'd done the same thing when Aaron had first died and everyone was telling her that the best thing to do would just be to sell up the flat and move on somewhere else, somewhere where there were no memories of him – good or bad – especially after the way he'd been found. At first, she'd been tempted to follow the advice, because every time she'd gone into the bathroom it had been all too easy to picture him there, but she didn't want to be somewhere that had no memory of Aaron. Instead, she'd had the flat reconfigured. What used to be the bathroom was now a small second bedroom, which she used mainly for storage, and the old second bedroom was a much bigger bathroom, with an old-fashioned style claw-foot bath instead of just a shower, so it looked totally different from the room where she'd found Aaron. She liked sitting in the sunny kitchen, though – which was a big reason why they'd chosen the flat in the first place – and remembering what it was like to sit down to breakfast with Aaron there.

For a while she'd taken to buying bottles of his old aftershave too and spraying it into the air when she was missing him most. Over time she'd needed to do it less and less, and it would be the same with Bobby; she wouldn't miss all the things she was going to miss about him forever. She'd got over a terrible loss once and she could get over this too. She was almost sure of it. She tried not to think about how much harder it was going to be this time. Seeing him every day at work and knowing for sure that the end of their relationship was her fault. In her rational moments she could admit to herself that Aaron's death wasn't something she could have controlled, but there was an internal voice that drowned that out more often than not. This time there wasn't any doubt; she'd hurt Bobby and it was all her fault, so the least she could do for him was cut him free.

There'd been a couple of guys she'd dated in the year before she met Bobby, but never anything serious enough for her to even feel like she needed to hide them from Aaron's parents, or from the rest of the world, and she'd never bought any of them home to the flat. They'd scratched an itch, that was all, a longing to fill the void Aaron had left in her life that had become almost a chasm by the time he'd been gone a year, when it had seemed impossible that she had to live the rest of her life without her best friend. She'd only ever been in love twice in her life and that was probably more than most people could say. If her punishment for letting Aaron down was losing Bobby, then she'd have to learn to live with it. At least she had the choice; Aaron's whole life had been ripped away without any warning.

'Come up.' As soon as Bobby buzzed the intercom, and she could see him on the doorbell camera, she pressed the button to let him in, her mind drifting back against her will to the first time she'd invited him over. She'd known what was going to happen then and she'd been terrified he might realise she was shaking, put two and two together and work out just how much he meant to her. She couldn't afford to let that happen then and she definitely couldn't afford to let it happen now. He'd stopped expecting her to casually respond in kind when he told her he loved her a long time ago, but controlling her words was the easy bit. Her body was much more likely to spill the beans using a language all of its own, it always had done.

'You're wearing my shirt.' There was a flicker of something in Bobby's eyes as she opened the door to the flat, but she couldn't quite read what it was. His tone was tight, though.

'You said you didn't want it any more.'

'I just didn't expect you to be ready for bed. It's only seven o'clock.'

'And I've been on call since five o'clock this morning, so it's been a long day. If it offends you, I'll put a dressing gown on.'

'It doesn't offend me.' The expression on Bobby's face softened and Toni had to force herself not to reach out to him, her fingers twitching at her sides with the effort of holding herself back.

'All your stuff is boxed up, in case you just wanted to take it.' Her muscles tensed as she waited for him to react.

'I don't want to just go, not without explaining...'

'You'd better come through then.' Stepping back, she let Bobby walk past her, breathing in the scent of his aftershave and suddenly wishing she was wearing a lot more clothes. This felt too intimate for the conversation he clearly had planned, outlining exactly why they needed to face up to the fact that this was never going to work. It didn't matter that she'd told him, and herself, all of that from the outset. At that stage, she'd never expected to feel the things she'd ended up feeling, things he didn't even know about, which made it a lot more difficult to be rational, even when the reasons for them splitting up made perfect sense.

'You know I don't want this, don't you?' The emotion on Bobby's face was even more naked than Toni felt. That was the thing about him, he never played games, or made her have to second-guess how he was feeling. He'd been the first to say 'I love you' by a long way. Even when she'd eventually said it back, it had come with a caveat: *I love you too, but...*

'That's not what it looks like from where I'm standing, seeing as you're here to collect all your stuff.' Even as she said it, Toni knew she wasn't being fair. It was only because Bobby couldn't live like this any more, and she couldn't blame him. She wouldn't have put up with being kept in the shadows for half this long, or being made to feel second best to someone who'd been dead for five years. Bobby was too nice for his own good and it had cost them both dearly. He'd put up with it and hung around for long enough to let her feelings for him get deeper and deeper. There was nothing she could do about that, and the truth was, it was all her fault really. Now, for the second time in her life, she was hurting the person she loved the most.

'All I want is for you to tell me this won't be forever. It doesn't have to be now or even next year, I just need to know that one day this will stop, and we can be together properly. All this sneaking around and pretending not to be a couple, even when our friends already know about us, is crazy.'

'They don't *know*, they just think they do.' Toni shut her eyes, so she didn't have to see the sadness reflected in his, but she could still have described every contour of Bobby's face. She hated the thought that she was the cause of his pain – not to mention her own. But Bobby could move on and find someone else. Aaron's parents couldn't replace their only child and that's why they were always going to come first. Toni was the closest link they had left back to Aaron and she couldn't take that away from them. Even if the thought of Bobby moving on and holding someone else in his arms, the way he'd held her, was enough to make her stomach churn so hard she was in danger of actually throwing up.

'Do you really think Judy and Simon expect you to be on your own forever?' Bobby's eyes were searching her face when she opened her eyes. If it was weird that he spoke about Aaron's parents as if he knew them too, it probably wasn't surprising, given the impact these strangers had had on his life. Toni hadn't spoken to anyone else about Aaron the way she'd spoken to Bobby about him, not even her closest friends. But now even he seemed to have reached his limit.

'Deep down I know they just want me to be happy and they wouldn't resent me for starting a new relationship, but I don't think they could bear to see it. And what would happen then? They'd lose me if they couldn't stand to have me visit, knowing I was with someone else, and they might even lose Mum and Dad. They've lived next door to one another for almost all my life and what if they couldn't even bear to see us pull up outside my parents' house? They might end up feeling like they had to move away, or we'd have to keep hiding, never visiting Mum and Dad in Port Tremellien and only seeing them if they came here. We could put them through all that and end up splitting up anyway. It isn't worth the risk.'

'But you can walk away from what we've got without a backward glance?'

'I don't want to, but what choice have I got?' Toni's voice cracked on the second half of the sentence, despite her best efforts. She knew what people thought of her, that she was brusque and closed off. Her emotions, if people thought she had any at all, were well controlled and dispassionate from the outside. The truth was that sometimes she felt raw from trying to hold it all in, to be strong for everyone else like she had from the moment she'd found Aaron lying in the bottom of the shower cubicle. She couldn't let those feelings out, because it would be like taking the cap off a bottle of Coke that had been shaken a thousand times over and expecting it not to flood over the top and end up unrecoverable, all over the floor.

'You could choose *us*. I know it would be hard, but I'd do it, if it was my choice. A hundred times over.' Bobby held her gaze and she nodded.

'I know you would.'

'But you're not going to, are you?'

'I'd choose you over any other man.'

'Except Aaron.' She couldn't avoid seeing the sadness in his eyes this time – she wasn't quick enough – and her gut twisted in response.

'It's not about Aaron.' She reached out for him, but he flinched away from her.

'It would be easier if it was just him and he was still around, at least I'd stand a chance of you picking me then.'

'I love you, Bobby. As much as I've ever loved anyone, that much I can promise you.' She was loosening the bottle top, but she couldn't watch him walk away without telling him the truth and for once her words didn't even come with the usual limitation. He deserved to know how hard this was for her, and she wanted him to.

'Toni, don't. This is difficult enough already.' Even as he protested, he was turning back towards her, his eyes widening as he saw how hard she was crying. 'Oh Tee, don't cry.'

'Don't be nice to me, please.' Bobby was the only person in the world who called her Tee and they'd used it as a secret code for their relationship. Everyone called him Bobby, but he was Robert really. It was okay for Robert and Tee to be dating, they didn't have any of the baggage Bobby and Toni had to cart around with them.

'I'm never going to be anything but nice to you, because I love you and I'm always going to love you. There's nothing either of us can do about it.' Bobby put a hand under her chin so that she had to lift her eyes to look at him, even though she was only a few inches shorter.

'I love you too.' Afterwards, Toni couldn't have said with certainty who made the first move, even if her life depended on it. Either way, ten seconds later she was kissing Bobby as if it was the last time and, the truth was, there was every chance it was. They were unbuttoning each other's shirts, fumbling like teenagers with all that same pent-up desire. The first time Bobby had lifted her off her feet, it had taken her by surprise – the fact that he could even do it had been part of the thrill. But as he did it now, her legs wrapped around him, almost automatically. She wanted to be with him and, in that moment, nothing else mattered. Not to either of them. She didn't want to think beyond the next little while. The closed-off and guarded woman, who everyone thought they understood, had a side to her that only Bobby knew about. And, in those moments, Toni belonged to him in a way she'd never quite belonged to anyone else.

4

Anna was still having a tough time with her pregnancy and the twins really were turning out to be double trouble in terms of the symptoms she was experiencing as a result. Ella had told Toni that the sickness was currently preventing Anna from doing much other than eating dry crackers and wishing the nine months were already over so she had her babies safely in her arms. In the meantime, Ella was standing in to run things for a while, as deputy head of the unit, and for the current shift she'd assigned Toni to cover the birthing suites with Gwen.

It was one of those days where they didn't dare to speak the truth of how quiet it was out loud. They'd spent most of the morning doing an audit of supplies, just to pass the time and to stop Gwen asking if there was 'anyone special' in Toni's life. When Bobby had said that their friends at the unit knew about him and Toni, he wasn't wrong. Most of them knew there was something going on between them, but they seemed happy to go along with the pretence that they were only friends, seeming to understand that there was a reason behind it.

Even when Toni had let the mask slip a bit, at Anna and Brae's wedding, no one had pushed it afterwards. Except Gwen. Her unsubtle questioning was no doubt well-intentioned. She probably thought if Toni would only say out loud what was going on between her and Bobby, the rest could all be sorted out. It would just have made it harder, though. Having interference from their colleagues – however well meant – would have compounded Bobby's view that she was crazy, sacrificing her happiness for someone who wasn't even here any more, but she doubted any of them would really have understood, even if they'd known the whole story. Not even Bobby did, no matter how hard he'd tried. Despite ending up spending the night with him, she still had no idea if he'd changed his mind about ending things between them and she wasn't sure she wanted to know. Whoever it was who'd said ignorance was bliss, had definitely been onto something.

'You know when I first met my Barry that we had to keep things secret, don't you?' Gwen looked up from where she'd been counting the boxes of bed pads.

'No.' Toni was hoping that the curtness of her response would shut down any elaboration of the story, but this was Gwen.

'Oh yes, it was because he was my brother's best friend, and Rhodri would have had Barry's guts for gutters, if he knew what we were getting up to behind the rugby clubhouse!' Gwen still sounded a bit giddy at the memory. 'I had to explain away the grass stains on my summer dress by saying I'd slipped, as it was. It was quite exciting all that sneaking around, but we were bound to get caught out in the end.'

'I suppose so.' Toni didn't even glance in Gwen's direction as she wrote down the number of boxes of surgical gloves she'd counted. Gwen would happily ramble away for hours with no apparent audience necessary anyway, so as long as Toni gave a vague response every now and then it wouldn't be a problem.

'I was right about how he would react. He chased Barry

around the pitch three times before he caught him and I was terrified Rhodri would beat seven shades of you-know-what out of him. I thought I was going to have to put my nursing training into action so my brother didn't end up getting done for murdering my boyfriend.' Gwen laughed.

'And did you?' Despite her best efforts, Toni found herself getting drawn into the story.

'They had a proper set-to, with Barry giving as good as he got in the end, but afterwards they got up, dusted themselves off and went to the pub together. By the time I saw them both again, a couple of hours later, they'd sorted things out and six months after that Rhodri was best man at our wedding. It just goes to show you that things are rarely as bad as you think they might be and everyone will come around in the end.'

'I'm glad it all worked out for you, but it's just easier being single.'

'Oh, it's definitely easier, but easier is not always best, is it?' Toni couldn't look in Gwen's direction, because if she did, the older woman would definitely spot the tears that had filled her eyes. She didn't even know if she was single, but right now it didn't feel easier or best. She just wanted Bobby to herself, the way they were when they were holed up in her flat together and nothing from the outside world could touch them. They were the easy moments, and the best ones, but that wasn't real life and she couldn't keep pretending it was.

'There's a call,' Toni stated the blindingly obvious, as the phone in the staff room started to ring, thanking her lucky stars that just for once an interruption had come at a welcome time. 'Hello, Port Agnes midwifery unit.'

'It's Lydia Yorke's husband, Tim. She's getting contractions every three minutes and she thinks it's time we came in, seeing as things moved pretty quickly from this point onwards last time around.'

'It definitely sounds like it's time.' Toni would have been tempted to tell Tim to bring Lydia in, even if the contractions had been more than twenty minutes apart. Anything to stop Gwen turning into an unwanted agony aunt and dispensing equally unwanted advice even more liberally than she dispensed tea and sympathy to the mums-to-be and their birthing partners. 'How long will it take you to get here?'

'About six minutes, based on the practice runs I've been doing for the last month and a half!'

'See you soon then.' Toni ended the call. 'Looks like we're finally being called into action. Lydia Yorke's one of your ladies, isn't she?'

'Ooh yes, that's good. She only had a couple more days before she was going to have to go to the hospital to be induced. She's at forty weeks plus four days already with baby number two.' Gwen smiled. 'She had the first baby in Truro hospital, but because the delivery was so straightforward, she wanted to have the second one at home. Her husband wasn't quite up for that, though, so a delivery at the unit was their compromise!'

'It's great that you're on duty for the birth.' Toni returned her smile. It was always good when the stars aligned and the primary midwife assigned to a patient was available for her delivery. Even so, the unit had a policy of trying to ensure that each patient met as many of the midwives as possible during their clinics and check-ups, so they'd stand a good chance of having met the midwife who delivered their baby before the big event.

'I know, I love it when that happens! We'd better get ready for them. Lydia said she wants to use the pool and at least we know we aren't going to run out of bed pads or gloves!'

Three hours later, there was no denying Lydia was in established labour, with her contractions getting closer and closer together, and she'd been in the pool for almost two hours by that point. She was handling it like a pro too and, if Toni didn't know better, she might have been able to convince herself that Lydia was floating around in a hot tub, her red bikini top protecting her dignity on the top half, and the gas and air, combined with the warm water, seeming to do a brilliant job of keeping her calm and managing her pain. Tim, on the other hand, was much more tense, jumping to his feet when Toni came in with the cup of tea she'd offered to make him, whilst Gwen monitored Lydia to see exactly how much progress she'd made.

'Tea – just what the doctor ordered, although in other circumstances I'm sure we'd all much rather have a gin!' Gwen dropped a wink in Toni's direction. 'Lydia's just had another contraction, so I reckon we've got time for a couple of mouthfuls of tea before the next one.'

'Never mind tea, right now I'd quite like to be knocked unconscious with a cocktail of drugs.' Lydia rolled her eyes. 'But for some reason I thought it was a good idea to have the baby where being numbed from the waist down by an epidural isn't even an option.'

'You're doing brilliantly; we'll take a look in a minute and see exactly how far along you are.' Toni handed Tim a cup of tea as she spoke.

'Will she need to get out for you to do that?'

'We can do it while she's in the water, but it might be more comfortable for Lydia on the bed.'

'I need a wee in a minute anyway and my mum always told me only naughty children pee in the pool!' Lydia smiled. 'I just can't wait until I can have a proper cup of tea too. Gwen's been telling me from the outset that decaffeinated tea and coffee taste just as good as the real thing, but she knows it isn't true either.'

'I like my tea builder's style, that's my problem!' Gwen raised her palms towards the ceiling. 'Talking of which, I can't be late leaving today because I've got a new plasterer coming over to quote for finishing off the extension. I couldn't have that other chap back.'

'Why, what did he do?' Lydia looked glad of the opportunity for a distraction whilst she waited for the next contraction.

'Wore my wedding dress.' Gwen was completely straight-faced and if Toni hadn't already heard the story, her mouth would have been hanging open in exactly the way Lydia's was.

'He did what?' Tim sounded outraged on Gwen's behalf.

'I came home earlier than he was expecting and caught him in my bedroom wearing my wedding dress, with a pile of my other clothes already tried on and discarded on the bed.' Gwen shrugged. 'I've got no issue with him wearing whatever he wants to on his own time, and I might even have sorted out some of my old clothes for him if he'd asked. But not when he's charging me a day rate for plastering my extension and not when it's my wedding dress, especially when he had the cheek to look better in it than I did back in the early eighties!'

'You've got to be joking?' Lydia widened her eyes, the shock as apparent on her face as it was in her voice.

'Nope, and it's the sort of thing that could only happen to me, isn't it Toni?'

'Definitely.' Toni smiled as everyone started to laugh, with Lydia's expression instantly being replaced by a grimace as another contraction took hold.

'Breathe into it, that's great. Every one of these is getting you a step closer, I promise.' Toni moved to the edge of the pool as Lydia dropped her chin to her chest, screwing up her face.

'You're nearly there with this one; it won't be long now my love.' Gwen stroked Lydia's hair away from her face, with Tim still hovering as if he might take flight at any moment. 'Like Toni said, every contraction is a bit closer to you having that baby in your arms.'

'It's easing off now. But between the contractions and Gwen's stories, I'm definitely going to have to get out of this pool for a wee before it's too late.'

'Let's help you out then sweetheart and, after you've been to the loo, we can see where we're at.' Gwen hooked an arm under Lydia's and Toni held on to her other hand as they helped her out of the pool. Five minutes later she was lying on the examination table and they had a verdict.

'The good news is you're at eight centimetres now, so it shouldn't be too long.' Toni smiled. 'The bad news is, I don't think baby's going to put in an appearance before Gwen has to go off and meet her new plasterer.'

'You'll be staying though, won't you?' Lydia gestured towards where Tim was standing, staring at the wall, with his back towards them. 'Because he might be the love of my life, but he's rubbish at all of this!'

'I've seen a hell of a lot less supportive partners, trust me. Not everyone is cut out for being in the thick of the action.' Toni looked towards Gwen who nodded her head.

'There are plenty of men who wish we were still in the 1950s when they weren't even allowed in for the birth. It's a brave man now who admits he doesn't actually want to be there.'

'I do want to be here.' Tim still didn't turn around. 'But I don't actually want to see *anything*, that's all.'

'We'll do our best to shield you from it.' Toni smiled at Lydia, who rolled her eyes again. 'But I can't promise the baby will agree to follow the rules!'

'I can't believe I'm going to miss all the fun! But I'll have to head off as soon as Bobby arrives for his shift. Getting a plasterer who doesn't wear your clothes is an opportunity that's too good to be missed!'

By the time Gwen left, Lydia was fully dilated and when Bobby put his head round the door to see if Toni needed any help, she waved him away. There was enough tension in the room already, with Tim as tightly wound as he was, without having to share the space with Bobby, still not knowing where they stood. This was Lydia's moment to be the centre of attention and Toni wasn't planning to let anything detract from that. Except, as it turned out, this was another moment where only the baby would get to decide what happened.

'Are you sure you don't want to try something different? Lying on your back is the worst position for encouraging the labour to progress.' Toni had already asked the question twice since Lydia had decided not to get back into the birthing pool, but the other woman was shaking her head.

'I don't think my legs would hold me up, even if I tried to kneel. I feel like I'm made of jelly.'

'Okay, it looks like you've got another contraction coming; just drop your chin to your chest and put all the energy you've got left into pushing this baby out. I've seen women defy gravity plenty of times before.' Toni silently prayed that she would soon be adding Lydia to that list, but she was losing power with every contraction.

'What's wrong?' Lydia barely mumbled the question as she collapsed back against the pillows after another attempt to push that hadn't yielded any progress. Furrowing her brow, Toni checked the baby's heart rate again; Lydia had been pushing for over an hour already. 'You look like you're starting to get really tired, and the baby's heart rate is fluctuating a bit more than I'm happy with. I think we need to arrange a transfer to the hospital for you, in case the baby needs some help getting out.' Toni pressed the call button without even waiting for Lydia to respond.

'How will they get the baby out at the hospital? Is there even going to be time to get her there?' Tim, who'd finally managed to sit down for a few minutes, was back up on his feet again.

'I'm going to talk it through with my colleague, but if we do need to arrange a transfer to the hospital, they'll probably use the ventouse. It's a kind of suction cup that attaches to the baby's head just to give nature a bit of helping hand. You were probably told about it at your antenatal classes first time around.'

'Like a sink plunger?' Toni couldn't help smiling as Tim raised an eyebrow. But his other question was still burning at the back of her mind. There was a good chance that the ambulance wouldn't come nearly as quickly as she'd like it to and then they'd have even fewer options to get the baby out safely.

'It's something like that, but the ventouse will be the quickest and safest way to get baby out if it needs some help.' She reached out to touch Lydia's arm. 'How do you feel about transferring to the hospital?'

'Anything that gets the baby out safely is fine with me, but will they need to cut me?'

'Not necessarily, but if it looks like there's a danger of causing a serious tear, then they might have to think again.'

'How long will the hospital transfer take?' Tim looked like he was ready to drive her there himself.

'About half an hour and they're very good at prioritising us, so the ambulance usually gets here within ten to fifteen minutes. If you need to transfer, I'll come with you in case things start to progress more quickly on the way.' Toni felt some of the tension leave her spine when she heard the knock at the door. 'Come in.'

'How are we getting on in here then?' Bobby brought an instant air of calm into to the room and Toni was sure she wasn't the only who felt it.

'The baby's heartbeat has been a bit erratic, and Lydia's been pushing for well over an hour now; she's getting exhausted. I think we might be looking at a transfer to the hospital for a vacuum delivery.' Toni's eyes slid towards Tim. 'But I just wanted a second opinion about whether we should wait a bit longer.'

'Okay.' Bobby turned towards Lydia and gave her one of his killer smiles, the sort that could light up a room, or even your life if they were directed at you. 'Do you mind if I examine you?'

'Right now you could wheel in the whole of the Port Agnes rock choir to take it in turns to have a look, and I wouldn't bat an eyelid!' No sooner had Lydia got the words out, than her face twisted in pain. 'Oh Christ, there's another contraction coming.'

'All right Lydia, just bear down with this one like you've been doing and we'll see if you and baby can prove me wrong. Keep going with the gas and air.' Toni stepped to one side, so that Bobby could check the baby's progress.

'I definitely think we need to give baby some help, but I don't think it's posterior, do you?' Bobby sounded as if he'd been doing this forever, but Toni could still picture the first time he'd walked into the unit, as a maternity care assistant, before he'd even decided to complete his training to become a midwife and long before they'd become more than colleagues. She'd been his mentor from the start, but she'd never dreamed they'd become as close as they had done.

'No, that's what I was worried about, but from what I can see, and from examining Lydia, I'm almost sure the baby's not lying back to back.' She met Bobby's gaze, his dark eyes drawing her in the way they had always done. 'You think we should sort the transfer then, for an assisted delivery?'

'Is there any risk from doing that ventouse thing to the baby?' Tim cut across them before Bobby even had a chance to reply.

'There might be some bruising and the shape of baby's head might look a little bit different initially, but it settles down really quickly.' Bobby gave Tim a reassuring nod. 'Sometimes the bruising can cause a bit of jaundice in baby too, but only for a very short time. And if the ventouse doesn't work, they can arrange a caesarean. I'm going to go and sort the ambulance now.'

Bobby left the room and Tim's pacing reached new levels. 'What about the risk to Lydia from using the ventouse?'

'Apart from the increased likelihood of needing some stitches, the risks are low.' Toni did her best to mimic Bobby's reassuring tone, but it didn't matter how hard she tried, she'd never have the natural bedside manner he had. 'There'll be a much greater risk to Lydia and the baby if we don't do something and I really do think the hospital is the best option.'

'We'd better get this show on the road then.' It was Lydia who spoke up with the sort of resolution that didn't allow for argument from anyone. 'Oh God, here comes another one.'

'Tim, why don't you go and hold Lydia's hand? You don't need to look down at the business end, but she really needs your support.'

'I just feel like I'll be in the way.'

'You won't, trust me.' Toni put a hand on Lydia's leg. 'Right sweetheart, we're going to try to pant through the contractions now, so we can get you to the hospital.'

'I don't think my body wants to cooperate!'

'You can do it, darling.' Tim finally seemed to have overcome his fear and he dropped a kiss on his wife's head. 'We need to get you to the hospital where it's safe.'

'I want to push!'

'But you're exhausted; just hold on.' Tim might have overcome his fears, but he was still incredibly naïve for a second-time dad. If the baby was as determined to come out as it suddenly seemed to be, then no amount of panting was going to stop it.

'If you can't fight the urge to push then don't; there's still a chance the baby might put in an appearance by itself.' Toni pressed the call button again. 'I know you're worn out, but, like I said before, if we're going to try to get this baby out, gravity could give us a helping hand. If you can get on all fours, or even try getting out of the bed and leaning over the side, it could make all the difference. And, if you get to the stage where you're actually ready to deliver, you could use the birthing bar to support you to squat down.'

'Okay, I'll give standing up a go, but I'm not going on all fours and I need to get up before the next one hits.'

'I'm here darling.' Tim put his arms around his wife, helping her out of bed. Toni then guided them through what looked like the world's most cumbersome slow dance, contractions still coming all the time. A couple of minutes later, he was holding her hands across the bed, from the opposite side, and whispering encouragement as she started to moan.

'There's another one coming and it's burning this time!' Lydia was barely getting a break between contractions now and, as Toni examined her again, the speed at which things were changing took even her by surprise.

'The baby's head is crowning.' She would have bet a month's salary that they wouldn't have got to this point as quickly as they had, given how tired Lydia was, and how exhausted her body had become. But the women she supported never ceased to amaze her and gravity was working its miracle too. 'I think a certain someone didn't want a trip to the hospital.'

'I knew you had this, darling. Just a bit longer and we'll have everything we planned all those years ago.' Tim had suddenly turned from a panicky mess to a motivational speaker and, as Bobby came back into the room, Lydia gritted her teeth with renewed determination, as another contraction took hold.

'I've arranged the ambulance, but I take it things have changed?' Bobby smiled as Toni looked up at him.

'It looks like the baby has decided to be born in Port Agnes after all and Tim's turning out to be an excellent birthing coach. No sooner were you out of the door and Lydia was up on her feet, than baby started crowning. I think using the birthing bar will give her the last bit of help she needs.'

'I'll move the gas and air round, in case Lydia wants it between contractions and I can administer the oxytocin when it's time.' Bobby swung into action and they worked together as effectively as they always had done, any tension between them left outside the delivery room. By the time the next contraction came, Lydia was in the squatting position and even Tim seemed to have overcome his fear of seeing the realities of birth.

'I think the next push could do it.' As Toni had suspected it would all along, the position Lydia was in now had helped to open her pelvis and her baby was finally ready to put in an appearance. Given the baby's earlier distress, Bobby had already checked over the resuscitation equipment in case they needed it.

'Come on darling, one more push and our family will be complete.' Tim stroked his wife's back as she let out a groan.

'Well done, Lydia, that's the baby's head delivered.' Toni was almost as desperate as Lydia to get the baby out and make sure everything was okay, as Bobby prepared the injection she'd be given that would help with delivery of the placenta, in line with Lydia's birth plan. 'Just let your body do its own thing with the next contraction.'

'Okay here we gooooooooo!' The last word lasted several seconds as Lydia bore down and Toni caught hold of the baby.

'Brilliant. We're going to clamp the cord straight away, so we can get baby checked over while we get you settled on the bed, then we can give you skin-to-skin contact. Okay, Lydia?'

'Uh-huh, I don't care, I just want to know if the baby's okay?'

'Everything looks good, although I'm not so sure about Tim.' Toni smiled as Bobby clamped the cord and Tim sobbed. 'Do you want to see what you've got?'

'It's a boy, darling, it's a boy!' Tim's sobbing increased as he took a proper look at his son for the first time, before Bobby carried him over the resuscitation unit to check him over.

'Okay little fella, let's just have a quick look at you before you meet Mummy and Daddy properly.'

'We've got a boy.' Lydia looked at her husband, laughing through her own tears. 'I want to get back on the bed to hold him.'

'Is it okay for her to do that?' Tim looked up at Toni.

'Of course.' Helping Tim manoeuvre Lydia to the bed, Toni smiled. 'It looks like you're about to have lots of cuddle time with your baby boy.'

'Everything looks spot on with this little man.' Bobby brought the baby, who had just let out his first cry, over to his parents, passing him to Lydia so they could have the essential skin-to-skin contact that bonded parents and their newborns, while they waited for the third stage of labour to complete.

'He's perfect, just like his mother.' Tim had finally stopped sobbing and was grinning from ear to ear instead. 'There were so many times when I thought this was never going to happen, but this is everything I ever wanted and more. Who'd have thought a plan we made back in uni would really lead to this?'

'You make it sound so weird!' Lydia smiled at her husband, despite her words. 'What Tim is trying to say, is that when we first started dating, and talking about what we wanted from life, we made a list of all the things that were most important to us. We wanted two children, one of each if we were lucky enough. The goal was to settle down and live somewhere beautiful that would be a great place to raise the kids, and run our own businesses, so we'd have the flexibility to spend time with them.'

'And with Evie back at home with Lydia's parents and this little one, we've got the final pieces of the jigsaw.'

'Congratulations again you guys, your little boy's absolutely beautiful, but I think I'd better go and cancel that ambulance now!' Bobby's voice was filled with warmth, but he still hadn't glanced in Toni's direction. Usually just after a delivery, they'd all be high on the adrenaline rush and he'd often mouth the words 'I love you' to her when they were certain the new parents were unable to take their eyes off their baby. Not this time though; they hadn't even exchanged a smile, let alone anything else. All the joy she usually felt at this moment had fizzled out. How was she supposed to contemplate a life without him in it, if it was already this hard not to be able to reach out to him?

'Thank you so much for everything.' Lydia stroked the baby's head as she spoke.

'My absolute pleasure, but Toni did far more than me.' Bobby finally caught Toni's eye as he turned to leave the room, and every part of her wanted to ask him if he'd really reached the limit on how long he'd wait for her. But how could she, when she couldn't promise it wouldn't be forever, or at least until Judy and Simon weren't around any more? It didn't matter how desperately she wanted to be the right person for Bobby, she never could be.

5

It was definitely beginning to feel like autumn now. There was a new chill in the air and the pavements were starting to be adorned with wet leaves in russets and burnt umber. There was something about the sunsets at this time of year too, they seemed more vibrant to Toni, like the summer sun was having one last big blowout before winter crept in. Heading back from Mehenick's bakery with the last of the day's loaves clutched against her chest as if it was one of the babies she'd delivered, she tried not to think about the evening that stretched ahead of her. Marmite on toast, or maybe a toasted cheese sandwich, if she felt like making the effort, and another night in front of Netflix binge-watching a series she already knew she wouldn't be concentrating on.

It might be lazy not to cook herself a proper dinner, but if it was, then she'd been nothing but lazy since the last time she'd cooked for Bobby. She didn't know if the night they'd spent together had changed anything and she was still in two minds about whether or not she wanted it to. Selfishly, she hoped he'd be willing to wait for her forever, but what was that old song? '(If

You Love Someone) Set Them Free', that was it. She wanted more for him than she could offer, but overriding that was the fact that *she wanted him.* She'd tried to be the bigger person and end things, but he only had to turn those dark brown eyes in her direction and all her principles went out of the window.

She'd tortured herself more than once with the thought of what she'd have done if she'd met Bobby when she and Aaron were together. If Aaron had agreed to the six months apart and they'd both still decided they wanted to get married at the end of it, she had no idea if she'd have been any more able to stay away from Bobby than she was now. She liked to think she would have done – and she knew for certain that she'd never have wanted to do anything to hurt Aaron – but what she felt for Bobby was totally different to anything else she'd ever experienced before.

She couldn't imagine choosing to go travelling for six months now and leaving Bobby behind; she'd be longing to get back to him before she even made it to the airport. What she'd had with Aaron felt safer, though, like the difference between driving a Volvo and a Formula One racing car. It didn't mean that one thing was better than the other, it just meant that one felt a hell of a lot more dangerous and out of her control. Marmite on toast and Netflix was safe too, but it didn't make it any easier to forget the thrill of another life, even when that ended up being the path not chosen.

'Toni.' Bobby stepped out of the shadows outside her flat, just as she was about to enter the passcode to access the main doors, nearly resulting in the bread she was clutching falling onto the flagstones beneath her feet, until Bobby caught it with one hand.

'Bloody hell, are you trying to give me a heart attack?' She could hear her heart thudding in her ears, but she refused to admit, even to herself, that it was only partly down to the fact that Bobby had made her jump.

'I just wanted to see you Tee, that's all.'

'I thought it was all over between us and that we were going to get on with the rest of our lives?' There might have been a chill in the air, but there was no way it could justify the way Toni's teeth were chattering against each other as she spoke.

'Did you? Because I didn't even take my stuff when I left last time, despite you boxing it all up for me, as if packaging me out of your life was as easy as having a spring clean.'

'Do you really think any of this is easy for me?' Toni widened her eyes, horrified that might be what he actually thought. She'd spent so long pushing down how she felt and shoving him away, there was a good chance he really had no idea how exhausting it was for her, when all she wanted to do was give in to her feelings.

'I'm sorry, I didn't mean that. Look, can we go inside for a bit and talk? I can take my stuff with me afterwards, if you still want me to, but maybe there's another way, Tee. I just want us to consider every option before we give up on this, because I don't think I'll be able to make myself let go until we do.'

'If you're hoping for a cosy dinner for two, you're out of luck. The bread you just saved represents my dinner plans for tonight, but you're welcome to join me for Marmite on toast if you've really got nothing else to do.' She was still holding him at arm's length and silently praying at the same time that there was nowhere else he needed to be.

'There's no place I'd rather be, but make it peanut butter for me and we've got a deal.' Bobby gave her one of his slow smiles and whatever it was he was about to suggest to give them another chance, she hoped to God it could actually work. She'd live on toast for the rest of her life if Bobby was the one on the other side of table, and she'd never ask for another thing.

* * *

'That might actually be the best meal I've ever had!' Bobby sat back after he'd polished off the last thickly cut slice of toast and smiled in Toni's direction.

'Don't let your mother hear you talking like that, or she'll never speak to either of us again.' Whenever Toni pictured Bobby's mother, Joyce, she couldn't help smiling. It was probably because the other woman permanently had a smile on her face too. Although she might not if she thought her son preferred peanut butter on toast to all her culinary efforts.

'Maybe it's because I didn't have the chance to eat all day, after leading on my first home delivery.'

'Really? How did it go?' Toni couldn't help smiling again at the look that crossed Bobby's face. It was one of the other things that made him so different from Aaron, he understood their shared occupation like no one who hadn't done the job themselves ever really could. There were massive highs, heartbreaking lows sometimes, lots of bits that were challenging, and sheer relentless hard work. To be a midwife, it took more than just the desire to do the job; you had to live and breathe it to be really good at what you did, and she'd seen that in Bobby from the day she'd met him.

'It was brilliant! Jodie, the woman having the baby, could have done it all by herself, I'm sure. It made it easier on me that she was so calm and by the time the agency midwife, Susie, joined me for the final stage, she was almost ready to deliver. It was Jodie's first girl after four boys, and she'd promised her husband this was the last one, whatever happened. She just kept laughing and crying afterwards, and when she found out it was my first home delivery, she insisted on giving the baby the middle name of Roberta! Poor little thing.'

'I think it's a nice name, but you should have suggested Betty.' The words were out of Toni's mouth before she'd thought them through. It had been so nice just spending time with Bobby and talking about the day they'd had, like normal couples, but then she had to go and open her big mouth and bring up the fact that to be a part of her life he was forced to go by a code name. If it bothered him, though, he did a good job of hiding it.

'I think Roberta is more than enough to be going on with. Maybe I could suggest Betty next time around, tell them it's my nickname or something? If I keep pretending every home delivery is my first, I could end up with a whole generation of local kids named after me.' Bobby laughed. 'Although Susie was a bit put out; she said she's been doing home deliveries for more than twenty years and hasn't once had a baby named after her!'

'You should have told her it's all down to your good looks.' Flirting definitely didn't come naturally to Toni, but then she'd never had to learn. She'd known Aaron since they were babies, and she'd got close to Bobby through work. The only flirting she'd ever experienced was from the two men she'd briefly dated in the year before she met Bobby, and she was the one on the receiving end. The fact that she was standoffish, and showed almost zero interest in response, only seemed to encourage them. All of which meant she'd never picked up the art of subtle flirta-tion; she had two techniques – completely ignoring someone or just coming out and bluntly saying what it was she liked about them. Bobby was beautiful – the word was actually far more fitting for him than handsome – the way his long, dark lashes framed his eyes, and the wide generous mouth that got her every time he smiled. So she meant every word when she said the baby being named after him was due to his good looks. Poor old Susie had never even stood a chance.

'I think it was down to the fact that having named four other children, each of whom was given a middle name after one of the grandparents or great-grandparents, they were struggling a bit to find something equally meaningful. Plus, Susie didn't actually get there until the last knockings, so it was only fair really.' Bobby dropped a flawless wink. 'I was glad she turned up, though. Not so much for the delivery, because Jodie didn't really need either of us that much, but because we had a great chat afterwards and it was that that got me thinking about a possible solution to all of this stuff going on with us.'

'Did you tell her about us?' Goose pimples were already prickling Toni's skin. It was evidence enough that she'd never have been able to cheat on anyone. Keeping her life with Bobby a secret from her parents and Aaron's was bad enough. There was no way of knowing if someone like Susie knew them somehow and could end up mentioning what Bobby had told them. It would probably seem far-fetched to anyone else, but the Three Ports area that stretched along the Cornish Atlantic coast was a small world and she didn't want to take any chances.

'Don't worry, I didn't say anything about us. I just asked her about the agency she worked for and whether she enjoyed it, because it occurred to me that I could do that – leave the unit at Port Agnes and go freelance – and it might be a way of taking some of the pressure off us.'

'But you love the team at the unit, and they love you.' Toni knew she was being unreasonable, but she'd have been lying to herself and Bobby if she didn't admit that a big part of why she loved working there so much was down to him too. She also knew that him not working there would make it easier for them to split up, and what he said next did nothing to reassure her that the thought hadn't occurred to him too.

'I know and I'll miss everyone, but I think having to keep the pretence up at work, as well as with your family, is too much for both of us. We need a space where were can just be ourselves and maybe then we can eventually find a way to break it to your family too. But if we can't... not working together would make that a lot less difficult as well.'

'I told Aaron once that we needed some space to make sure that we wanted to be together.' Toni bit her lip. When she'd said those words to Aaron and planned to suggest a six-month break, she'd already been pulling away from him. If that was what Bobby was doing too she only had herself to blame, but he was reaching for her hand.

'I think this will give us our best shot and despite all the things I said before about not being able to keep waiting, I want to know I've done that. Otherwise, I don't think I'll ever get over you, Tee.'

'I don't want you to.' Looking him in the eyes, she suddenly felt naked, exposing the truth in a way she so rarely did, even with him. The vulnerability was uncomfortable, but not trying everything they could to find a solution was going to hurt a hell of a lot more. He was right, they had to try this or they were never going to move on. But the painful truth was that they'd have to draw the line somewhere and, if this didn't work, it had to be the end. For both their sakes.

* * *

When Bobby had suggested a trip further down the coast on their next day off together, Toni hadn't needed any persuasion. St Ives was big enough, busy enough and far enough from Port Agnes for no one to notice Bobby and Toni walking along together hand in hand, just like the hundreds of other couples wrapped up against the autumn breeze, wandering the pretty streets that led down to the wide, sandy bay and the expanse of turquoise sea beyond it.

They had lunch in a little restaurant with a view of the

harbour and when Bobby suggested a drive up to Land's End afterwards, Toni felt like a proper tourist taking a day trip with the man she loved, and she couldn't help looking at the faces of some of the other people walking along the headland towards the furthest point of the peninsula before you hit the Celtic Sea. How many of them were hiding secrets like she was and wishing that they didn't have to? Even as she tried to enjoy the moment with Bobby, the wind coming off the sea making her hair fly across her face as she clung on to his hand, there was part of her that was watching the time slip past like sand through an egg timer and longing for it not to be time to go home again or to be able to grab hold of Bobby's hand whenever she wanted to.

'I've loved it here ever since I was a kid.' Bobby wrapped an arm around her, pulling her close to his chest. 'There's something about looking out and just seeing endless open water that makes me feel like anything's possible. Anything could be over the horizon, any life we choose, we just need to be brave enough to head over there.'

'What do you mean, "over the horizon"?' Toni shivered, all at once longing to cling to the warmth that Bobby offered, but at the same time wanting to run in the other direction so that she didn't have to hear what he was about to say.

'When I started looking at other agencies, some overseas ones came up on the search and I contacted one in America, just to see whether working out there was a possibility.' He turned her to face him, with that same look of excitement he'd had on his face when he'd come to see her at the flat after his first home delivery. 'They said they'd love to have us work out there with them and they'll sort out all the visas and any training we'd need to do to transfer our qualifications. They'll even sort out some temporary accommodation until we find our feet.'

'We?' Toni was already shaking her head, but Bobby was doing his best to talk over any protests she might make.

'They're desperate for people with our skills and it could be a whole new start for us, Tee, somewhere that no one knows us and where we don't have to pretend we're only colleagues. You always said you wanted to see the world. This could be your chance – our chance – to make that happen and, more than that, to be together. Properly.'

'I can't leave, you know that; it would kill Judy if I went.'

'No, it wouldn't.' Bobby held her gaze for a long moment, as the same words she'd said to Aaron hung in the air between them. 'But it will kill us, our relationship, if we stay. Because I can't be around you and not with you, not when I know we could have a whole lifetime of days like today. It's not just about what that would do to me, watching you do that to yourself is even more unbearable. I'd go anywhere with you Tee, just so I can be with you, properly, but I can't stay here.'

'I know and I can't ask you to.' A single tear rolled down her cheek and she brushed it away with the back of her hand. There'd be hundreds more to come, she knew that, but right now she was almost glad of the wind stinging her eyes. She could blame the tears on that and try to hold herself together until she was on her own again. She'd been holding herself together for more than five years now, but it suddenly felt as if the last piece of her was unravelling and, without Bobby, she wasn't sure she wanted to put herself back together this time around.

6

'Are you feeling any better?' Toni greeted Anna as she walked into the staffroom; she might only have been four months pregnant, but she was already walking with the sort of gait that a penguin would be proud of.

'Since I started taking the supplements for anaemia it's been a bit better; I only feel like a wrung-out dishcloth about 90 per cent of the time now!'

'Well, you're looking much better than you were. Can I get you a drink, we've got plenty of caffeine-free tea and coffee?'

'Tea would be great thanks, but we'd better do a round of drinks, if you don't mind? I've asked Gwen and Jess to come in before they start home visits, and Bobby and Ella are going to come in too, before they start their clinics.'

'Is there a special occasion?' Toni and Anna were covering the delivery suite, and Jess and Gwen could be pulled off home visits for an unexpected home delivery, although none of the patients who'd requested a home birth were due that week or the next.

'I've got the new MCA, Emily, starting today, and Isabella, the midwife who's starting next month, has also said she'll pop in to meet everyone. I just want to get everything set up, in case I have to finish earlier than planned.'

'I better get the kettle on and open one of the six tins of biscuits that Tim Yorke dropped off to thank us for delivering Lydia's baby.'

'That sounds like a good plan, but remember I've got to have three times as many biscuits as anyone else, given I've got the twins on board!'

'I thought we always advised our ladies not to eat for two?' Toni grinned at the expression that crossed Anna's face.

'We do, but my new rule is that if you're carrying twins or more, then you can do whatever gets you through the day.'

Ten minutes later, the core of the day team had arrived at the unit to meet the new staff. There were other midwives and MCAs, who tended, for various reasons, to prefer covering the night shifts and so the team in the staffroom were those who Toni most often worked with. Ella's phone had pinged at least ten times already.

'Is someone trying to get hold of you?' Toni put a cup of tea in front of her as she spoke.

'Only Mum, she's lined up about twenty wedding venues she wants to go and look at. We're not even planning on having the wedding until the year after next, but Mum seems to think if we don't get it booked in now, we won't get anywhere we want.'

'Doesn't she know about your skills?' Anna grinned. It was only thanks to Ella's tenacity that Anna and Brae had managed to get married at all, after the hotel they'd booked their wedding at had been badly damaged in a fire the night before, along with Anna's dress, all the bridesmaids' dresses, the cake and even the flowers. They'd ended up getting married on the Sisters of Agnes Island, in an old chapel that was part of the former convent and had fallen into disrepair. It was due to be renovated before any weddings were supposed to have taken place there, but fate clearly had other ideas. Ella's fiancé, Dan, and Anna's husband, Brae, had pulled off a minor miracle in securing the venue. It had been Ella who'd sorted the dresses, the cake, the flowers and some of the catering, though, and the night had been finished off with fish and chips from Brae's shop. All of the midwives had pulled together to give Anna the day she deserved and so if anyone could sort a last-minute wedding out, it was Ella. She certainly had form.

'If you want a particular venue, even booking it two years before might not be early enough.' Jess took her cup of tea from Toni's tray. 'Just don't get married where I did, it's unlucky! Although I'm feeling more and more like I had a lucky escape.'

'How are things progressing with the fostering?' Toni put the tray down as she waited for her friend to answer.

'I've started to have social worker visits to complete the assessment. I've got some more training coming up too, which is always really interesting, but a bit nerve-wracking at the same time, because whenever I'm at one of these things, I know they're judging me and deciding whether they think I'm up to the job.'

'You'll be brilliant and doing respite to start off with will give you a really good idea of whether you want to look at other types of fostering eventually.' Anna smiled. 'It also means you won't be leaving us any time soon.'

'Yes, and definitely don't give my job away any time soon, either! I've got to get approved first and they could easily turn around and say no.' Jess had applied to be a respite foster carer at weekends when she wasn't working, and in pre-planned holiday periods from work, with a view to longer-term fostering at some point in the future. That would mean giving up work, though, and Toni knew how big a decision that would be. She had nothing but admiration for her friend, even if she couldn't bear the thought of Jess leaving the unit, especially not now that Bobby had decided to leave. As far as she knew, he hadn't told any of the others yet and it wasn't her place to either, but she was definitely going to need all her friends around her if he went through with it. The silence in the car on the way back from Land's End had been painful. They both knew it was over this time, their last option for making it work exhausted, and now it was just a matter of time until she had to say goodbye. She wasn't sure she'd survive saying goodbye to Jess as well; everything was changing and there was nothing she could do to stop it.

'They won't say no, and we definitely want to hang on to you for as long as possible. We need you.' It wasn't like Toni to say anything so deep and meaningful, and the words surprised her as much as anyone else when they came out of her mouth. But just lately her emotions appeared to be much closer to the surface and there didn't seem to be anything she could do about that, so she'd just have to try and cover it up by making a joke of it. 'I mean Anna's already leaving us and it'll be Ella next. Plus Gwen's been threatening to retire. I don't want to be the last of the old gang still standing.'

'What about Bobby?' Jess raised an eyebrow. He'd gone down to reception with Gwen to collect the new team members and bring them up to the staff room.

'He's not part of the *original* team.' Toni kept her voice deadpan. If they said anything else there was a danger of her blurting out that Bobby was threatening to leave too and, if she did that, there was an even bigger risk of her bursting into tears.

'He was here before I was!' Ella had hit on an unfortunate truth and Toni was having to bite down hard on her lip. Bobby was part of the fabric of the unit and everyone knew it.

'Me too.' Jess wrinkled her nose.

'But he was an MCA then, not a midwife.'

'Don't let the new MCA hear you saying that. We're all one team.' Anna's tone was gentle, despite her warning. 'And if Frankie wasn't still over in New Zealand, she'd be reminding you exactly how vital our MCAs are!'

'I'd never argue against that.' Toni was digging herself a hole, trying to justify saying something there was no justification for, other than wanting to bury her feelings for Bobby for the millionth time. Maybe if she changed the subject they could stop talking about him and there was a chance she could hold it all in. 'Speaking of Frankie, when's she due back?'

'Given that she was only supposed to be going for a month and she's already been gone for six *and* missed my wedding, I'm starting to wonder! She's promised to come back before these two arrive, she just wants to make sure her daughter's properly back on her feet. I think everything that happened was a shock and it was just lucky Frankie was out there at the time. But I'm going to need as much advice as I can get on how to handle the twins.' Anna rubbed her stomach. Frankie had been an MCA at the unit since it had opened, but she'd gone to New Zealand to visit her daughter after her own marriage had broken down – and then her daughter's marriage had gone the same way almost as soon as she arrived. It meant her stay kept getting extended and Toni had only been half joking when she'd talked about being the last one standing.

'And this is the staffroom.' Gwen made the announcement as she walked in ahead of Bobby and the two new team members.

'Ah brilliant, it's great to see you both!' Anna got to her feet as the others came into the room. 'I wanted everyone from the day team to be here when you arrived. 'Everyone, this is Emily, our new permanent MCA, and Isabella, who's joining the midwifery team next month.'

'Hi, I'm Ella, and this is Jess, and Toni.' Ella gestured towards each of them in turn. 'We're all midwives on the day team. As I'm sure Anna told you, we've got a couple of agency MCAs covering the role at the moment, but we're hoping Frankie, our most experienced MCA, will be back soon, and we're looking to make another permanent appointment in the not too distant future as well.'

'Yes, Anna explained that there are a lot of changes coming.' Emily smiled and Toni suddenly wished she was standing next to almost anyone else. The new MCA looked like she was only in her early twenties and was naturally pretty and petite, like Jess, making Toni feel like an old cart horse standing between the two of them. 'It's so lovely to meet you all.'

'It really is.' Isabella, who was standing next to Gwen, stepped forward. 'I know I'm not starting for a few weeks, but it's lovely to come in at the same time as Emily to meet you all and not feel like the only new girl on the first day of school. Everyone usually calls me Izzy and I'll know I'm in trouble if you opt for Isabella!'

'Izzy it is then. We're really excited to have you both joining us.' Anna smiled again. 'And the reason I wanted Gwen and Bobby to come down and meet you, is because they're going to be your mentors. There's no one as experienced as Gwen when it comes to midwifery, and Bobby was an MCA before starting his midwifery training, which I know is something you're interested in Emily?'

'Absolutely! Lucky me to get Bobby to show me the ropes and hopefully I can follow in his footsteps.' Emily's laugh had a sort of tinkle that most people would probably consider charming, but Toni was already finding it really irritating.

'You might think you've got the short end of the stick, Izzy,' Gwen gave the new midwife a bit of a nudge, 'but I've looked up more vaginas than you've had hot dinners, so there's nothing I haven't seen.'

'Exactly.' Anna grinned at Izzy. 'I think I've found the perfect match for both of you.'

'It's definitely the perfect match for me.' Emily was actually looking at Bobby through her eyelashes now and, when he favoured her with one of his beautiful smiles, it was all Toni could do not to launch herself across the staffroom and wipe the stupid look off the younger woman's face. The worst thing was, Emily and Bobby really did look like the perfect match and, even if he thought so too, Toni had absolutely no right to pass comment on it any more. It almost made her thankful for the prospect of him leaving, because not even Toni could keep up the act of pretending she didn't care if she had to stand by and watch him move on with someone else.

The cemetery at St Jude's church had gravestones that were over four hundred years old and these days there wasn't much space left at all. It was what Reverend Sampson had told Toni and Judy when they'd gone to see him to talk about Aaron's funeral. Whether it had been Judy's hysterical sobbing that had made him change his mind, or Toni's stoic pleas that at least this way Aaron would still be able to glimpse the sea at Port Agnes, the same way he'd been able to do from their flat, she'd never know.

The church at Port Tremellien might have seemed the obvious place, seeing as it was where he'd grown up, but the church in Port Agnes was where Judy had been determined to hold their wedding and so St Jude's was the natural choice. They'd secured a spot for Aaron in a quiet corner of the church-yard, under a horse chestnut tree, which had beautiful flowers in late spring, shade in the height of summer, and which was currently depositing shiny conkers and their spiky casings on the ground all around Aaron's grave. If he'd still been alive, he'd definitely have been collecting them, even at thirty-five years old. She could still remember the conker fights he'd arranged at school, the undefeated champion of the playground. Maybe they'd even have had their own kids by now, if things had been different, kids he could have taught his overarm swing to. Or maybe they wouldn't have made it that far. That was one of the hardest parts, not knowing if things would have ended up being perfect, or a disaster. But she couldn't imagine ever having got to a point where she'd choose not to have Aaron in her life in some shape or form; even if things hadn't worked out romantically, she was certain they'd have found a way to stay best friends. He'd always been around to pour her heart out to and now she needed him more than ever.

'Hello you.' Toni brushed a hand along the top of the headstone as she reached Aaron's grave. 'What have you been up to? Is there much going on up there, wherever it is you hang out these days?'

Toni wasn't even sure if she believed in an 'up there' of any sort, but if there was one, then Aaron would definitely have a prime spot.

'What's going on with me?' Toni had become so used to the one-sided conversations over the years, she could almost hear Aaron's voice. 'Well, you know Bobby, right? I've told you about him lots of times before.'

She jumped as a leaf fluttered down in front of her eyes. It was just autumn making way for winter that was all, not a sign that Aaron was actually there – somewhere – listening to everything she was saying, and dropping leaves into her line of sight so she'd know it was true. She spoke to Aaron as a way of getting her thoughts in order, processing things and making sense of it, that was all.

'Well, he's finally had enough of sneaking around and keeping things a secret. At first, I think he quite liked it, you know, keeping things just between us. Maybe it was like the thrill people get when they have an affair.'

When she'd first started telling Aaron about Bobby it had felt weird, sharing her relationship problems with her fiancé, but he'd always been her closest friend too and there was no one else she could turn to. Not when she had to pretend to the rest of her friends that she and Bobby weren't even a thing.

'And now there's this new girl at work, Emily.' Toni was vaguely aware that she was saying Emily's name with the same sort of contempt that most people usually reserved for describing tax returns, or someone else's cat doing its business in their back garden. 'She's all over him like a rash and absolutely thrilled that he's her mentor, batting her eyelashes at him and simpering like feminism isn't even a thing.'

She stared at Aaron's shiny black headstone again, the dash between the two dates marking a far shorter time span than it ever should have been.

'How did Bobby react? He just smiled and yes, I know, I haven't got any right to even comment on what they do or don't do now, but it bothers me, Aaron. Okay? It bothers me! And you're the only one I can tell.'

Looking at the gravestone, she tried to imagine what Aaron would say if he was there, but the trouble was she already knew. She'd always known. He wouldn't want her to live her life the way she was, still engaged to a ghost. He'd tell her to grab the life he'd never had the chance to live and to tell Bobby how she really felt. But then Aaron hadn't been there to see his parents' distress when he'd died. He hadn't heard his mother say that the only thing keeping her going was the fact that they'd never lose Toni, or those memories of Aaron and Toni together, unsullied by anything else. So how could she expect Aaron to understand? This time, not even he could help.

'You need a haircut.' Toni took a pair of scissors out of her handbag. The edges of grass around Aaron's grave always seemed to get missed by the church mower and there was something strangely intimate about taking out the scissors and cutting the blades of grass by hand – as if she could still show him how much she cared for him in some tiny way. It was therapeutic too, snipping away at them until they looked perfect. They'd grow back again, probably by the next time she visited, when the grass would look scruffy and unkempt until she neatened it up again. Whatever happened between her and Bobby, life would go on, the grass would keep growing and the world would keep turning. She'd just have to find a way to keep going too, without Bobby in her life. At least she'd always have Aaron, and if that was as much a curse as a blessing, she'd just have to keep living with that too.

7

'Thanks so much for coming over to help out with the decorations. I'm not sure whose stupid idea it was to have a Halloween party at almost five months pregnant with twins!' Anna looked from Bobby to Brae and back again.

'A Penrose Halloween party is a new Port Agnes tradition.' Brae shrugged. 'And when we've got access to the sort of muscle Bobby can provide, we'd be stupid not to accept it.'

'If I didn't know you better, I'd think it was you enjoying having all that muscle around.' Anna was teasing her husband and Bobby couldn't help smiling too. They were such a great couple, able to laugh with one another and tease each other, but they always had each other's backs. Anna and Brae belonged together and, even though they hadn't been a couple all that long, he couldn't imagine one without the other. He and Toni had been seeing each other for longer than Anna and Brae, but in that time their friends had got married and now they were expecting not one, but two babies to make their family complete.

What had he and Toni done in all that time? There'd been plenty of nights hidden away in her apartment, and even a few in the little studio flat he hadn't really been able to afford when he was still an MCA, but he'd wanted somewhere he could cook her dinner and not feel like he was a guest in Aaron's home. He'd thought that qualifying as a midwife would change things and that maybe then Toni would finally relax her attempts to keep their relationship secret. The idea that she might be ashamed of dating him because of his job was a depressing one, but at least there was something he could do to fix that. The reality of why she wanted to keep things secret had nothing to do with his job, but it also meant the reason she wanted to keep their relationship under wraps was completely out of his control. Not being able to do a single thing about it was far more depressing than thinking Toni might just be a bit of a snob.

'I'm more than happy to help out with the decorations and Emily's cooking enough to feed the whole of Port Agnes from what she's told me.'

'She's certainly doing her best to integrate with the team, isn't she? She must have brought something in for you almost every day.' Anna gave Bobby a knowing look. 'She's giving Gwen a run for her money in the baking stakes, but I get the sense that not everyone is quite as keen on her.'

'She's lovely, but I suppose she can seem a bit full-on until you get to know her.' Emily was certainly confident; she hadn't hesitated for a second when she'd asked Bobby if he wanted to go out for a drink with her one night after work. He'd been the one left stumbling over his words and trying to come up with an excuse that didn't sound as lame as it felt. He didn't owe Toni anything. What they'd had – whatever that had even been – was over, she'd made that perfectly clear after their trip to Land's End. He'd been prepared to give up everything to be with her and start again thousands of miles away, but Toni hadn't even needed to think that idea over. Now he had no idea what he was supposed to do. The offer to take the job in the States was still on the table and Susie, the midwife from the agency, had said she could get him in there straight away if he wanted to stay local. The sensible thing to do would be to decide which of the offers he wanted to go for and get away from the Port Agnes midwifery unit as soon as he could. The trouble was, he still loved Toni and he couldn't just turn that off, no matter how much he might want to. It would be so much easier not to love her and, God knew, sometimes she made it hard.

'Emily's really enthusiastic. Anyone who can be as upbeat as she is after a shift definitely has what it takes to be a midwife.' Anna gave him a level look. 'What do you think of her? Would you be interested in getting involved?'

'She's nice, but I'm really not looking for that sort of thing, especially with someone I work with. Far too many complications.'

'Sorry! I meant what do you think of her plans to follow your example and apply for a midwifery degree? Would you be interested in getting involved in supporting her application, as her mentor?' Anna raised her eyebrows and she looked as if she was trying not to laugh.

'Oh, yeah, I think so, I mean, I haven't seen any reason why not.' Bobby couldn't remember blushing since he'd been about fifteen, when Daisy Ryan had told him he had sexy arms. But right then, if the ground had opened up and swallowed him, he'd have considered it a merciful act of God.

'We can review it at the end of her probation and if you still think she'd be a good candidate, we can put her forward.'

'Sounds like a plan.' Bobby gestured towards the string of Halloween decorations, made from black metallic skulls. 'But shall we stop boring poor old Brae with all this shop talk and get some of these decorations hung up?'

'We better had, because I need to supervise the pair of you and it's been a least ten minutes since I last needed a wee, so I probably haven't got long left before the next visit.' Anna shrugged. 'Just one of the joys of a twin pregnancy!'

'I don't know how you do it, Bobby.' Brae dropped a wink in his direction. 'Worrying about one pregnancy is stressful enough for me, but you do it day in and day out.'

'It's a brilliant job, but it's different when you can leave it at the door and go home at night. I count myself lucky to do the job I do every day, though.' Bobby stepped up onto the chair to secure his end of the string. It was true, he wouldn't swap his job for the world. But what he couldn't bring himself to tell Brae – or anyone else for that matter – was that he'd give anything to have what Brae and Anna had. But if he didn't find a way of getting over Toni, he was *never* going to have the chance of that. Maybe it was time to stop making excuses and go on a date with Emily, or at least reply to the emails from Susie and the job offer in America and let them know he was thinking them both over. He had to start somewhere, after all.

* * *

'Can I get you some punch?' Emily was wearing an animal print catsuit and the only thing that was scary about it was how little it left to the imagination. Toni could begrudgingly admit that, if she'd had a figure like Emily's at her age, she might have been tempted to wear the same thing. But she'd always been solid – even at her thinnest, in the wake of losing Aaron, when trying to eat just the tiniest morsel of food had felt like she was swallowing a boulder.

'I can't drink, I'm on call with Ella in case there are any more home deliveries.' Two of the team who usually covered nights were already out on a call to a home birth, so Toni and Ella were on standby in case a second woman went into labour.

'No problem. Brae's briefed me about all the soft drinks on offer, so I can just pop to the kitchen and get you something fizzy, or some fruit juice. What would you like, apple, orange, pineapple or mango?' Emily had the sort of energy and tone of voice that Toni would have expected from a children's TV presenter. If it was wrong to feel an urge to flick the end of her perfect little upturned nose every now and then, Toni couldn't help it. Deep down she knew her resentment of Emily had nothing to do with her personally and everything to do with the fact that she seemed capable of flirting up a storm with Bobby without even trying. Toni had tried holding eye contact with him when she'd spotted him earlier, just to see what his reaction would be, but she'd ended up with watery eyes and had made herself sneeze. By the time her vision had cleared again, Bobby had disappeared completely.

'Apple, thanks.' She didn't even want a drink really, but anything to get rid of Emily for five minutes. Every time she looked at her, she couldn't help picturing Bobby and Emily together, as if they were already a couple.

'What about you two?' Emily turned towards Ella and Dan, who, like Toni, were dressed in Ghostbusters' boiler suits. She and Ella had decided it would be the easiest thing to whip out of if they ended up being called out, but it made her feel like more of a third wheel than ever. Most of the couples were dressed in a joint theme, but there she was, hitching her wagon to Ella and Dan's, and feeling completely unlovable as a result.

'Punch for me please, Emily.' Dan smiled.

'And I'll have some mango juice please.' Ella touched the younger woman's arm. 'If you're sure you don't mind running around after us. You don't have to wait on everyone.'

'Anna's feeling more exhausted than ever.' Emily held up her palms. 'And she's been so lovely to me since I started at the unit, you all have, so it's the least I can do. I'll go and get the drinks now. I'll just check on the way whether the Bobster wants anything.'

'*The Bobster*?' Toni waited until Emily was out of earshot to repeat the word, unable to stop herself from rolling her eyes at the same time, as Anna came over to join them.

'She started calling him that a couple of days ago.' Ella wrinkled her nose. 'I'm not sure he's that keen on it though.'

'Sounds like a term of affection to me.' Dan shrugged and Toni didn't miss the look that Ella and Anna exchanged.

'She's just a friendly sort of person.' Anna kept her tone casual. 'And she's been brilliant tonight, helping out. My back's been killing me all day, but even if it hadn't been, between her and Bobby, they've hardly let me and Brae lift a finger. She cooked almost half the food in the buffet; everyone should have an Emily.'

'It looks like Bobby might have already staked his claim.' Dan was looking across the room and Toni followed his gaze – taking a deep breath as she caught sight of Bobby and Emily standing just inches apart. She was leaning into him, whispering something in his ear, and for a moment the world seemed to stop. All Toni could see was the man she loved talking to a woman who could no doubt snap her fingers and make any guy run in her direction. She probably couldn't have stopped what was unfolding in front of her eyes, but the worst part was that she couldn't even try.

'Can you hear me, Toni? Is that your phone ringing?' Ella actually had to shake her arm to get her attention.

'Oh, yeah, right, it is.' Grabbing her phone, she hit the answer button. 'Hello, Toni Samuels speaking, Port Agnes midwifery unit.'

'It's Annie White. I'm sorry to call you, I'm not sure if this is even real labour, but the pains I'm having in my back certainly feel like the real thing.'

'No problem at all, I'll be straight over to check you out. It should only take me about ten minutes. See you soon.' Toni had been out to see Annie several times before, so she knew the address without even asking.

'I take it that was the call-out we were hoping to avoid?' Ella looked at Toni after she'd ended the call.

'It was Annie White, but she's not even sure it's actually labour, so you don't need to come with me. I'll go over and see how she's getting on and I'll call you if I need you.'

'Are you sure?'

'Definitely, there's no point both of us leaving the party early.' Toni was absolutely certain and she'd never been happier to get a call-out in her life. If Bobby was about to move on with Emily, she didn't want to be around to see it. Just the thought of it made her feel nauseous and despite all the years of practice at hiding how she felt, this was one time Toni wasn't sure she'd be able to pull it off. She was only human after all.

8

Jess had managed to get the first Monday after the Halloween party off to attend some more pre-approval training with the local authority, after Ella had offered to step in and cover her clinics. She'd been due to spend the morning seeing some of the unit's expectant mothers for routine check-ups, and the afternoon running a healthy eating workshop for women who were struggling with too much or too little weight gain during pregnancy. But when someone had dropped out of the training course the local authority was offering and Jess had the chance to attend, Ella and Anna had insisted she didn't miss it

'Thanks so much again for taking over my clinics, how did they go?' Jess had called Ella straight after the training to make sure nothing had happened to cause Ella more work.

'They were absolutely fine, although Faith Baxter came in and she was a bit agitated when she realised she wasn't going to get to see you.'

'Were all her checks okay, though?' The skin on the back of Jess's neck prickled. Faith Baxter was more than halfway through her second pregnancy, a few weeks ahead of Anna, but her first pregnancy had ended in tragedy, after she noticed a drop in movements just two weeks before the baby's due date. Faith had been living in Truro, but by the time she'd seen the midwife to get the baby checked, it was already too late. Baby Archie was stillborn at thirty-eight weeks, apparently looking perfect in every way. Unbeknown to Faith, her placenta had failed and Archie just hadn't got the blood supply he needed to survive. It was no wonder her second pregnancy was proving terrifying rather than exciting, and Jess had offered Faith as many appointments as she felt she needed to manage the panic that often threatened to overwhelm her. Jess hated the thought that her not being there for clinic had caused Faith even more distress.

'Her checks were fine, and I've booked her in to see you again the day after tomorrow.' Ella laughed. 'I don't think she believed a word I said, but she certainly seems to have confidence in you.'

'She'd have been the same with you if you'd been the first midwife at the unit to see her. I'll have to make sure Anna keeps her on my list if I actually get through the foster panel and drop my hours before Faith has the baby.'

'If they've got any sense the foster panel will sign you up in a heartbeat. What are you doing tonight?'

'I think I might drop in to see Faith on the way home.' Jess could picture Ella screwing up her face even before she heard the sigh. 'I know you're going to tell me that I'm not on duty, but I want to take the coast road back from Port Kara anyway and I'll have to drive straight past Faith's door if I go that way.' It wasn't an excuse; nothing cheered her up more than the sight of the lights on the Sisters of Agnes Island, twinkling out at sea as she drove back down into the village. It was when she knew she was home.

'Nothing I say is going to make you change your mind anyway, is it?'

'Probably not.' Jess laughed. 'I'll see you in the morning and breakfast is on me, to say thanks for covering for me today.'

'I'm supposed to be starting a diet so I can eat what I want over Christmas, but I might just let you twist my arm! See you in the morning.'

* * *

'How are you?' Jess smiled up at Faith as she walked through the door of her consulting room, one hand cradling her bump protectively as she always seemed to do. It had been less than forty-eight hours since Jess had dropped in to check on Faith, but she was obviously on edge, her right foot tapping repeatedly against the laminate flooring as soon as she'd taken a seat.

'I had a panic attack in the baby department of Marks and Spencer yesterday.'

'What happened?' If it had been a full-blown panic attack, it would be new territory for Faith and a sign that her anxiety was ramping up to the next level.

'I felt as if I couldn't breathe, and the rails of clothing seemed to be moving closer together and closing in on me. I knew if I didn't sit down, I'd pass out. And by the time the first aider got there, I'd convinced myself I was having a heart attack – that's how bad the pains in my chest were. Thankfully she realised it was a panic attack and managed to talk me down to a point where I could breathe again. But I'm terrified if I go out now that it's going to happen again.'

'I can imagine how scary that felt, but the most important thing is to try and find a way to stop you worrying about it happening all the time. The best way of doing that is probably to work out why it happened in the first place.' Jess kept her voice even, doing her best to sound like one of those voice-overs on the mindfulness apps she sometimes used – calm and melodic, with ocean sounds playing in the background. 'Can you think of anything that might have triggered it?'

'I was looking at the baby clothes, but I couldn't bring myself to actually pick up an outfit, let alone take it to the till. I bought loads of stuff last time, but Archie never got to wear any of those clothes. I couldn't bear to look at them afterwards, so Michael took them all to a charity shop. But there was an outfit on one of the rails yesterday that looked exactly like the one I'd picked out for when I brought Archie home from the hospital. In the end it was the only outfit he ever wore.'

'Oh Faith, that must have been so hard.' Jess was fighting to keep her own emotions in and she had no idea how Faith was holding it together at all. Discovering she might never have a baby of her own had been devastating for Jess, but what Faith had lost was so much worse than that. She might have had the chance to see Archie's face and hold him in her arms, but she'd never got the chance to take him home. Now Faith was terrified the same thing was going to happen all over again.

'I just wish I could control the way I feel, because it can't be good for the baby when I get like that. I don't want to let this one down the way I let Archie down.'

'What happened to Archie wasn't your fault. We're monitoring you really closely and if your placenta starts to fail this time, we'll be able to pick up on it and do something about it. But I think it's important to make you feel as in control as possible.'

'You're going to suggest I make a birth plan again, aren't you?'

'I know you're a bit reluctant, but I really think it would help. If you don't want to go through it with me, maybe it's something we could get your therapist to help you with?' Jess had got Faith a referral to a therapist early on in her pregnancy and she'd been having CBT sessions at least once a week to try to help her visualise a positive outcome for her pregnancy.

'I had everything planned out with Archie and not one thing in my birth plan turned out how I wanted it to. I'm just trying to do everything differently this time.'

'I understand that, I really do, and there are ways to do it differently, but still make your preferences clear. Rather than writing down exactly what you want to happen and then feeling even more stressed when it doesn't, why don't we make a list of the things you definitely *don't* want? Like not having the staff talk to Michael instead of you, so you know what's going on the whole time, and not being in the same delivery suite at the hospital. I know that's important to you.'

'I think I could work with that.' Faith smiled for the first time. 'I just hope when the baby finally gets here that I'll actually be able to enjoy being a mum, instead of wishing I could change what happened.'

'You might not think so, Faith, but you're doing really well, and I promise I'll be here for you every step of the way.'

'You've been amazing, and I know I've had far more appointments with you than I should have done.'

'Not at all, I'm happy to see you as often as you need. Now shall we have a little listen to baby?' Jess helped Faith onto the examination table so that she could carry out the necessary checks. But she couldn't shake the feeling that Faith wasn't the only one who needed to start letting go of the past. She'd been separated from Dom for almost exactly a year now, so maybe it was time Jess made a plan of her own and pushed ahead with divorce as soon as possible.

* * *

Aaron had liked to joke about being Toni's toy boy, when the truth was he'd been born just twelve hours after her. It had meant a lifetime of joint parties, growing up living next door to one another and with mothers who'd developed a bond when they were babies that couldn't be broken. Both families had only wanted one child, a decision that cemented their parents' friendship. Toni's mother had told her once that they'd been determined to stay close so that Aaron and Toni would always have one another, because they didn't have siblings, but that she'd never really dared dream they might end up together. It was weird because to Toni it had always felt like an expectation, rather than a distant dream.

The joint parties they'd had growing up had been the source of the biggest rows she and Aaron had ever had, most of them before they'd even reached the age of ten. One year Toni had wanted a Ninja Turtles theme, but Aaron had wanted the Flintstones, for some reason that she'd never quite been able to fathom. They'd actually come to blows over it and they really had bickered like siblings for a long time. It was a game of truth or dare that had finally changed things, at the birthday party they'd had when they'd become teenagers. A party they'd involved their parents in as little as possible. Illicit bottles of horribly cheap cider that one of their friends had snuck in, had resulted in both of them having their first ever taste of alcohol. It had only taken a few sips – which was more than enough when it tasted as bad as it did – and an empty bottle spun in Aaron's direction to be the catalyst. He'd kissed Toni, as a dare, to avoid telling the truth to his group of mates about who it was he fancied. It was only later, when they were on their own again, that he'd admitted his truth would have featured Toni too. She'd never thought of him that way, until he'd kissed her, and there was no going back after that. That kiss had changed everything for both of them.

Even after five years it felt really weird to have a birthday cake that didn't have two sets of candles on. There'd have been two threes, and two sixes, to mark their joint thirty-sixth birthday if Aaron had still been around. Judy would have made his favourite dinner of lasagne, but he'd have let Toni pick every other part of the day. After they'd got together, there'd been no more arguments about the choice of birthday theme. '*Whatever makes you happy*' had been Aaron's stock phrase and sometimes she'd pushed it to the limit, just to test out if he really meant what he said. Even when she'd pretended she wanted to spend their twenty-first trawling around a designer outlet centre, he'd gone along with the idea. Although he'd definitely known her well enough to know it was her idea of hell too. They'd ended up going on a seal spotting boat trip instead and, even though most twenty-one-year-olds would probably have thought it was terminally boring, they'd loved every minute.

It was still her favourite birthday memory; they'd had a meal with their family afterwards, and a night out with friends the day after. The Crab and Winkle pub in Port Tremellien was hardly a week clubbing in Ibiza, but it had been more than enough for Toni. Maybe they should have been more adventurous and had those holidays and rites of passage you were supposed to have in your late teens and early twenties, but they'd always been so focussed on saving for their six-month around-the-world trip. When his mother's health had meant the trip was cancelled, they'd fast forwarded into a life of mortgages and eventually decisions about where to have their wedding list. They should have grabbed every chance when they'd had it and saving so hard for a day that had never come – instead of just enjoying the moment more – was something she'd always regret, for Aaron's sake.

Some regrets were all the more poignant once he died. Had they been too comfortable? Holding each other back and settling for what they already had, instead of looking for more? It wasn't a question she'd been equipped to answer back then and she'd really believed that six months away from each other would have told them all they needed to know, but the truth was she still had no idea now.

'Happy birthday.' Toni reached out to touch the headstone that marked Aaron's grave, in the way she always did when she came to see him. 'How did we get this old? I've started to wake up with backache in the mornings. Although I suppose you're forever thirty.'

Judy and Simon had obviously been to visit already. There were fresh flowers in the vase in front of the gravestone and a card, still in the envelope, was wedged behind it. For a few moments Toni wasn't sure whether she should open it. It felt intrusive somehow, but if Aaron had still been alive she'd have read the card, so why not now?

Happy birthday darling Aaron,

Another birthday without you is hard, but then every day without you is hard. We miss you and love you as much as ever. Toni keeps us going, we don't know what we'd do without her. Sharing her birthday makes it feel like you are still with us too and each year brings us a year closer to being with you again.

All our love, as always, Mum and Dad xxxx

The card didn't say anything Toni hadn't expected it to. Judy had told her before that sharing the day with her was the only thing that made it bearable. She'd never had the chance to spend it with friends, or even just by herself somewhere, trying to pretend the day didn't belong to Aaron much more than it did to her now. Instead, she painted on a smile for everyone else and, even when Bobby had begged her, the year before, to spend at least part of the day with him, she'd told him she couldn't.

It wasn't even true. There'd have been plenty of opportunity to grab an hour or two with him if she'd wanted to, even in amongst Judy's plans, but it would have felt more than ever like she was cheating. Not on Aaron, she'd already told him all about Bobby as soon as things between them had started to progress, or at least she'd said the words out loud at his graveside. No, it was his parents, and hers, who had no idea about Bobby's existence and now they had no reason to ever know. Emily would be a much better fit for Bobby; she almost certainly didn't have the kind of problems Toni had loaded onto him. He deserved someone like Emily and just because the thought of what might be developing between them had left Toni with a now almost permanent feeling of nausea, that didn't make it any less true.

When Aaron had first died, she'd barely been able to function, and Judy had been the only other person who seemed to understand. Neither of them could eat or sleep much at all and the only time Toni ever felt a sense of calm was when she was with Aaron's mother. They could talk about him into the early hours of the morning and rake over and over the same ground, going through what had happened in the run up to his death, without either of them ever losing patience with the other.

Toni must have asked her a thousand times in those early days whether Judy thought she could have done anything differently to stop things turning out the way they had, but Judy had never tired of reassuring her that she wasn't to blame. She'd asked Toni just as many times whether she thought Aaron had known just how much his mother had loved him. It had been easy for Toni to offer reassurances. Judy's love might have been overwhelming at times, but it had never been in doubt.

It meant they'd formed a sort of co-dependent relationship,

which had just heightened Toni's determination to be there for Aaron's mother. She'd needed Judy's support to stop herself being eaten alive with guilt and it was Judy who'd encouraged Toni to apply for the job at the Port Agnes midwifery unit, six months after Aaron had died. Without Judy, she wasn't sure if she'd ever have been able to stop going over that last conversation with Aaron, as if she could somehow change the things she'd said if she thought about it often enough. Making the promise to Aaron to look after his mother, whatever the personal cost to Toni, went some way to assuaging her guilt, but the truth was she'd needed Judy's reassurances every bit as much as Judy had needed hers. It was a bond that doubled back on itself, even if after five years it sometimes felt like a stranglehold.

'I've bought you a present.' Toni pulled the pickled onion flavour bag of Monster Munch out of her bag. They'd always been Aaron's favourite and, whatever else she'd bought him over the years they'd been together, there'd always been a packet of Monster Munch tucked into one of the present bags. If anyone had been around to see her scatter the crisps on his grave it would probably have looked really weird. Although she'd seen another mourner pouring beer on a grave once and there were all sorts of tributes left by the headstones of Aaron's neighbours in his corner of the churchyard.

'And don't worry, I'll eat your portion of lasagne for you, although I'm starting to get middle-aged spread, as well as a bad back. I was hoping to get to at least fifty before that happened.' She could still tell Aaron anything and, just lately, it seemed there were even more things she'd only shared with him than there had been when he'd been alive.

'I'm going to have to get going in a minute, otherwise your mum will start to worry, and you know what she's like when she worries, especially since... well, you know.' Toni touched the headstone again. 'Love you lots and I'll forgive you for not wishing me a happy birthday too. I know you would if you could.'

Toni was lucky, she knew she was. There must have been thousands of people out there who didn't receive a single good wish on their birthday. And she was always overwhelmed; Judy, Simon and her own parents always made a fuss, then there were her friends from the midwifery unit, not to mention a few old school friends and one or two from university who still remembered her every year. Bobby had sent her flowers too, with a note telling her he missed her. He'd been right, though, when he'd said that starting over afresh, somewhere else, had been their final chance. But she'd blown it once again.

Telling her he missed her was like a slither of light filtering through a gap in the door and, if she pushed on it, they'd be right back where they were. It would have been so easy and every time she saw him face-to-face, her resolve to set him free crumbled. One of them needed to start afresh and if she had to push him away more firmly than she ever had, this time she was determined to do it. Regretting waiting for a day that had never come with Aaron had already burdened her with guilt, she wasn't going to be responsible for doing the same thing to Bobby. It might have been the actions of a coward, but it was so much easier by text.

Thank you for the flowers, but I think we both know it's time to move on and that job in America could be perfect for you. If you don't take it, maybe I should leave the unit instead. One of us needs to pull the plug for good.

She could have written a lot more, but she'd read an article recently that said only 'old people' sent text messages that were more than a few lines long and she couldn't bring herself to tell him the truth either way. If she'd said what she wanted to say, she'd have told Bobby that she missed him too, but that more than anything she wanted him to be happy, even if that meant she never could be. Not without him.

* * *

Toni had kept her word to Aaron and eaten enough lasagne for both of them. If she was going to end up on her own anyway, it didn't matter if middle-aged spread had hit her almost fifteen years earlier than she'd anticipated. At this rate, it wouldn't be long before she was having to tuck her spare rolls into pants the size of a pillowcase. That still didn't mean she could face cake straight away, though, not after two portions of Judy's lasagne. Luckily Aaron's mother seemed to have read her mind.

'I thought we could go through to the lounge for a bit and look at some old photos?' It was a rhetorical question and her parents were already heading out of the dining room, with Simon and Judy close behind them. For a split second Toni wondered what they'd all do if she didn't follow. Would they even notice? But she didn't put it to the test. Instead, she followed them into the lounge, where two huge silver metallic balloons in the shape of a three and six bobbed gently in the centre of the room. And both sets of parents were already poring over the photographs spread out across the coffee table.

'Look at this photo Mandy, can you believe that was thirty-six years ago?' Judy slid a photograph towards Toni's mother. 'Although strictly speaking it was taken thirty-six years ago tomorrow, as Aaron didn't arrive until just before midnight.'

'In some ways it seems like yesterday and in others it feels like a lifetime ago.' Mandy gave her friend's arm a squeeze.

'Do you remember this?' Steve, Toni's dad, picked up another of the pictures that was laid out on the table, in which she and

Aaron were both dressed as elves. 'They look like they're about four in this one and Netty doesn't look too happy to be dressed up!' Her father was the only person who called her Netty, a derivative from her full name of Antoinette that he'd used for as long as she could remember.

'It was when we took them on the Santa train at Bodmin, I think.' Simon took the photo to have a closer look. 'I've got a horrible feeling that there's one of us somewhere too, wearing the sort of Christmas jumpers that should be against the law!'

'I'd wear anything and do anything to have another Christmas like that again.' Judy sniffed, wiping her eyes with the back of her hand, despite promising all of them that she was going to do her absolute best to make the evening a celebration and not to cry. Not that Toni had ever really expected her to be able to keep that promise.

'At least we can all be together at Christmas as Toni's not rostered on call this year, and we can raise a toast to Aaron then too.' Mandy squeezed Judy's arm again and Toni took a swig of the wine she'd carried in from the kitchen.

Judy sighed. 'We've never minded having to celebrate it on whatever day Toni has off nearest the twenty-fifth, but to be able do it on the big day itself... that's really special and I feel like I've got more energy and motivation to plan things as a result. It isn't always easy to find that, especially with the MS.'

'We'll have a wonderful time and I know Toni wouldn't dream of being anywhere else.'

Toni's mother smiled at her as she spoke, but no one had thought to ask her if she had other plans, not for her birthday, not for Christmas, and sometimes, it seemed, not for the rest of her life. She was never going to stop missing Aaron, but she hadn't realised when he'd died that she was never going to be allowed to stop mourning him. Back then, she hadn't anticipated that she'd ever want to, which was why it had been so easy to make the promise, but it hadn't occurred to her that she wouldn't even have the choice. Bobby's parents had invited her, more than once, to spend part of Christmas in their noisy, joy-filled home, where it didn't feel as if you were stepping into a shrine to someone who was no longer here. But even if she and Bobby had managed to work things out, spending Christmas with him would never have been an option. Judy would only have needed to mention one extra symptom of her MS occurring as a result, and Toni would have dropped her plans in an instant.

'You're very quiet tonight Netty. Are you okay, sweetheart?' Her father had come out to the kitchen to find her an hour after they'd started to look through the photos and ten minutes after she'd made the excuse to go and get a glass of water. The term of endearment almost weakened her resolve.

'I'm fine, just tired from work, that's all.'

'It's more than that, isn't it?' Her father scanned her face. 'You're tired of all this too, aren't you? Having to share your life with Aaron, even after he's been gone for all this time?' Part of Toni longed to scream out that her father was right, or to slump to the floor in relief that someone else had finally noticed what the strain of trying to fill Aaron's shoes was doing to her. She could never replace him and sometimes trying to fill the void he'd left was like bailing out a sinking boat with a thimble. It was relentless and she couldn't envisage a point where it was ever going to stop, not with Judy's health as fragile as it was. She might not have had a serious relapse in almost three years, but that didn't stop the threat of it lurking around every corner. So as much as Toni wanted to lean into her father's shoulder, burst into noisy tears and tell him just how much misery trying to take Aaron's place had caused her, she just shook her head.

'Of course not, I just need a few days off work that's all. Some different staff have joined us and you know what it's like with people who are new to the job – for the first little while helping them get settled in is harder going than just doing the jobs you allocate to them yourself.' Toni screwed her face up as she pictured Emily, hanging off every word Bobby said.

'You can tell me if this all gets too much. I can have a word with your mum and Judy about their plans for Christmas too, if you want. I know Simon will understand; he told me he was worried about you after Aaron's anniversary.'

'It's not that, Dad. Honestly.' Toni held his gaze. It wasn't even a lie, not really. Work was getting on her nerves when it was usually her salvation at times like this, and it *was* down to the new members of staff – or at least one of them.

'I don't want you to spend another five years like this, pretending Aaron might still come through the door one day and deep down I don't think Judy and Simon do either.'

'Did I hear my name being taken in vain?' Judy raised her eyebrows as she came into the kitchen.

'No! Dad was just saying he doesn't really think you and Simon want to get stuck with doing the cooking at Christmas this year and having to entertain us all.' Toni had said the first thing that had come into her head. 'Maybe we could book a restaurant to give you a break?'

'Don't be daft! We love doing it the way we always did when Aaron was here. Smoked salmon and scrambled eggs for breakfast and the full trimmings for lunch, he'd never have wanted to swap that for a restaurant.' Judy opened a drawer and took out some candles. 'Come on then, it's time for cake and birthday wishes. I don't know what you'll be asking for, but I'll be making the wish I always do on Aaron's behalf – that we'll all be together again next year, to do this all over again. The Famous Five and Aaron here with us in spirit.'

'Who could ever wish for more?' Toni forced a smile. It didn't matter what her father said or how right he was about how damaging this was for all of them. They were stuck in this collusion, keeping up the pretence that no one could have done anything differently to change how Aaron's life ended up. Maybe it was true that no one could have changed how it *ended*, but what none of them were brave enough to say out loud was that they could have changed how Aaron spent the time he had on this earth.

If Toni stood up and told Judy she couldn't take this any more, and that she could see now what living his life for someone else must have done to Aaron, then Judy would have the right to call her out too. She hadn't been honest about her doubts and if Toni let herself go back over the time running up to Aaron's death, she'd have to admit it had been easy to use Judy's demands as an excuse, a get-out-of-jail-free card until she made up her mind whether marrying Aaron was what she really wanted. What neither of them had done was tell him the truth. Judy's health wouldn't suddenly have deteriorated if Aaron had been allowed to make a few of his own choices, and Toni should never have agreed to marry him only to look for a way to slow things down the second his grandmother's ring was on her finger. Nothing was ever going to change, because none of them could admit the truth, even to themselves, and Toni couldn't imagine a time when they ever would.

Anna was still finding it difficult just to get through the working day and had cut her hours down to about two thirds of what she'd been doing before she got pregnant. Running the infertility support group was a voluntary role, but she'd confided to Toni and the others that she didn't want to let that go, despite having fallen pregnant herself not long after setting the group up. Jess had been a founder member too, but now they'd asked Toni if she'd mind starting to come along as well, in case there were times when neither Jess or Anna were able to go, with everything they had going on. It probably seemed an odd thing for a group of midwives to agree to do – setting up a group for women who were having trouble falling pregnant – but with Jess and Anna's own issues, they'd wanted to reach out to others and Toni couldn't think of a reason why she shouldn't help. She hadn't been feeling great lately, but it was all down to stress and having too much time to keep overthinking things with Bobby. She'd even woken up with a nosebleed in the night and her blood pressure was probably sky high, so getting out and listening to other people's problems might be a good idea.

Anything that helped her get her own issues into perspective had to be positive.

There hadn't been any other infertility groups already up and running in their corner of rural Cornwall and, although she didn't have any experience of the pain of trying to fall pregnant and not being able to, in a weird sort of way Toni was infertile too. Only, in her case, it was a result of circumstances that meant she'd never be able to admit to dating someone else, let alone having a baby with them. Not that she'd ever talked about feeling that way with Anna, Jess or any of the other midwives. They'd probably just assumed that she had a lot of time on her hands, no family, no partner and not much she even talked about doing outside of work. She had wanted to be a mother, she'd always known it, even when she wasn't sure of whether she wanted to marry Aaron. But it was part of what she'd lost when he died, the chance to have a child with him or even with someone else, if they'd decided to just be friends. Even if she'd considered going it alone, with a donor, Judy would never be able to cope with that. It would just be another thing that Aaron could never have and so, by default, she could never have either. Maybe it was just as well. There was no way Toni wanted to bring a child into the world if she couldn't put their needs first and she'd never be able to do that while she was still trying so hard to fill Aaron's shoes.

Keeping yet another secret wish to herself was how she found herself at The Cookie Jar café in Port Agnes, waiting to be introduced to the members of the infertility support group which had increased in size since Anna and Jess had first set it up. Weirdly, Anna wasn't the only original member who'd fallen pregnant in that time and there was a good chance that the women who'd joined since had done so in the hope the group had cottoned on to some secret formula for beating infertility. If it had been drinking only nettle leaf tea and sticking to a diet solely consisting of root vegetables, Anna had told Toni that some of the women would probably still have been desperate enough to give that a try. Lucy was the other original group member who'd been told that she'd almost certainly never fall pregnant, but had since discovered she was expecting a baby, due a couple of months before Anna, and Toni had recently been assigned as her primary midwife.

Jess had already briefed Toni about the other members of the group. Jacinda was in the process of pursuing surrogacy overseas, after being born without a womb, and Tara, a former professional athlete, was about to start her second round of IVF with eggs she'd had frozen ten years before. The newer members were Jennie, a single woman in her late thirties who'd joined the group to try and work out if she should go it alone with a sperm donor; Rachel, who had endometriosis; and Ellen, who'd recently discovered that her partner's sperm count was less than 2 per cent of what the doctors had said it should be.

'Is it your usual order ladies?' George, the owner of The Cookie Jar came over to where Anna, Jess and Toni had taken their seats at the reserved table in the window, which was separated from the rest of the tables by enough distance to ensure that their conversation wasn't overheard by other customers. Anna had told Toni it was why they'd chosen to keep having all their meetings there, after George had promised to reserve that table for them.

'That would be great, thanks, George, plus another pot of tea for Toni, and I've been craving one of your cinnamon buns all week, so we'd better have some of those. Just don't tell Jago Mehenick, whatever you do!' Anna smiled at George, who dropped a wink in return. Jago, Ella's father, ran the bakery by the harbour and he would probably consider it a personal insult for any of the midwives to get their cake fix from anywhere else.

'It's okay, Jago makes all our bread and pastries, so I think he'll forgive me for baking the one thing I can compete with him on.' George winked again and disappeared to fill their order, Anna's little secret clearly safe with him.

'You don't think the other women will resent me covering for you two, when I've got no understanding of the issues they've been through?' Toni couldn't help feeling like a fake. She'd taken the mini pill religiously since she'd got together with Bobby, so there was no chance of falling pregnant. How was she supposed to support women who were desperate to have a baby, instead of being desperate to avoid having one like she was? Having a baby with someone other than Aaron would be a sure-fire way to tip the balance of the carefully woven illusion that she and Judy had fabricated between them. The recriminations that would be bound to come would result in things being said that could never be taken back and the fallout from that was a risk Toni just couldn't take.

'Of course they won't resent you.' Anna shook her head to emphasise the point. 'They just want a space to talk about how they're feeling. They've all said they like having a midwife running the sessions, even if we just did it initially because we were having fertility issues too.'

'It's true.' Jess, who was sitting opposite Toni, shrugged. 'They like the fact that we've seen everything there is to see and won't be shocked about the mention of any of the biology. We've also seen babies arrive to women who've been told they'd never have children, through fertility treatment and even naturally, like Anna. So I guess that gives them hope too.'

'I suppose I've got my share of stories like that to tell.' Toni smiled. 'And cinnamon buns are just an added bonus.'

'You'd better get in before Lucy does.' Anna grinned. 'I might be the one having twins, but she told me if there aren't at least two buns with her name on them when she gets here, she won't be held responsible for her actions – and she'll just blame the whole thing on pregnancy hormones!'

'Oh, here comes Jacinda.' Jess gestured towards the door as the first of the support group members arrived. Within twenty minutes, everyone else was there too, and Toni had been introduced to them all.

'So that's it, we're definitely settled on working with the agency in Georgia.' Jacinda, who'd been updating the rest of the group on her surrogacy journey, dropped a cube of sugar into her tea. 'With the surrogacy agreement being legally binding in that part of Europe, it just gives me that bit more reassurance that the host won't end up wanting to keep my baby.'

'Can they even do that, if it's your eggs that are being used?' Rachel knitted her eyebrows together, leaning forward to hear Jacinda's response. It held all the more weight for her, as she'd shared with the rest of the group that surrogacy might be something she'd have to think about too.

'In most countries, the woman who gives birth to the baby is its legal mother, regardless of whether she's biologically related to that child or not. So, if a surrogate changes her mind, she has all the rights in the UK.' Jacinda's mouth turned down at the corners. 'Which means I'd have to adopt the baby or get a parental order after the baby was born to be recognised as its mother.'

'That's crazy.' Rachel sighed. 'To be honest, I'm still hoping I'll get a miracle like Lucy or Anna, but this group is so great for learning more about the options, if we do need to look at other routes.'

'I think we're all hoping some of that luck rubs off on us.' Ellen smiled. 'Talking of which, can we have an update on how you're both doing? And don't leave out the bad bits, it'll help remind us that there will be some upsides to not having to put in all the work it takes to grow a new human!'

'The good news is I'm now well past the bit where they say sickness eases off.' Anna rolled her eyes. 'The bad news is they lied! And, if I tell you the next bit, you've got to promise it doesn't go beyond these four walls...'

'You can trust us. We won't breathe a word.' Ellen stepped in to make the promise, backed up by several murmurs of agreement.

'Okay, here goes... The other morning, I woke up feeling sick and needing a wee in equal measure. I just about made it to the loo, but I knew I was going to have to make a decision about which to prioritise. But then the sickness made the decision for me, a split second before I wet myself.'

'Ah the glamour, no wonder we're all so desperate to be pregnant!' Jennie laughed. 'How about you, Lucy? Please tell me you're spending all your time floating around designer baby stores, planning the perfect nursery, and the sort of baby shower that could feature on the cover of Hello! magazine.'

'I don't want to tempt fate by doing all of that, just in case something happens.' Lucy had been very quiet, but Toni didn't really know her well enough yet to know whether that was normal.

'Is everything okay? You look like you're blooming. Although for the first time since I met you I think your bum might actually be bigger than mine!' Tara, who'd already flashed a hip to the rest of the group – showing off the bruises caused by her fertility injections – nudged her friend, but Lucy didn't smile.

'It's fine, all my checks have been normal, but I don't know... Maybe it's just because I didn't think I'd ever fall pregnant naturally, I can't let myself believe that nothing will go wrong. Anyway, that's enough of the pregnant woman whinging when she's got nothing to whinge about. I know how lucky I am, but one of you must have something far more interesting to say.' Lucy gave the rest of the group a half-smile, but Toni had a feeling there was a lot more going on than Lucy was prepared to admit in front of the group. She'd text her after the meeting and ask her to set up an extra appointment. At least that way they'd have the opportunity to talk through whatever it was that was bothering her; assuming she wanted to, of course.

'Well, you could all help me with something.' Jennie's smile looked a lot more convincing than Lucy's had. 'Choosing a sperm donor is not like they show in the movies. You don't flick through an album of potential donors, but I have got to make a list of characteristics I'm looking for. I've got about twenty things listed so far, but I think I'm going to need some help to narrow down the list and decide what's *really* important.'

'Hit us with what you've got then and I'm sure we can help.' Lucy seemed far more comfortable discussing the group's shared fertility issues than she did discussing her pregnancy, but maybe that just came down to the nature of why they were all there. There was a good chance she felt guilty about falling pregnant at all, when it was something the other women in the group so desperately wanted, but Toni couldn't help worrying if she was okay. Whether Lucy felt she was whinging or not, Toni was going to do her best to get her to open up and share what it was that was really on her mind, even if she had to force Lucy to make the extra appointment she had planned.

* * *

'Thanks for coming over.' Lucy opened the door, the dark circles under her eyes convincing Toni that she'd been right to push for an extra check-up. 'Sorry I couldn't make it to clinic, but I'd only planned the scheduled appointments around my work commitments.'

'It's no problem at all. I know I sprung this one on you.' Toni's scalp prickled with guilt. She'd ended up having to tell Lucy a white lie to try to persuade her to make another appointment, saying she'd been sent some new information about exercise plans which would help Lucy prepare for the birth and lessen the chance of needing an assisted delivery. The truth was that the pregnancy yoga exercises she was planning to share were nothing particularly new, she just wanted to check on Lucy in person after she'd had no luck in getting her to open up over the phone.

'I've put a couple of mats down in front of the TV and Henry's promised to stay out until I tell him the coast is clear.' Lucy led the way into the room. 'This surely has to be going over and above the scope of your role. You can't tell me that all your patients get this level of support!'

'You got me. The truth is that Anna is thinking of extending our prenatal classes and offering some pregnancy yoga at the unit as part of that, so we're talking to a select few patients about it and seeing what sort of feedback we get before taking it forward.' It was another white lie, but it was probably the sort of thing Anna would want to start offering, if she could think about anything other than just getting through the day right now.

'I'm happy to be a guinea pig if it helps someone else. It feels like a bit of payback for all the luck I don't deserve to have.'

'What do you mean the luck you don't deserve to have? Most people would say you'd been through the mill, trying for as long as you did to get pregnant.' Lucy had told her at their first consultation about her husband Henry having a low sperm count and everyone's shock when she'd fallen pregnant naturally, after two years of trying, just before they'd been due to start ICSI IVF.

'That's true.' Lucy took her position on the yoga mat with far more elegance than Toni, despite being the pregnant one. 'But most people don't know what came before those two years of trying and that's the bit that makes me think I don't deserve this.'

'Whatever it was, it doesn't mean you need to feel guilty about being pregnant now.'

'Even if it was a late termination?' Lucy's eyes had filled with tears as she turned to look at Toni. It wasn't the first time a mother-to-be had told Toni a similar story; a subsequent pregnancy tended to bring even long-buried emotions about a previous termination back to the fore, as if it had only happened the day before. And in Toni's experience, women very rarely treated a termination casually, so it was no wonder Lucy was looking so wrung out. Either way, the last thing she wanted to do was bring her own emotions into it, even if hearing it from someone who'd struggled with infertility, and who Toni might not have expected to have to make that sort of choice, was more of a shock. There were so many reasons a woman might choose a termination and it wasn't up to Toni to decide on the rights and wrongs of that. Her job was to support women – the origin of the word midwife meant 'with woman' – and whatever Lucy wanted to tell her, that's what she was going to do.

'Like I said, it doesn't matter what happened, it's not for anyone else to judge you. And you don't have to tell me unless you want to.'

'That's the trouble, I'm the one who judges myself the most harshly, and not telling anyone else just makes it worse.' Lucy pulled her knees up towards her chest, at least as far as her bump would allow. 'And I didn't tell Henry until we found out about his sperm count, because I was terrified the reason we couldn't fall pregnant was to do with my termination.'

'Infertility makes people blame themselves, but most of the time it's just bad luck. Do you want to talk about it?'

'I was at university when I found out I was pregnant. It felt like the end of the world and I wasn't with the dad. He'd only spent six months at the same uni on an exchange programme and he'd already gone back to Spain by the time I found out.' Lucy's voice caught in her throat. 'All my friends thought I should have a termination, but I was determined to go through with it. I wasn't great at going to my appointments, though, and I think I was in some sort of denial about it all, which was how I ended up missing my twenty-week scan. It meant I was twenty-six weeks by the time they found out the baby had anencephaly, and that most of his brain and skull were missing.'

'Oh Lucy, it must have been horrendous going through all of that on your own.' Anencephaly was a severe birth defect in the neural tubes of the brain, and babies suffering from the condition were either stillborn or died within a few days of delivery. Having to make the kind of decision Lucy had been forced to make didn't bear thinking about, especially making it alone.

'It was awful, but I couldn't stand the thought that he might be born and suffer for hours or even days before he died, so terminating the pregnancy seemed like the best thing to do for him. At least that's what I told myself, but I can't help thinking that I really did it to protect myself from the pain of getting to know him for a few days, holding him in my arms and then having to watch him die and let him go. I also keep wondering whether all the times I wished I wasn't pregnant, when I first found out, were the reason why he had the condition. I never even told Matias about the baby and a big part of me tried to pretend Oscar had never existed, until Henry and I started trying for a baby. Since I've fallen pregnant, every stage is like a reminder, and I keep expecting someone to turn around and tell me something's wrong as my punishment for not giving my first baby a chance.'

'They must have told you, with Oscar's condition, that his chances of surviving beyond a few days were minimal.'

'They did, but if I'd been more careful... If I'd have been taking folic acid when I fell pregnant, it might not have happened. Or maybe if I'd gone to the other checks and the twenty-week scan, something could have been done to prevent what happened to Oscar.'

'It couldn't Lucy.' Toni kept her tone as gentle as possible, all the time trying to emphasise the point. 'Sometimes these things just happen, they're not fair and no one knows why, but they just happen and it's not your fault.'

'I spent at least the first six weeks after I found out about the baby wishing him away, though! That has to mean something.'

'It means you were in shock, but that's not why things turned out the way they did, and it doesn't mean you don't deserve to be happy and enjoy your pregnancy this time.'

'That's exactly what Henry keeps saying, but I don't think anyone understands that sort of guilt unless they've been through it themselves. My first baby didn't even get a chance at life, so why should I get a second chance at motherhood now? Just because I've met the right person and I actually want a baby? That's not how it works. It was almost easier when I felt like I was being punished by not being able to get pregnant. I don't deserve to be happy, not when Oscar didn't ever get the chance.'

'You deserve it more than you realise, Lucy, and I really think it would help you to talk to someone about all of this, someone who's a lot more qualified than I am to help you try and work through it.' It had been on the tip of Toni's tongue to say that she understood much more than Lucy would have believed. She knew exactly what it felt like to be riddled with guilt for feeling happy and seeming as if she was moving on with life, when there was someone she loved who'd never got that chance. But Toni's story was completely different to Lucy's and it would have been wrong of her to even try to compare their experiences. She was just glad that Lucy had opened up to her, and much more quickly than she'd expected. Now, at least, she could make a referral for Lucy to get the support she needed and have the opportunity to really start enjoying this second chance at motherhood. Everyone deserved a second chance – as long as that didn't pile on the pain for someone else. That was where Lucy and Toni's stories were so completely different.

* * *

Toni hadn't meant to walk to the tiny studio flat that Bobby called home, but after leaving Lucy's place her feet almost seemed to do their own thing and he was the only person she wanted to see.

'Thank you for the flowers.' She blurted the words out the second he opened the door.

'You already said that in your text, along with something about us both knowing it's time to move on and suggesting I bugger off to America.' Bobby stood framed in the doorway, looking far more qualified to run a yoga workshop or fitness class than she ever would. She'd never have got bored of looking at him, even if they could have had the next fifty or so years together.

'I was trying to do the right thing.'

'Who for?'

'For both of us, but mostly for you, because we keep saying we're going to end this and finish things for good, but then we see each other again and—'

'I don't need anyone to make my decisions for me.' She tried to stop staring at his lips as he spoke, but it was too easy to remember what it felt like to kiss Bobby – his mouth on hers making her feel like she was the only woman in the world he ever wanted to kiss, without him having to say anything.

'Okay, how about a truce? I could really use a friend right now, that's all.'

'You'd better come in then.' Bobby stepped to one side, but the hallway was narrow and she couldn't help brushing up against him as she walked past; it was what she told herself anyway. She was also trying to tell herself that the almost overwhelming desire to reach out and touch him would pass too. It was harder to lie to herself than she ever would have believed, though, and it just hammered home how impossible it was going to be to distance herself from him, as long as they still worked together. 'So, what's up?'

'I've just had a tough time with a patient, that's all, and I'm not sure I said the right thing to her.'

'You will have done, don't worry.'

'What, me? The only midwife with all the emotional warmth of a frozen fish finger.'

'That's not what people think of you.'

'How do you know?'

'Because it's not what *I* think of you, and I know I'm not the only person who sees the real you.' He fixed her with a look, his dark brown eyes still holding all the warmth for her that they always had. He didn't hate her and that was a start towards friendship, surely? 'Do you want to talk about it?'

'It'll all go on the patient's records, so I wouldn't be saying anything that you couldn't read at one of the clinics. She had a late termination more than ten years ago because of a foetal abnormality that was incompatible with life. She's stricken with guilt because she was single at the time and didn't want the baby when she first found out she was pregnant. She thinks that somehow made things turn out the way they did.'

'And what did you say?'

'That nothing she did could have changed the situation and that she shouldn't feel guilty for being happy now. It's not her fault and she's been through more than enough already.'

'Sounds like it was the perfect thing to say to me.' Bobby flicked the coffee machine on and turned back towards her. 'I just wish you'd take your own advice.'

'Bobby...'

'I know, I know, we've had this conversation a million times already, haven't we? At least that's what it feels like.' Bobby sighed so deeply, it was as if half the air had been sucked out of the room, and his voice had an edge to it. 'But sometimes you make me feel like tearing my hair out. If it was Anna, Jess, Ella – or anyone else – still punishing themselves, five years later, for something they didn't even do, you'd want to shake them until they saw sense, wouldn't you?'

'It's not that simple.' Even Bobby didn't know the whole story of how much stress she'd put on Aaron, making him choose between what his mum wanted and what he thought Toni wanted, when she hadn't even known herself.

'It could be that simple, Tee, it really could! All you've got to do is tell them and, if they can't deal with it straight away, we can go elsewhere, even if it's just for a little while. In my experience people tend to come to terms with these things.' Bobby held her gaze for moment, his tone softening. 'You know that Dad dated my Mum's sister for a few weeks until he met Mum one night when he came to pick Auntie Yvonne up to go to the cinema. For about six months afterwards, Yvonne wouldn't even be in the same room as them, but now it's like it never happened.'

'And how long have they been together? Forty years?'

'A bit more than that.' Bobby gave her a half smile. 'But it didn't take that long for Yvonne to get over it. Wouldn't you rather have six months, or even six years, of things being a bit difficult with your family and Aaron's, than a lifetime of wishing we'd taken a chance.'

'If I was going to take the chance of doing that with anyone, you know it would be you, don't you?' Her hands were actually twitching to reach out for him now, her fingers curling over on themselves to stop herself from giving in to it.

'But you aren't, are you?' Bobby didn't even wait for her to answer as he sighed again, and it was as if all the fight had gone out of him. 'I think the only question now is which one of us leaves the unit. What do you want to do, rock, paper, scissors?'

'I don't want either of us to have to go.'

'Well I should warn you I'm unbeaten at rock, paper, scissors competitions with my nephews and nieces.' He was trying to make a joke of it now and maybe that was the only option they had left, because if she didn't laugh, she was definitely going to cry.

'You're also the one with job offers coming out of your ears.' Even as she said it, she wanted to beg him to stay, but she knew for certain now that she was never going to be able to stop herself from running to him all the while she still could.

'If I'm leaving there's no point in me trying to impress the senior midwives any more and, given that we're not together either, you do know that means you only get the basic biscuits from now on, don't you?' He smiled, immediately lifting some of the tension in the room and revealing the matching dimples on either side of his beautiful mouth.

'I can live with that.' Toni leant against the kitchen counter like her back was glued to the wood. If she'd taken even a half step towards him, her resolve would have crumbled all over again and suddenly, despite all her determination to try and hold on to her sense of humour, she felt like crying harder than she'd done in years. She could never be just his friend, because she loved everything about him. So how was she supposed to work with him and keep things strictly platonic? But if she couldn't work with Bobby, then all of this was no joke and one of them really was going to have to leave the unit, which meant she'd never have the excuse to see him. It was an impossible situation and so she stayed frozen to the spot, terrified that the smallest move would give her away. For now, she just needed to be with Bobby for the next half an hour or so; she couldn't think about what came next. That would just have to wait.

10

Meeting up with the carers who'd been on Jess's Skills to Foster course with her was a mixed bag. There were some of them she hoped she'd stay friends with, so they could support one another if they eventually got approved to foster, but there were others who she'd happily never see again. Pulling up in the car park outside the building where their latest pre-approval training session was taking place, she took a deep breath. It was show time.

'Woo hoo, we're at the halfway point!' David called out to Jess as she got out of her car, walking towards her with his husband, Richard. The last time she'd seen them had been before they'd started their assessments. Now it was all beginning to feel a bit more real.

'Are you ready for this?' Richard kissed her on both cheeks. His aftershave smelt like sandalwood and he was as immaculately groomed as he'd been the first time they'd met. Jess, on the other hand, had managed to end up running late, after Luna had gone AWOL for a whole twenty-four hours, and she felt as if she'd been dragged through a hedge backwards. Three circuits of the harbour later, she'd finally spotted the cat stretched out on the deck of one of the trawlers, making the most of the morning sunshine. Risking life and limb – or at least a damn good soaking – Jess had jumped straight on board and Luna had looked singularly unimpressed. Showing no intention of moving, the little cat had stretched out even further, looking like a doorstop that had been fed through a mangle. Even when Jess had picked her up, the cat had barely reacted, and she'd been terrified that Luna had eaten some rat poison from a trap on one of the boats.

It was only when Jess had carried her all the way back to Puffin's Rest that Luna had finally decided to stop playing dead and make short work of the bowl of mackerel that Jess had lovingly prepared for her. God knew why she made so much effort when Luna would happily eat mouse guts, and 90 per cent of the time had nothing but disdain for her owner. It was that 10 per cent of the time that swung it, though, when Luna purred contentedly on Jess's lap, as though there was nowhere else in the world she'd rather be. One-sided relationships seemed to be the story of Jess's life, but then if she'd wanted unconditional devotion she'd have got herself a dog.

'I'm about as ready for it as I'll ever be.' Jess gave Richard and David a half smile, before turning her attention to a streak of what she hoped was toothpaste smeared across her black top. Although there was always a chance it was a gift from a passing seagull. It would be horribly bad form to lick her finger to see if she could get the stain out, but as soon as she had the chance to get to the ladies, she was definitely going to give it a go with a paper towel. 'How have you guys found the assessment so far?'

'We kept panicking that we'd say something to mess it all up, or more accurately that I would! I lost count of the times that

Rich said "he doesn't need to know that, Davy", when I was going into *way* more detail than anyone wants to hear!'

'It's pretty terrifying, isn't it? Thinking that the next word out of your mouth might derail all your plans.' Jess was still second-guessing herself every time she had an assessment visit from Dexter, but there was something about him that made her spill almost every single secret she had. As hard as that had been, it was probably for the best. After all, her mum had always said that you couldn't go far wrong if you told the truth, and following her advice was the next best thing to having her around in person.

'Trying to only show your best side is such hard work, especially when you've got a mouth as big as mine!' David laughed. 'Although we were pretty lucky to be given Dex as our assessing social worker. He's been an absolute sweetheart.'

The back of Jess's neck prickled at David's use of the short-ened version of Dexter's name, as if he and Richard had somehow developed a deeper bond with their shared social worker than she had. David did that to everyone; he even called himself Davy for heaven's sake. It didn't mean anything, and it didn't matter either way; even if Dexter was closer to them, it wouldn't affect the likelihood of her getting approved. At least she hoped not.

'Yeah, Dexter's great.' That was the end of the conversation as far as Jess was concerned and she definitely didn't want to get into comparing notes about which parts of the assessment were the hardest to talk about. Just because she'd managed to open up to Dexter, it didn't mean she'd suddenly become the sort of person who wanted to share the details of her difficult childhood in a council car park. 'Do you know if any of the others from our Skills to Foster course are coming today?'

'I'm not sure.' Richard turned towards his husband. 'Have you heard from any of them, Davy?'

'Mo and Tima are definitely going to be here; she Whats-Apped me last week.' David was doing it again, shortening their names. Fatima was just lucky he'd used the second half of her name; no one wanted to be called Fati. 'She also told me some red-hot gossip.'

'I thought you were trying to rein that in, the all-new Davy whose mind is on far higher things than gossip.' Richard shook his head, but David just grinned.

'Some gossip is just too good to pass up, especially when it involves know-it-alls like Sally and Ian, Mr and Mrs Perfect Parents from our training course.'

'Now you've got my attention.' Jess wasn't usually one for gossip – she'd been the subject of it far too often over the years – but sometimes you had to make an exception. Sally, another prospective carer, had seemed to delight in belittling Jess at their last training session for being single, childless and – in Sally's opinion – wholly unqualified for a career in fostering. If she was having to miss today's training because she'd stubbed her toe on the door of her Aga, which she must have mentioned was the centrepiece of her kitchen at least four times, then Jess certainly wasn't going to feel sorry for her. Although she'd hardly call that red-hot gossip.

'Apparently their assessment was stopped after the second session, because she said something racist.' David imparted the information in a stage whisper that could have reached right to the back of the car park.

'Really?' Jess had pegged Sally as a pain in the proverbial, but not a racist.

'Tima wouldn't even repeat what Sally said, it was that bad apparently.'

'And who exactly told Tima this?' Richard raised an eyebrow.

'I hope to Christ Dexter isn't going around telling everyone all the things we've said.'

'Sally and Ian didn't even have Dex as their assessing social worker.' David rolled his eyes. 'Look it doesn't matter *how* Tima knows all this stuff, she just does.'

'We'd better get in, or none of us are going to make it to the next stage of the assessment.' All of a sudden Jess was desperate to get inside, before there was any chance of the conversation being steered back to her.

David was right, it didn't matter who'd told Fatima about Sally and Ian: someone had. However great they all thought Dexter was, he must have told people about their backgrounds as part of his job. If she made it as far as the end of the assessment, a whole panel of people – and God knew who else – would be invited to read every tiny detail of Jess's life story and debate whether or not that made her worthy of being a foster carer. It was like having one of those horrifying dreams, when you're walking naked down the pasta aisle in Sainsbury's, and suddenly realising it's not a dream after all. So if she didn't go inside now, she never would.

'I suppose you're right, Jessie J, we'd better get this show on the road.' David linked an arm through hers. She'd been waiting for him to come up with a nickname for her, but it must have killed him to end up lengthening it. At least it wasn't JJ, which is what Dom had always called her, because the way she was feeling, hearing that would definitely have been the final straw.

* * *

Jess scribbled down another line of notes in the pad she'd bought to the training:

With foster children, it's important to remember that their functioning age is sometimes very different to their chronological age. Don't miss the chance of being matched with the right child by being too limited about the age range you'll accept.

Dexter was leading the session by himself this time, but Jess had to admit that he looked as if he could have done with some help, even though he was doing a great job. His eyes were bloodshot and he had much more than his usual grazing of stubble, not to mention the shirt he was wearing didn't look like it had seen an iron for a while. He hadn't completely let his standards slip – when he'd said hello to Jess on her way into the training centre he'd smelt of fabric conditioner and soap – but he obviously hadn't had time for the finishing touches.

He didn't seem quite his normal self either, checking his mobile phone every chance he got and disappearing altogether at break time, instead of hanging out and chatting with the group. He probably had some important work on the go, or maybe there were problems at home. Although she couldn't imagine Dexter being the sort to have long drawn-out rows with his other half via text message.

Whatever was going on, Jess couldn't help being disappointed when Dexter didn't even join them for the final coffee break of the day. She'd wanted to tell him how useful she'd found the session and that it had made her think again about the approval terms she wanted the panel to consider. She might just be doing respite at first, but that didn't mean she wanted to shut down the chance of helping more children in the future.

'What do you think of the training?' Mohammed, or Mo as David insisted on calling him, smiled as Jess walked towards him, a snack-sized packet of ginger nuts in one hand and some bourbon biscuits in the other. Mo and his wife, Fatima, had years of experience working together in a children's residential home, so as far as Jess was concerned they had a head start on everyone else. 'Even more importantly, which biscuits do you think I should have?'

'Both?' Jess laughed as Mohammed raised his eyebrows. 'It's really not that shocking a suggestion and it's been a long day; you deserve both packets.'

'Fatima said I could have one packet at each break. She doesn't want me putting on too much weight, in case it goes against us.'

'And because I'm looking out for your health!' Fatima walked over to join them and nudged him in the side.

'The regime she's got me on has got to be good for me, Jess, because it's flipping awful.' Mohammed grinned. 'You didn't say what you thought of the training, are you in desperate need of biscuits too?'

'My trouble is I always fancy a biscuit.' Jess ran a hand through her blonde hair. 'But the training's been really good. It's made me a bit more open about the different sorts of placements I might be able to support. Maybe I should be more nervous now I know about the possibilities, but for some reason I feel more confident this time around.'

'You always seem so confident to me.' Fatima was straight-faced, but Jess was still struggling to believe the other woman was serious. Jess felt like she was a seething mass of insecurities and the idea that it didn't show on the outside was almost impossible to comprehend.

'Appearances can be deceptive, I guess.'

'They definitely can. Take our social worker, Nigel, for example.' Fatima leant in conspiratorially. 'He looks like he sits quietly at home crocheting his own jumpers when he's not working, and he barely ever cracks a smile, but he's one of the biggest gossips I've ever met.'

'Doesn't that worry you, when you're sharing all the details of your life with him, if he's telling you about everyone else he's assessing? Maybe you should report him?'

'No way! I'm finding out way too much.' Fatima moved closer still. 'Take Dexter for instance, there's a lot more to him than meets the eye.'

'Really?' Jess desperately wanted to tell Fatima she wasn't interested, and that Dexter's private life was his own. But she wasn't that saintly.

'Well, for a start, he's resigning after he's finished the assessments he's doing at the moment. He's been working all hours to get them done apparently and finish off all his other commitments with the local authority.'

'That's a shame, he's a really nice guy.' Jess was fighting hard to try and keep a neutral expression. It was more than a shame, but at least Dexter would be seeing her assessment through to the end. That was something and she'd learnt the hard way that, sometimes, you had to be thankful for what you could get. 'Do you know why he's leaving?'

'His wife died.'

'Oh my God, that's terrible.' Jess's hand involuntarily went to her throat. Poor Dexter, no wonder he looked like he'd forgotten how to iron a shirt. It was a miracle he was even up and dressed.

'Oh no, not recently.' Fatima was shaking her head. 'It was about eighteen months ago, but apparently she had a little boy who was obviously a big part of Dexter's life. He wants to be able to see a bit more of his stepson, pick him up from school and things like that, but working such long hours makes it difficult when his stepson lives with his biological father.'

'That's really sad.' Even as she said it, Jess wasn't sure that sad was the right word. There were parts of the story that were sad – Dexter losing his wife and the little boy losing his mum – but there were parts of the story that were beautiful too. There was a child out there whose dad and stepdad were putting aside any differences they might have and working together to support him. That little boy had two dads who wanted the best for him; Jess hadn't even had one who was prepared to do that for her.

11

Brae had gone all out for Anna's fortieth birthday, just a fortnight before Christmas, hiring one of the boats on the harbour that was decked out with fairy lights. He'd told Bobby that the original plan had been for it to sail around the Sisters of Agnes Island, but Anna's sickness still hadn't fully abated and Brae had decided not to risk anything that might spoil her night. It was obvious he adored her, and something twisted in Bobby's gut when he went to the boat early to meet Brae, to help him set up for the party. He and Dan, Ella's fiancé, were helping to hang up the black and white photographs that Brae had had made into bunting, documenting Anna's first forty years on earth and her relationship with Brae, right up to the scan photos of their babies.

'I'd love to do something like this for Ella when we finally get around to organising the details of the wedding. If it doesn't just seem like a blatant rip-off of your idea!' Dan turned to Brae, as he hung up the end of the final piece of bunting.

'Rip me off all you want! It's not exactly an original idea – I looked it up on Google.' Brae laughed. 'I just wanted to make things as special for Anna as I could and, if I'd relied on my own imagination, we'd probably be having a buffet at home with a karaoke machine I bought from Argos!'

'That doesn't sound too bad to me.' Bobby grinned. 'Although given that you've heard what all the midwives sound like on the karaoke nights at Casa Cantare, I can understand your reluctance!'

'It's not that I don't like your singing.' Brae laughed again. 'It's just that I'm hoping, after tonight, there'll be enough new photographs for a whole other string of bunting full of memories for Anna. I never thought I could be as happy as she's made me and I just want to make sure she's happy too. Dan knows what I mean.'

'I do, but be careful, Brae, we might make Bobby more nauseous than Anna with all of this lovey-dovey stuff.'

'You'd have to go a long way to beat my parents.' Bobby shrugged. 'They still hold hands all the time and they want to sit next to each other at every opportunity, even after more than forty years of marriage. As for the public displays of affection, it's no less of a cringe-fest at twenty-seven than it was when I was seventeen. They've been together more than forty-five years, ever since they were about eighteen.'

'That's impressive, although you and Ella got together first time around when you were even younger than that, didn't you?' Brae looked at Dan, who nodded.

'We were a bit younger, in the sixth form, and I didn't think we'd get another chance, but that bond was what helped us find common ground again second time around.'

'Do you think growing up together meant you'd always have been closer to Ella than anyone else you might have dated?' Even as he spoke, Bobby wasn't sure he wanted an answer. He already knew that he couldn't compete with Aaron, he didn't need Dan to tell him that.

'I don't think there's any one thing that trumps everything else. It's just different when it's the right person and you find a way of getting past all the other stuff.' Dan laughed. 'Surely we should be doing shots or downing pints, three blokes on our own. Not hanging up bunting and talking about our feelings!'

'Probably.' Brae pulled a face. 'But I'm soppier than ever since we found out that Anna is pregnant. What about you, Bobby? I bet you never thought you'd be spending your Saturday evening hanging up bunting and talking about your feelings, did you? You've got a few years on both of us and I don't suppose settling down's top of your agenda just yet.'

'I definitely want all of that one day, but like Dan said, it's got to be the right person.' Bobby busied himself moving some of the chairs and, if Brae replied, he didn't hear it. There was no way he wanted to get into a conversation about his experience of relationships, or what he was looking for in a woman. He'd already found everything he was looking for. The tragedy was that circumstances had taken the chance to be with Toni away from him, before they'd even met.

'Did you get everything you wanted for your birthday?' Ella put the lid back on one of the gift boxes that Anna had opened while the audience had been watching the birthday girl's every move. Toni would have hated to be in that position, with the party guests scrutinising her facial expressions, to see if she really liked the apron with 'This is Forty' emblazoned across the middle. Anna had genuinely seemed to love everything, though, and now it was just the three of them, as the other guests had gone back to drinking and dancing.

'I didn't expect any presents and I don't need anything. The best thing was having you all here and knowing that the twins are doing okay. After the latest scan, it's the best gift I could possibly have got.' Anna had told Toni and the others how terrified she'd been, at her twenty-week scan, when the sonographer hadn't been sure if one of the twins had an issue with their heart. She'd had to have a couple of repeat scans before they'd been able to be certain everything was okay. Thankfully, a week before her birthday, they'd finally been given the all-clear, and Anna was smiling now as she turned to Ella. 'What do you think about having your wedding reception on a boat like this? Dan seemed pretty keen.'

'I'll definitely think about it. The main thing is that we've managed to book a slot for the wedding itself at St Jude's. Dad is absolutely over the moon. And seeing as it's where me and Dan first admitted we still had feelings for each other after I moved back, it seems fitting.'

'It's such a lovely setting and if we'd been willing to wait a bit longer, I'd have loved to get married St Jude's too. The view down to Port Agnes is lovely from there, don't you think?' Anna turned to Toni this time and for a second the question hung in the air before she realised she was actually supposed to answer it.

'Yes, it's great.' Her voice sounded flat, and it was no wonder everyone thought she was standoffish, but what they didn't know was that if she thought too much about the view – the same one she looked at every time she visited Aaron's grave – she'd probably have burst into tears. The fact that Emily had hit the dance floor as soon as the music had started up wasn't helping. She looked as if she was having the best time ever and it didn't seem to have taken much persuasion for Bobby to join her. It was none of Toni's business, but she kept going hot every time she glanced in their direction. It would be just her luck to find out she was going through the menopause at least ten years early, just to ram home the fact that she was a clapped-out old hag compared to Emily.

'I was amazed we managed to get Valentine's Day, even the year after next, but I think Dad bribed Reverend Sampson with as many pasties as he wants between now and then. Although I'd never have gone for that day in the first place if Mum and Dad hadn't been so keen.' Ella laughed and Toni tried not to think about Judy trying a similar trick when she'd been engaged to Aaron. It was no wonder the vicar had to sit on a chair during services these days; all that bribery with baked goods over the years hadn't done him any favours. Last time she'd seen him, when she'd been visiting Aaron's grave, the vicar had told her that both a double knee replacement and retirement were looming, he just wasn't sure which was going to come first. So there was a good chance he wouldn't even be around to conduct the service by the time Ella and Dan tied the knot.

'I'm just glad I'll have time to shift the baby weight before I get to be matron of honour. Otherwise you'd need to ask your photographer to use a wide angled lens!'

'You look great, especially as you're doing double the work with twins.' Ella smiled. 'So come on, tell us what you think the worst symptom of pregnancy is; after all, we must've heard them all over the years. Actually, let's guess... I'm going for bloating and being absolutely knackered! What about you Toni, what's your best guess?'

'Sickness, sore boobs, needing to pee every ten seconds?'

'Nope, I've got all of those, as you'd expect with double trouble, but the worst symptom of all has been the constant worry that something might go wrong – especially with the bleeding early on and then the panic that there might be a problem with one of the babies' hearts.'

'I totally get that,' Ella squeezed her friend's hand, 'but, come on, tell us what the worst physical symptom has been for you, so that we can empathise with our patients when they list everything that sucks about being pregnant. Even when we're at the end of a twelve-hour shift and our sympathy has all but done a runner!'

'I can tell you what the worst symptom is *going* to be,' Gwen called out as she and Jess came over to the others with a tray of drinks. Dan and Brae were still busy out on the deck, supervising the delivery of a four-tier cake that had been another of Brae's treats to mark his wife's fortieth birthday.

'I can't wait to hear this!' Jess exchanged a look with Toni and the others as they waited for Gwen to enlighten them.

'It'll be the day you go to the loo and realise you're going to need an inflatable rubber ring to ever sit comfortably again because you've got haemorrhoids like dangly earrings – in a place where dangly earrings should never be!'

'Please tell me that's not going to happen!' Anna pulled a face. 'Not everyone gets them...'

'It's a lot more common with twins, sorry.' Ella had pressed her lips together, obviously trying not to laugh, and even Toni could feel a smile tugging at the corner of her lips, despite the fact that Emily was still stuck to Bobby's side like glue.

'This just keeps getting more and more glamorous! Luckily I'm willing to take it all.' Anna laughed. 'First it was a constant feeling of nausea, then hot flushes that came out of nowhere, a horrible metallic taste in my mouth that made everything taste the same, nosebleeds, and then the texture of all my favourite foods making my stomach churn. Now I'm just waiting to get piles!'

'Nosebleeds aren't something many pregnant women get, though, are they?' Toni's smile slid off her face and her eyes widened in response to Anna's words, as she tried not to make links with the other symptoms her friend had listed and some of the things Toni had been experiencing recently but had mostly put down to stress. Like the constant nausea, the fact she hadn't been able to face swallowing her pasta at lunchtime, even though most of the time she couldn't stop eating, and the hot flushes she thought had signalled the start of an early menopause. She hadn't even factored in the nosebleeds she'd been getting lately. It couldn't be down to pregnancy, it just couldn't.

'It's certainly a less common one, but it's not all that unusual. Why?' Ella waited as Toni did her best to arrange her face into a neutral expression.

'It's just that none of my patients have ever mentioned it, that's all.' Her stomach was suddenly swirling like it would if the boat had set out to sea in a storm, rather than staying firmly moored in the harbour. She couldn't be pregnant, it wasn't possible… Except that – even as she repeated the assurance to herself over and over in her head – she already knew that she was.

12

The fact that the staffroom at the midwifery unit was almost always stocked with cake was both a positive and a negative for Toni. It meant there was never any risk of going hungry, even on the longest of shifts, but it also meant she'd gone up a dress size for almost every year she'd worked at the unit. The size eight uniform she'd been able to wear when she'd started wouldn't even go over her shoulders now, but then she'd only ever been that thin because of losing Aaron. Months of feeling as if she was struggling just to swallow had taken their toll and everyone had begged her to start eating.

Starting work at Port Agnes had been the beginning of everything changing and she'd been able to reinvent herself, so that she wasn't just *Toni, the girl who'd lost her fiancé on the night of their engagement party.* Within a couple of months of working alongside Anna and the others who'd started in the early days of the unit, her passion for the job had come back and she'd begun to feel as if she was living again and not just existing. Her appetite had gradually reappeared too and now she could just about squeeze into a size fourteen. On a good day at least.

'Oh my God, Gwen, that smells divine.' Jess lifted the lid of the cake tin that had been set down in the middle of Anna's desk. 'Would it be really wrong to have a piece of lemon drizzle cake for breakfast?'

Gwen had brought in what could only be described as a masterpiece and left it on the empty desk. Anna had cut down her hours again, after her latest tests had shown that the fluid around the babies had reduced, so there was even more cake on offer than before.

'This will count as one of my five a day, won't it? Lemons are fruit after all.' Jess grinned as Gwen passed her a slice of cake that was big enough to bend the paper plate it was sitting on and Toni tried not to inhale the zesty aroma that was making her stomach rumble. She'd tossed and turned for half the night in an attempt to convince herself that there was no need to even take a pregnancy test to rule out the possibility. She was stressed, that was all. Every symptom she'd looked up on her phone – even the recurring nosebleeds – could be put down to stress. But she was going to have to get a handle on it – and her eating – otherwise she'd be up another dress size before Christmas. The trouble was, she was still struggling with the smell, taste and texture of so many of the foods she usually loved, including anything remotely healthy, but cake was one thing she'd never have any problem with. Especially when it was one of Gwen's.

'You're not supposed to worry about healthy things when you're eating cake, my love. It won't taste nearly as good if you do.' Gwen was originally from Wales, but she'd lost a lot of her accent over the years and it definitely had a West Country twang now. She'd been a midwife for nearly four decades and Toni loved hearing her stories about what the job used to be like. She might not hold much truck with some of the new ideas – they all knew better than to even say the word 'doula' in Gwen's presence – but she was the definition of a safe pair of hands.

'Jess has got to eat healthily to set the kids a good example.' Toni whipped the slice of lemon drizzle cake off her plate just as she was about to take the first forkful, laughing at the look of incredulity that crossed her friend's face. Thank God for the job and the chance to surround herself, day in and day out, with her closest friends. It meant that for at least a part of every day she didn't have to think about everything else. 'I'm only doing my bit to help you out by eating it for you.'

'If I stick a fork in your forehead, that's not going to go down very well with the foster panel either!' Jess laughed as Toni dropped the cake back onto the plate and held up her hands.

'Can I draw your attention to the laminated signs in the corridor – *aggression towards the midwifery staff will not be tolerated.*'

'That's only for the general public. There's nothing to say we can't fight to the death over Gwen's lemon drizzle cake. It's worth it after all.' Jess finally put a forkful of cake into her mouth. 'Oh my God, it really is good. So, so good.'

'Someone sounds like they're having a good time!' Ella came back from checking on the progress of a woman in the early stages of labour in the birthing suite, just in time to hear exactly how much Jess was enjoying the cake. 'Are you having a *When Harry Met Sally* moment?'

'Nope, this cake's *definitely* better than sex.'

'You're obviously having it with the wrong people then, Jess.' Gwen might have been a grandma several times over, but that didn't mean she'd couldn't drop a bawdy one-liner when the mood took her and more than once Toni had found herself wishing that Judy, or even her own mother, was more like Gwen. Maybe if they'd been even half as open, she could have told them how she felt and she'd have known they'd understand why she didn't want to be on her own forever. Gwen shot a look in her direction. 'I love cake as much as the next person, but it's never made my legs shake after I've eaten a slice. You know what I mean, don't you Toni?'

'The only thing that makes my legs shake is the yoga class that Ella roped me into.' Toni screwed up her face; there were definitely some things she was glad her mother and Judy had never wanted to discuss with her. 'Downward dog is the closest I've got to a sex position since I turned thirty.'

'What about Bob—' Gwen had been about to mention the elephant in the room, the open secret the whole team knew but no one talked about. But then Jess gave her a nudge.

'Frankie's the one you need to talk to when she gets back from New Zealand. Since her divorce she seems to be making up for lost time and apparently she's got enough unsolicited dick pics to paper her downstairs loo.' Jess wrinkled her nose. 'It's all of that stuff that makes me think I'll be single forever, if that's what internet dating has to offer.'

'Why do they do that anyway?' Ella shook her head. 'I mean, there's absolutely nothing pretty about a willy, is there?'

'You clearly haven't been looking at the right ones either, my love.' Gwen dropped a perfect wink.

'Much as I hate to leave before Gwen fills us in on her idea of the perfect willy, I've got my first home visit in twenty minutes with Maxine Murphy.' Toni was already checking her bag, making sure she'd have everything she needed.

'How's Maxine doing?' Jess furrowed her brow as she spoke, clearly realising how worried Toni was. She'd told Jess about Maxine living in shared accommodation, which essentially wasn't much better than a squat, and the tell-tale signs Toni had spotted of drug taking in the room that Maxine's boyfriend and his mates seemed to hang out in all day long, playing the PlayStation and smoking more than just cigarettes. Even Maxine's clothes had smelt of weed. So, whether Maxine herself was involved or not, she and her unborn baby were still being subjected to the second-hand risks at the very least.

Toni had managed to get Maxine to open up in the end, after scheduling several extra visits and finally hitting on a time when her boyfriend, Kai, and his mates had apparently gone out to get burgers. Maxine had admitted she wanted to get the baby away from the situation, but that she was terrified of leaving because she had nowhere to go. Her parents had apparently disowned her after her second arrest for possession of drugs and she was clinging on to Kai because he was all she had – even though she and the baby came way down his list of priorities. Toni had managed to put Maxine in touch with a social worker, who'd arranged some temporary accommodation for her just outside Port Tremellien. Technically, it put Maxine outside the unit's catchment area, but Anna had agreed to make an exception because of how much Maxine wanted Toni to remain as her midwife, and the fact that the accommodation was only tempo-rary until the council could find somewhere to house her permanently.

'She seems to be doing okay. It's only a one-bedroomed place, so she'll have to move again when the baby needs its own room.' Toni shrugged. 'But she's looking a lot happier already and appar-ently her mother has even been over to visit. They didn't believe she'd got clean when she first told them about the baby, because she was still living with Kai, but now her mother has seen things with her own eyes, Maxine is hoping it's the start of them rebuilding their relationship.'

'It's hard to imagine someone turning their back on their child like that.' Jess sighed. 'But sadly we know it happens.'

'Maxine only told me about the drug arrests at first, but since she's been in the flat, she's started to say a lot more about what went on. Kai had her stealing from her parents and trying to set up loan arrangements in their names, all to get the money for more drugs. Maxine was sucked into it, but somehow she stopped it all overnight when she found out she was pregnant. That takes real strength and I've told her that. I really admire what she's done.' Toni's eyes met Jess's for a moment and she swallowed hard. If there was any chance she was pregnant, that was what would make it such a disaster – the fact she wouldn't be able to break the cycle. She'd still have to find a way of putting Judy first, or at least far higher up her list than she should be, otherwise the guilt would overwhelm her and that wasn't fair on any child. Jess was someone who was determined not to replicate the experiences she'd had as a child, though, and as much as she might not always be able to find the right words, Toni wanted her to know how special that made Jess in her eyes. 'The women who manage to break the cycle of what they've been through, to do the best for the next generation, are always the ones I admire the most.'

'Having you as her midwife has helped Maxine no end and I know what a difference having a good social worker can make too.' Jess was obviously determined not to take any credit, but then that was just the sort of person she was.

'Jess is right, you'll have helped Maxine more than you even realise.' Ella moved to stand next to Toni as she spoke. 'Not every midwife would have pursued things with social services as tenaciously as you did. You deserve to give yourself some credit too, Toni.'

'I just did what any of us would have done.' Toni wasn't that different to Jess when it came down to it, and she found it difficult to take credit for doing her job at the best of times. But when part of the reason she'd spent so many hours ringing round to try and get Maxine the help she needed was so she wouldn't have to think about her own life, it was even harder. If she'd had a family of her own, she wouldn't have had the time to help Maxine as much as she had, but it had filled the days when she wasn't working. She was almost as scared of having too much time to think as she was of getting a message from Bobby to say he'd made a decision about taking one of the job offers. She'd got so jumpy every time her mobile pinged, she'd had to put it on silent when she wasn't on duty or waiting for a call back from Social Services. As for the internal voice that told her she really should take a pregnancy test... she couldn't give that any airtime at all.

'However much you might protest, Toni, you've been a star and we all know it.' Jess put another paper plate on top of the one with her half-eaten cake on it. 'That said, if you get back to the staff room before me and eat my cake, there will definitely be some fork in the forehead action.'

'At least that way you and Toni will get some action at last!' Gwen was out in the corridor before Toni could even respond. It came to something when your love life made someone over the age of sixty laugh, but that was the least of Toni's worries. The internal voice was at it again, reminding her she'd be driving right past the chemist in Port Agnes and there was absolutely no reason not to stop and buy a test. If she was so certain it was going to be negative, why didn't she just find out for sure? Shaking her head, she grabbed her bag. Maxine needed her and even a short stop off at the chemist's was out of the question. That was the only reason she wasn't doing a test and, if she told herself that often enough, she might even start to believe it.

* * *

Jess had one more clinic appointment before she could get ready for her date… with the rest of Gwen's lemon drizzle cake. She'd been running to time all morning, but the last appointment was with Faith Baxter and there was no telling whether it would be straightforward or not. As far as Jess knew, Faith was still seeing her therapist twice a week and having regular CBT sessions to help her deal with the extra worry of being pregnant after a still-birth. But she also had a weekly appointment at the midwifery unit and, more often than not, her anxiety levels were still pretty high.

'How have you been since I last saw you?' Jess helped Faith onto the examination table. They'd agreed, as soon as it had been a possibility, that the first thing Jess would do at each appointment was to find the baby's heartbeat, after Faith had admitted she couldn't concentrate on anything Jess said until she'd done that.

'I bought a home Doppler.' Faith wriggled down the table. 'I know you told me it might not be a good idea, but I couldn't stand waiting between appointments.'

'It's not that it's necessarily a *bad* idea, as long as it lowers your stress levels rather than making things even worse. You've just got to be careful that you aren't picking up the sound of your own blood vessels, or the blood flowing through the placenta. And if you can't pick up the heartbeat, it probably isn't because anything terrible has happened. You just need to make sure you've got a way of managing your anxiety and getting checked over, if anything worries you.'

'If I had the choice, I'd spend the next couple of months hooked up to an ultrasound machine until the baby arrives.'

'That might not be very practical!' Jess smiled, tracing the Doppler over Faith's stomach, the sound of the baby's heartbeat coming through loud and clear almost instantly. Faith's body visibly relaxed in response.

'Ah there he is.'

'*He*?' Jess's money had been on Faith having another little boy, but she'd said they didn't want to find out.

'We had a private 4D scan on Wednesday and I decided I wanted to know after all.' Faith sighed. 'I thought not knowing the baby's gender might make things easier and I wouldn't get so attached until I was sure that he or she was going to make it. But it was a stupid idea. How are you supposed to stay detached from something that's growing inside you and getting up to all sorts of tricks to remind you of the fact? The latest little gift is extra body hair in places I've stopped being able to reach!'

'There's a story for his wedding day!' As soon as the words were out of her mouth, Jess wished she hadn't said them. The last thing she wanted was to trigger Faith's anxiety by expecting her to think too far ahead, but her reaction was the last thing Jess expected.

'I'd be more than willing to share that story with everyone I meet between now and then to make it to that day. Thank God I'm finally starting to feel like it's going to be okay and that Michael and I will get to bring our baby home this time.'

'That's brilliant! Everything's looking great from my point of view too. All the blood tests we ran last time look good, the baby's heartbeat is really strong and with you feeling much calmer, I've got a feeling your blood pressure will be spot on too. But we'd better just get it checked.' Jess tightened the blood pressure monitor around Faith's arm. 'One hundred over seventy. That's fantastic.'

'I'm trying not to imagine what kind of state I'm going to get myself into once Titus arrives, worrying about every little thing that could possibly happen to him. Not to mention the big things.

I'm just hoping that all the monitors, thermometers and purifiers I've bought will give me a bit of reassurance, otherwise Michael is going to be hairless by the time the baby's six weeks old.'

'Every new mum feels like that and you've been through a lot. Don't be too hard on yourself if you struggle with any of it. I'll be around to support you for a couple of weeks too and then you'll have the health visitors to turn to for advice. What about the rest of the family, are they going to support you after the baby's born?'

'Mum's coming to stay for two weeks; hopefully it'll work out that she ends up being here for a little while before Titus arrives and for the first week afterwards.'

'How lovely to have your mum with you.' Jess swallowed the lump in her throat that could still lodge itself there when she least expected it. She'd never be able to share the experience of bonding over a newborn baby with her own mum, even if by some miracle of IVF she managed to give birth one day. Maybe things really did happen for a reason. Not having her mum around when she started fostering was sad, but at least it didn't feel like she was missing out on some kind of rite of passage of mother and daughter bonding. 'I've never looked after a baby called Titus before; it's a really strong sounding name.'

'You don't think it's a weird name then? I chose it because apparently it means hope and the true son of faith. When I read that I couldn't think of anything more fitting. It helps me believe I'll actually get to keep my second son.'

'It's perfect.'

'He's our rainbow baby, so we're going to go for Indigo or Blue for a middle name. I'd like both, but Michael thinks it'll make us sound like the Kardashians!' Faith laughed, making the tape measure slide down her bump as Jess tried to gauge the baby's growth. 'I didn't realise he even knew who the Kardashians were.'

'It's nice that he can still surprise you!' Jess shook off the image of Dom that had suddenly popped into her head. Even though they'd separated, he still had the power to surprise her, given the text he'd sent her the night before.

Let's try again

As if it was that simple. He must have forgotten all the promises he'd broken, and the reason he'd given for leaving hadn't suddenly disappeared either.

'He's definitely still got the odd surprise up his sleeve. He wants us to have a babymoon before Titus arrives, just a couple of nights over in the hotel on the Sisters of Agnes Island. Do you think it'll be okay?'

'Like I said, all your checks are looking great and the baby's growth looks spot on for his dates. Not to mention you'll only be a boat ride away if you do need to come back. You can still call me or one of the other midwives at any time if you're worried.' The old convent on the tiny island, less than half a mile from the harbour at Port Agnes, had been converted into a hotel when the last of the nuns had left. It was such a beautiful place. It was also where Jess had realised there was no hope for her and Dom, the last time they'd met face to face. She'd caught him at the hotel with his boss's secretary, who'd been stupid enough to post pictures of them on Instagram, tagging Dom. But he still wouldn't stop pushing to meet up again, as if none of that had even happened.

'Thanks, Jess. You always make me feel so much better. I think I'm going to tell Michael to book it.' Faith pushed herself into an upright position with Jess's help. 'It'll be lovely to spend a few days together, now that I'm finally starting to let myself look forward to Titus arriving. A lot of that's down to you and I really can't thank you enough.'

'My first cuddle with Titus will be more than enough reward.' Jess smiled. 'Now get yourself home and tell Michael to get the hotel booked.'

'I will. Thanks again and I'll see you next week.'

'Definitely.'

Picking up her mobile after Faith had gone, Jess read the message from Dom again. She'd promised Dexter when she'd started the fostering assessment that she wasn't going to start a new relationship. Her relationship with Dom might not be new, but seeing him again still felt like it would be a big mistake, so she had no idea why she couldn't just delete his message. For a second her fingers hovered over the screen and then she started to type.

* * *

'Now that's what you call a biscuit.' Dexter lifted the chocolate chip cookie off the plate in front of him.

'They came out a bit larger than I expected. They just seemed to treble in size in the oven.' Jess felt herself go hot. Wanting to impress her social worker with the smell of home baking when he arrived meant that she had to serve up the results, even if the biscuits were almost as big as the plates she'd put them on.

'Trust me, I'm never going to complain about the size of a biscuit, unless it's too small!' He grinned. 'You'll have to give me the recipe for Riley, he'd absolutely love these.'

'Is that your stepson?' Jess held her breath, hoping she hadn't overstepped the mark. It was her second to last fostering assessment and Dexter still hadn't said much to confirm whether everything Fatima had said at the training day was true. He had mentioned being a widower, but he'd never spoken about his late wife's son. Until now.

'Yes, he's five, and chocolate chip cookies are just about his favourite thing in the world at the moment. His dad has been struggling to manage caring for him full time, which is why I've decided to reduce the amount of hours I'm out working to give Riley a bit more stability. But I think I'm going to have to learn how to sneak some vegetables into the cookie dough when he starts staying with me a lot more often.'

'You'll have to share the recipe for that if you manage to pull it off.' Jess was almost having to sit on her hands to stop herself from asking more questions. If Dexter wanted to tell her then he would, but she needed to find a way that was less obvious than just blurting out the million or so questions racing through her head.

'Someone did mention that you were handing your notice in. Will this be your last assessment before you leave?'

'It'll be a race to the finish line between yours, and David and Richard's. Single carer assessments are usually a bit quicker, so they'll probably be the last.' Dexter broke off a bit of biscuit. 'I need a bit more flexibility in the job than the local authority could give me, so I can take Riley to school and pick him up at least some of the time. I'm going to go freelance instead, doing assessments for fostering agencies and setting up a training company so I can work as a consultant. I volunteer with the lifeboat too, so something had to give.'

'That sounds really exciting, although I've got to admit it would have been nice for you to be my supervising social worker. If I get approved, that is.'

'I don't say this very often, but if you don't get approved I'll be very surprised. Not to mention more than a little bit...' He hesitated, frowning as he looked at her. 'I'm searching for the right words here, but what I really want to say probably wouldn't be appropriate. So I'll just say I'd be gutted if the panel turns you down, because it means there'll be children out there who'll miss out on having you as their foster carer and that would be a real shame.'

'Thanks.' Colour was already rising up Jess's neck, so she might as well go for it and ask the question that could embarrass them both if he shut her down. 'Is Riley's dad okay with you taking more responsibility for him?'

'Connor's done his best by Riley, but he's not coping with trying to follow his own dreams and putting Riley first.' Dexter shrugged. 'Sometimes a hard decision is the best one. When Connor met Chloe, that's Riley's mum, they were both struggling with addiction and they ended up splitting soon after Riley was born. Chloe managed to turn her life around and we had Riley with us full-time, but when she died Connor wanted to step up, so I just had him for a few days a month when Connor asked me to help out. He's been doing great, but he's training to be a sound engineer and he's a musician too, playing in a band at nights, and it's all just got too much for him lately. He started using again. Nothing major, but enough for him to decide he needs to step back a bit. So at least for now, Riley will be with me more or less full time and Connor will get to see him whenever he wants to.'

'I wish I'd had someone like you in my life when my dad decided he couldn't cope with me. Thank God Riley has you.' Jess bit her lip. Her life and Riley's mirrored one another's, but for the fact that there'd been no one – other than social services – to step into the breach for her. Riley was going to have a different story and he wouldn't need to make the mistakes she had, searching for love in all the wrong places.

'All that stuff you've been through is exactly why you'll make such a great foster carer, Jess, and I don't think I've ever seen a reference from an ex-partner as glowing as the one that Dominic gave you.'

'It was nice of him and I'm glad we've managed to stay friend-ly.' Jess might not be telling the full story, but it was complicated for anyone outside her relationship with Dom to understand. She'd also been only too aware that Dom had the potential to scupper all her plans with a negative reference. So although 'friends' might not be quite the right word, she couldn't sever all ties with him either.

'I know we've talked about this already, but you're absolutely certain that's all you are, friends? There's no chance you'll get back together? It's just that I'd hate to take you all the way to panel and for that to be what stops you getting approved. Especially when he still seems to think the world of you.'

'Don't worry, I'm 100 per cent sure that's all we'll be.' Jess nodded. Dom was her past, but if everything went okay then fostering would be the biggest part of her future. It didn't matter how nice Dom was being, she wouldn't let herself fall for him again. There was so much more on the line now. If she had to spend every meeting she had with Dexter promising him that things were over between her and Dom, then she would. Whatever either of them might think, there was absolutely no chance of her backing down.

13

Toni was doing the same thing she did every year, rushing around Port Agnes looking for extra Christmas gifts for Judy and Simon because she wasn't sure she'd bought them enough. It was as if she somehow had to make up for the fact that Aaron wasn't around to buy his parents a gift himself. Buying a little something extra for Judy was fairly straightforward; a pair of earrings, a scented candle and a box of truffles had already been paid for and safely stashed in her bag. Simon was a lot harder to buy for, and Port Agnes was hardly a sprawling metropolis of options. She'd already bought him a new shirt, the mandatory socks, some golf balls and his favourite aftershave, which meant she'd officially run out of ideas. Although there had been some after-shave balm in the same brand and things were getting desperate.

The only chemist in Port Agnes wasn't part of a chain, but it sold everything from birthday candles to table napkins, along with the aftershave balm it now seemed imperative for Toni to buy before closing time. There was also a shelf of pregnancy tests on the left-hand side of the wall as she went in, promising instant results before a period had even been missed. Toni didn't need one, though, because she hadn't missed a period; she didn't even have them on the mini pill, so she couldn't be pregnant. No. Absolutely not. No way. All the so-called symptoms she was having had to be caused by something else and she wasn't about to spend ten pounds on a test just to prove what she already knew: she wasn't pregnant. Except it didn't matter how many times she tried to tell herself that, the internal voice was winning. All the signs pointed to the fact that in every likelihood she was and no amount of denial would make it go away. The only thing that not knowing for sure did was allow her to sleep at night, at least for a few hours.

But even that didn't stop her waking up and staring into the darkness, trying to work out how she felt. There was a tiny flame of excitement flickering inside her, as if it was mirroring the tiny heartbeat that was almost certainly flickering away inside her too. When she laid her hand on her stomach, in the darkness of the bedroom, she allowed herself – just for a moment or two – to picture the future she'd have chosen if things were different. Bobby was an integral part of that, but so was a dark-haired child, reaching up for Bobby's hand on one side and Toni's on the other. The problem was that she couldn't stop another image coming into her head, no matter how hard she screwed up her eyes and tried to will it away; Judy tortured by grief and betrayal, and the impact of that on her illness, leaving her a shell of the person she was. Then there was the image of Aaron, sorrow in his eyes as he realised she'd let him down on the one promise she'd been determined to keep. Guilt was always going to snuff out the flicker of excitement and there wouldn't be a dark-haired child that she and Bobby shared, no matter how much she might want there to be. It was why denial was so much easier; even a tiny slither of hope that she might have got this all wrong was easier than facing the alternative. But she couldn't deny things forever and she couldn't risk leaving it too late.

'I thought that was you through the window, but you looked like you were a million miles away.' Scott, Bobby's father, almost made Toni jump out of her skin as he touched her shoulder, her face flushing with heat at the prospect of him seeing her staring at the pregnancy tests.

'It's lovely to see you.' She had no choice but to be folded into Scott's embrace; Bobby's parents were those sort of people. It was really lovely to see him, though, even if it did make her want to burst into tears. The whole of Bobby's family had welcomed her from the moment he'd first brought her home. Toni had insisted that they tell his family they were only friends, too. After all, Port Agnes was only a few miles from Port Tremellien, where her parents and Aaron's lived, and news had a way of travelling.

'When I saw you, I knew I had to try and get you to change your mind and come to our Christmas Eve party. Joyce has already started cooking up a storm in preparation for it and, you know her, there'd be enough to feed the whole town if they showed up, but she'd be so thrilled to see you.'

'I can't, I—' Toni was desperately trying to remember what Bobby had told his parents about why she couldn't come to their party this year. If everyone had known they were a couple, it would have been easier to explain why she wasn't there. Couples who split up didn't go to each other's family parties. But it was harder to explain away why a friend wouldn't turn up for the first time in three years.

'Bobby said you were going away yesterday to visit family in Devon for Christmas, but your plans have obviously changed.' Scott had an open, friendly smile and it was his dimples Bobby had inherited.

'Oh yes, my aunt's not well. So my plans ended up changing

last minute and I'm just seeing my immediate family in Port Tremellien now. I'm going on Christmas morning and I'm staying until Boxing Day, seeing as I'm not on call for once.'

'What about on Christmas Eve, are you on call then?'

'No, but—' For the second time in less than a minute, she couldn't finish the sentence and Scott didn't miss a trick.

'I don't know what's gone on between you and Bobby, or why you've spent the last three years insisting to us that you're just friends.' Scott held up a hand when she started to protest. 'But whatever is, you need to get past it. We've all seen the way you look at each other and I'm guessing it's other people keeping you apart. I know what that's like. When I married Joyce, there were plenty of people on both sides of the family who weren't happy about it. You wouldn't believe it, but my uncle even told me I should "stick to my own kind". We actually got into a physical fight and he still doesn't talk to me now, but he's no loss to my life. Not with that sort of thinking. Anyone who doesn't want you to be happy doesn't deserve to be a part of your life either. Especially if it's because of the colour of Bobby's skin.'

'It's nothing like that; we *really* are just friends.' Toni sounded desperate even to her own ears and she blurted out what she said next without thinking about it. 'There's another girl at work, Emily. I think they've started seeing each other and I thought maybe he'd like to bring her this year. I just didn't want to cramp his style, that's all.'

'He hasn't mentioned wanting to bring anyone else.' Scott touched her arm again. 'Come on, come over and see us. Bobby's not even coming until later in the evening if you'd rather not see him.'

'I really don't know if I can.' Even as she said it, part of her was trying to work out a way to make it possible. Bobby's parents' house was like an explosion in a tinsel factory at Christmas and his nieces and nephews spent the whole time hyped up on selection boxes and adrenaline, powered by sheer excitement. It was the opposite to five adults sitting quietly in Judy and Simon's tastefully decorated home, reminiscing about Christmases past and, the truth was, there was nowhere else Toni would rather be. She was desperate to see Bobby too, but that equation was more difficult to balance. Spending any amount of time with him now, even at work, was a mixture of heaven and hell. Like staring through a shop window at the most delicious cake you've ever tasted and finding out the shop was shut for good. It would be easier not to see him at all, especially at Christmas, and hide out at Judy and Simon's place instead, pretending that the rest of the world didn't exist, just like Judy always did.

'It would make Joyce's Christmas, *please*.' Scott's expression suddenly made him look so much like Bobby all the times he'd pleaded with her to put them first and give them a proper chance. The longing to see him again, outside of work, and try to explain one more time that she'd do anything for him that was in her power to do, was almost overwhelming. She couldn't turn down Scott's invitation, even if it was the sensible option.

'Okay, but I'll just pop by for a quick drink, that's all, and then I'll have to go.' If she set out the expectations now, she might not be so tempted to stay any longer than that, especially as there was no guarantee that Bobby would be pleased to see her.

'Great, we'll see you at seven on Christmas Eve, then. Bye sweetheart.' As Scott disappeared back out of the door, Toni's body almost sagged with exhaustion and she had to lean up against the display of hair dyes for a moment to steady herself. The constant rows between her heart and her head, with that pesky internal voice barely seeming to pause for breath, not to mention the broken sleep, were making her bone-tired. Catching her breath, she picked up a pregnancy testing kit and a tub of aftershave balm and headed to the till. She might as well know for sure, even if the prospect of finding out the results make her legs go weak all over again.

* * *

Watching the turntable of the microwave spin around as she waited for her frozen curry for one to finish cooking, Toni seemed to have hit rock bottom. It was two days before Christmas and she'd picked up her ready meal on the way back home after seeing Scott. She could have been out with the girls from work. Izzy, the new midwife on the team, was throwing a Christmas party at her flat in Redruth, but the thought of being crammed into a small space with that many people was making her hot flushes go into overdrive. She was on call until 6 a.m., so she had a reason she could give for turning down a glass of something bubbly to celebrate the festivities and at least the others might think she was simply giving Scrooge and the Grinch a run for their money. Maybe it was just as well she couldn't drink, though, because she'd never felt more like she needed a large glass of something alcoholic than she did right now and she might not know when to stop. Once she did the test, there'd be no pretending any more that there was a chance she might not be pregnant and then she'd have to start making some impossible decisions.

Looking around the flat, there was nothing to even indicate it was Christmas; she hadn't felt like bothering when there'd been no one but her to see it. Bobby was a chip off the old block when it came to Christmas, albeit with slightly more of a low-key style than his parents. When he'd found out, in their first December together, that Toni wasn't planning to have a tree, he'd stepped in. Coming home from work one day, three weeks before Christmas, she'd found Bobby waiting for her. Somehow he'd lugged a five-foot potted Christmas tree up the stairs, after discovering the lift was out of order. He'd bought some beautiful wooden decorations too and he'd encouraged her to pull out the box of decorations from the back of a storage cupboard, where they'd been left since Aaron had died. Having not been able to go travelling, they'd settled instead for weekends and day trips away; always close enough to be able to rush home if Judy's health took a turn for the worse. They'd got into the habit of buying quirky Christmas decorations when they found them on their trips, everything from an angel made out of welded antique cutlery, to a star made out of a mosaic of broken stained glass pieces, salvaged from a deconsecrated church further up the Atlantic coast.

'You shouldn't hide all these away.' Bobby had turned the star over in his hand, the glass catching the light and creating a rainbow of colour. 'You need to remember the good times you had with Aaron and focus on those, otherwise you'll never really get over the rest.'

She loved him more than ever in that moment. He could quite easily have kept quiet and not had to look at reminders of her life with Aaron every time he glanced at the tree. But he'd wanted what was best for Toni, there'd never been any question of that. If he looked around the flat now, he'd have been horrified, but he would have had it transformed within the hour if he got half the chance. She couldn't even bear to think about how amazing he'd be at creating the perfect Christmas for a child; every day of December would be filled with excitement and fun. What could she offer a baby, in comparison, though? If the flat was anything to go by, then the answer was nothing at all.

Suddenly the microwave pinged, making her jump. The curry somehow looked even less appetising than it had when she'd put it in ten minutes before. *Do the test, do the test, do the test.* The words were starting to repeat in her head on a loop, spinning around and around like her plate had in the microwave, and she was never going to get them to stop unless she took the test.

'Oh, for God's sake. Okay, I'll do it.' Toni mumbled the words to herself as she went through to the sitting room, where her handbag was. Unzipping it, she hesitated and then zipped it straight up again. She'd waited this long, so she could carry on waiting for a bit longer. If she found out before Christmas, she was going to have to hug the secret she'd been keeping to herself all the tighter, just to make it through to New Year. Whatever she tried to tell herself, there was a difference to being almost sure and knowing the facts with 100 per cent certainty.

Walking back through to the kitchen she looked at the curry again, a wave of nausea swirling in her stomach at the sight of it. *Just do the bloody test!*

'All right!' This time she didn't hesitate. Grabbing the box out of her bag she ripped off the wrapper and headed straight for the bathroom. It was the sort that would not only tell her whether she was pregnant or not, but also by how many weeks, up to as far as three weeks plus. If that was the result that came up, she'd need a scan to work out just how far along she was. Other than getting a negative result, it was the only one of the three options that was possible, because there was no way the one week or two week outcomes were an option; she hadn't slept with Bobby since October. If three weeks plus appeared on the display, it would mean she was somewhere between ten weeks and about sixteen, otherwise she'd have had more of a bump. For now, she was still crossing her fingers, against all logic, that the test would come up negative. Less than five minutes later she was staring at the display.

Pregnant 3+

'Shit.' Toni stared at the result for at least ten more minutes, trying to process what it meant – even though it was spelt out in digital simplicity. A thousand thoughts were rushing through her head and she didn't know how to even begin making sense of them. What the hell was she supposed to do now? She wasn't with Bobby and there was no guarantee that he'd want anything to do with her after all she'd put him through, although he was too family-focussed to ever walk away from that sort of responsibility. He'd step up, if she gave him the chance, she was almost sure of it. But it was harder to work out if he'd really want to and whether she could even let him try. She hadn't been able to put him first, not once in their whole relationship, and she'd seen what it had done to him. It wouldn't be fair to even contemplate doing that to a child. She was always going to be pulled in two directions and every child deserved to be the centre of its parents' world. Anything less just wasn't good enough.

Tears were streaming down Toni's face as she stared at the test again, the words merging into an incomprehensible blur. Nothing made sense and none of the solutions she was desperately trying to grasp were going to work. The only thing she knew for sure was that she had to tell someone, and there was only one person that could be.

* * *

It was barely light by the time Toni headed out. She hadn't slept for more than about an hour, in fifteen-minute bursts, ever since she'd seen the result on the pregnancy test. She'd kept hoping for a call-out, anything to take her mind off the fact that she was pregnant. She was too old and in the wrong job to have let this happen by accident. When she'd thought about calling one of the other girls at work to talk about it, she couldn't do it. What was she supposed to say to Jess, who would desperately have loved to be able to have a baby on her own? Or to Anna, who'd needed to take fertility medication to fall pregnant and had been terrified it might never happen?

So here she was, about to tell the only person she could, that she was pregnant. It was cold and misty in the churchyard of St Jude's, like something out of a black-and-white horror movie, but somehow it fitted her mood perfectly.

'Happy Christmas, Aaron.' Toni touched the headstone, the way she always did when she came to visit him. 'I've done something really stupid. I'm pregnant.'

Even saying the words out loud was difficult, like trying to pronounce a complicated word in a foreign language, instead of one she dealt with every single day of her working life.

'What am I supposed to do? I'm not with Bobby any more, but I could do this on my own, couldn't I?' Toni stared at the words etched on Aaron's gravestone, as she waited for an answer she knew would never come.

Beloved son, much loved fiancé, missed by all and simply irreplaceable

'It would break your mum and dad's heart, though, wouldn't it? Thinking that I'd replaced you. They wouldn't be able to stand me being around any more. Then Mum and Dad would have to divide their time between their best friends and their daughter, and however close they might be, your parents might decide they need to move away, so they could be left with no one. I can't do that to them.' Toni gave a shuddering sigh. 'Can I?'

A robin landed on a branch of the tree above Aaron's grave, studying her intently. *Robins appear when loved ones are near.* She remembered reading that somewhere, once, maybe on one of the plaques that hung in Pottery and Paper, the art gallery and gift shop in the centre of Port Agnes. Not that she really believed in all of that, but what if it *was* Aaron trying to send her some kind of message?

'What should I do, Aaron, tell me, please?' The robin was still staring at her, but it wasn't helping at all. If she had this baby, she was going to break at least two people's hearts and she had no idea how her parents would feel about it, especially if they ended up losing their oldest friends over it. If she decided not to go ahead with the pregnancy, Bobby would be none the wiser, and the only heart she'd end up breaking would be her own. There were so many things against the idea of going ahead, it was hard to think of the positives, except that she wanted a baby. She'd wanted a baby one day for as long as she could remember. This wasn't just any baby either, it was Bobby's baby. The picture she'd had in her head of the two of them, with a child holding their hands, had crystalised into a much clearer image in the dead of the night and she'd recognised it immediately – as everything she'd ever wanted, but hadn't dared believe she'd have. She could visualise the baby's features and it all felt so real, it was almost as though she could have reached out and touched it. But however hard she tried, she couldn't make that picture fit into the wider landscape of her life. She was going to have to choose and she still had no idea how.

'I wish you were here, so you really could tell me what to do and because I still miss you so much.' A single tear made its way down Toni's face and once she'd started crying she couldn't seem to stop. Whatever she did, someone was going to be hurt in a way they'd never get over and, as much as she still missed Aaron, she missed Bobby even more. He was the love of her life. But Judy and Simon had already lost the love of both their lives too. It wasn't just about them any more, though, it was about doing what was right by the baby. She'd already made Bobby's life a misery and made her own so narrow and claustrophobic that it sometimes felt like she could barely breathe. She couldn't do that to a child; bring it into a world where there were people in its mother's life wishing it had never been born and resenting it from day one. She couldn't have a baby unless she was certain that she would always, without failure, be able to put that child first, no matter what. But if she could do that, she wouldn't be here now asking Aaron a question he could never answer. And that should tell her all she needed to know.

14

Toni had turned back to her flat no less than three times before finally deciding to put in a very brief appearance at Scott and Joyce's house, before Bobby turned up. She'd checked the rotas and he was working the Christmas Eve shift at the unit until seven o'clock, so there was no way he'd make it before eight, even if there were no deliveries. She couldn't risk bumping into him because there was always a chance she might blurt out that she was pregnant and then all of her options would be taken away from her.

Scott and Joyce only lived a few roads away from Toni's flat, so even with the three abandoned attempts to get there, she could still make it by quarter past seven. No one wanted to arrive bang on the start time for a party, anyway.

Port Agnes was bathed in the glow of thousands of sparkling lights as Toni finally made her way through the streets. The lights strung between the narrow roads that led down to the harbour were themed to display the twelve days of Christmas and most of the cottages had been decorated to celebrate the festivities in one way or another. There were Christmas trees on display in the front windows of a lot of the houses Toni passed, but she was still a few doors down from Joyce and Scott's place when she saw the glow of their outside Christmas lights. The pièce de résistance was a life-sized Santa Claus, complete with sleigh and eight reindeer, stretching from one side of the roof of their double-fronted cottage to the other.

Even at the last minute Toni had almost doubled back to the flat for a fourth time. The thought of looking into Scott and Joyce's eyes knowing she was keeping an enormous secret from them, was already making her stomach churn. During the night, she'd run through every possible solution in her head. She'd even considered the possibility that Judy and Simon might welcome the baby into their lives. The trouble was, if they did, it would still come with a caveat. Everything in Judy's life came on her terms and there was every chance she'd start dictating how Toni parented and the decisions she made about her child's life. Bobby would never stand for that and Toni knew she shouldn't either, but it was easier said than done when the stakes were as high as Aaron's death and Judy's illness had made them. Toni and the baby would end up being pulled in two different directions until something snapped. There was too much resentment on Bobby's side and too much history of control from Judy for them ever to get along. Judy was never going to change and Toni knew she'd never be able to live with herself if she cut her out of her life. As much as she didn't want to accept it, because even considering it was too painful to dwell on, there really was only one solution to her unexpected pregnancy.

'You came!' Scott opened the door wearing an apron emblazoned with the words '*Mrs Claus's Little Helper*' and a headband with two antlers, which kept knocking against the low ceiling. Something that smelled delicious was obviously busy being concocted in the kitchen and Toni's stomach gave a low growl before she even had a chance to answer Scott, reminding her that she hadn't eaten since she'd abandoned her microwaved curry the night before. But she couldn't carry on like that and it was a relief to feel like she might actually want to eat something, instead of having to force it down.

'Sounds like you're hungry, sweetheart; go straight through and I'll make you up a plate from the buffet before we set it out. You midwives need looking after, I know how often you forget to put yourselves first!'

'I'm not going to fade away from missing a meal or two. Let's face it, I could do with losing some weight.' Toni's face had gone hot and it was nothing to do with the warmth inside the cottage or the fact that her growling stomach could have woken the dead. Scott's words had echoed the ones that Bobby had said to her so many times, but it was the uncomfortable truth that she was already forgetting to prioritise the baby's needs that really hit home – like a slap in the face that would have made her cheeks even redder than they already were.

'Nonsense, you're perfect as you are. Go through sweetheart and bring the plate in. What would you like to drink? We've got white wine, red wine, rosé, cider, beer, Prosecco, mulled wine and every flavour of gin known to man, or at least Joyce!'

'Just a fruit juice would be great, thanks. I'm on antibiotics for an ear infection.' She shrugged, the lies already tripping off her tongue far too easily. Maybe it was stupid avoiding alcohol in the same way as she would have done if she was planning to go through with the pregnancy. But no matter how much sense it made, she was nowhere near coming to terms with the decision yet and, until she was, she was going to follow the advice she'd have given any other new mother-to-be.

* * *

Toni had hoovered up the food that Scott had brought to her with embarrassing haste in the end, but her stomach seemed determined to keep howling in protest and she had to get it to stop somehow. She'd have been horrified if one of her mums-to-be had gone without eating for more than twenty-four hours, so she was just doing what she'd promised herself and following her own advice for once.

Joyce had greeted her with every bit as much enthusiasm as Scott and had enveloped her in a hug that immediately felt like coming home. There was no chastising her for the fact that she hadn't visited in ages; all Joyce had wanted to hear was how Toni was. No wonder Bobby struggled so much with understanding Toni's interactions with Judy and Simon, and even her own parents, when his so clearly put other people, but especially their own children, at the top of their list of priorities.

She was chatting to Bobby's sister – after his mother had gone to put another tray of puff pastry cheese whirls into the oven – and thinking about how she could end the conversation and make her excuses to leave, when Bobby walked through the door.

'I wasn't expecting to see you here.' He found Toni before she had a chance to formulate an escape plan, despite her telling his sister that she needed the loo and then making her best attempt to disappear altogether by wedging herself in the gap between the Christmas tree and the bookcase in his parents' lounge.

'I wasn't expecting to see myself here either, but when I bumped into your dad at the chemist, he wouldn't take no for an answer.'

'He's very persuasive when he wants to be.'

'You don't have to tell me, but I've missed seeing your parents.'

'They've missed you too. They've been driving me mad asking what's gone on between us. They don't buy it that we're just friends you know.' His eyes met hers for a minute and her stomach flipped over. 'Ironically, now that we're actually telling the truth about that, they believe it less than ever.'

'Are we friends again? I wasn't sure if you'd want to be after... well, you know, everything. Especially with you planning to change jobs and maybe even move to the States just to get away from me.' Toni's heart was thudding in her ears, a sudden realisation of how much she wanted Bobby – in any form she could get – in her life. But if he found out what she was keeping from him, he'd have every right to hate her. She couldn't stand the thought of him doing that, so whatever it took, she was going to have to make sure he never found out that she was lying to him by omission.

'If friends is all I can get, then I'll just have to take it.' Bobby attempted a causal tone, although his body language looked anything but relaxed.

'And what about your plans to move?' The blood was still rushing in her ears and for a couple of seconds she swayed to and fro before reaching out to grab hold of the bookshelf to steady herself.

'I'm not going anywhere.' He held her gaze and she had to grip the bookshelf even more tightly to stop herself from throwing her arms around his neck, as her body flooded with relief. If he'd gone to America, there was a chance that she might never have seen him again and that was something else she wasn't ready to come to terms with. 'I don't want to miss out on seeing my nieces and nephews grow up, or be the sort of uncle that they only ever see on FaceTime. I don't want to miss out on time with Mum and Dad either, they aren't getting any younger. Although they told me I shouldn't turn down the opportunity, if I really wanted to go. Even if Mum was trying desperately to pretend she wasn't crying when she said it.'

'She just didn't want to stand in your way.' It was another

stark example of how different Bobby's parents were from Judy. He'd never really understand how lucky he was. 'What about the other offer, from the agency?'

'I'm still thinking it through, but they've given me until the new year to decide.' His voice was low now, barely more than a whisper, so that no one but her would be able to hear what he said next. They'd spent so long trying to keep things secret that even now every conversation felt like part of a covert mission. 'Are you really okay with this ending, Toni? Because I'm not.'

She wanted to tell him that she was terrified. Terrified of saying something that might give away a secret so big that it made the one they'd kept about their relationship seem like nothing in comparison. She was also terrified that she'd never get over their relationship. Never get over *him*. But she didn't say any of that.

'I'm trying to be okay.'

'I guess that's all either of us can do, if this is how it's got to be. Like I said, friends is better than nothing, right?' Bobby suddenly sounded exhausted and he drained the glass of wine his father had pressed into his hand as he'd walked towards Toni, as if he had an unquenchable thirst. 'Can I get you another drink?'

'Thanks, it's just apple juice. I've got to head off soon anyway. I've got all my presents still to wrap and I need to be at Judy and Simon's in time for breakfast at ten-thirty tomorrow.'

'The same old traditions, eh? Nothing ever changes. Don't you ever wish you could just change one or two of them?' Bobby's tone was tight, a muscle going in his cheek. He'd run out of patience with the situation a long time ago and the mention of Aaron's parents seemed to have compounded what Toni already knew. Bobby wouldn't be able to make any space in his life for the people he blamed for driving a wedge between the two of them. She couldn't keep her promise to Aaron and ever be anything more than faux friends with Bobby. There was no way they could be real friends; there was too much tension between them and just a passing comment about Aaron's parents would always be enough to drive him crazy. So she'd never be able to open up to him about her home life now, the way she might to Anna, Ella or Jess.

'Those traditions mean so much to Judy and Simon.'

'And what about you, Toni. What does all of it mean to you?'

'It means I'm doing right by Aaron.' It also meant she'd be doing right by Bobby, but she couldn't tell him that. Staying away from him as much as possible, ever since their trip to Land's End, to give him a real chance of moving on and having the life he deserved, had been one of the most difficult things she'd ever had to do. Until now.

'My favourite couple, back together again! This is all I wanted for Christmas.' Joyce was heading towards them, clutching a bunch of what Toni had a horrible feeling was mistletoe. Everyone else in the lounge had stopped chatting to each other and they were already looking in their direction. If Toni had seen a clear path to the door she'd have shot forward before Joyce even reached them, but the other guests were blocking her only means of escape.

'Mum, if that's what it looks like, don't even think about suggesting it.' Bobby's protests might as well have been in Lithuanian for all the notice Joyce took.

'Come on then, have a kiss and really make my Christmas.' It was like Joyce was channelling her inner Judy and manipulating the situation in the most embarrassing way possible. Toni wasn't into public displays of affection at the best of times, but the idea of kissing Bobby in front of a room full of people, especially with the way things were between them, was like a form of torture. For a split second she thought about diving head first into the

Christmas tree and knocking it flying – anything that might create a diversion, so she could get away.

'Please Uncle Bobby.' His youngest niece suddenly appeared like a genie from behind where her grandmother was standing, still brandishing the bunch of mistletoe. She was wearing a yellow dress, which, if Toni wasn't very much mistaken, was a miniature version of one of the Disney princess dresses. 'You'll be like Beauty and the Beast at the end of the film!'

'Are you calling me a beast?' Bobby grinned at his niece, twin dimples appearing in his cheeks and making Toni's chest ache with longing for things to be different. If they were alone in her flat and he'd turned up with a bunch of mistletoe, she wouldn't even have tried to stay strong. She loved him so much and she always would, but she was betraying him in a way that might be even worse than the way she'd betrayed Aaron. Lying by omission seemed to have become her modus operandi, but that was what happened when you were trying – and failing dismally – to keep everyone happy.

'You're only like the beast after the curse is broken Uncle Bobby!' His niece wagged a finger at him. 'But I'm wearing Belle's dress 'specially and I really want to see a real-life prince and princess kiss!'

'You know I'm not a prince and that Toni's not a princess, don't you?'

'You think she's pretty enough to be one, though, Uncle Bobby. I've heard you say to Nanny that Toni's beautiful.' Bobby's niece fixed him with a stare filled with all the unwavering honestly and determination that only a six-year-old could muster. For her part, Toni was starting to feel like death would be a welcome relief – not just from the embarrassment of the situation, but from the knowledge of what she was throwing away with Bobby. She didn't deserve him to love her the way he did – or at least the way he had – and she was never going to find anything like it again. She didn't even want to try.

'You're right, she is beautiful.' Bobby's eyes met Toni's and her legs turned to jelly; she couldn't have run away now even if the option had been open. 'And I suppose if this is the one Christmas wish of my mother *and* my niece, I'll just have to grant it.'

'Yay!' Joyce and her granddaughter called out at the same time, as Bobby finally accepted the mistletoe from his mother.

'I'm sorry if this is the most embarrassing thing that's ever happened to you.' Bobby whispered the words, his mouth inches away from Toni's ear. 'But the truth is, I want to do this too, in case it's the last time.'

She didn't answer. She was rooted to the spot by a combination of horror and longing that was impossible to unravel. When Bobby kissed her it was gentle and low-key, like the sort of kiss the heir to the throne might give his new bride on the balcony of Buckingham Palace – entirely appropriate when there was an audience watching. Despite the circumstances, if she could have frozen the moment and stopped the world's most awkward kiss from ever ending, then she would. Kissing him, even like this, still beat every other kiss she'd ever had hands down and she had to fight to stop from wrapping herself around him in a way that would have been anything but PG. Bobby had already said that this could be the last time and as he pulled away from her, Toni's eyes filled with tears. She'd already lost so much and she was about to sacrifice even more. That had to have repaid the debt she owed Aaron, because it had cost her absolutely everything.

15

Toni hadn't slept for more than about twenty minutes at a time and whenever she'd woken up, she'd reached straight for her phone to check whether there was anything from Bobby. All it would have taken was one tiny message, a handful of words, or even the right emoji, and she'd have snatched up the phone and replied, told him everything and asked what he wanted her to do. But there was nothing. When the phone had pinged with a text message alert at 4 a.m., she'd snatched it up, her heart thundering with anticipation. It had just been Gwen, though, who was on call overnight, wishing the rest of the team merry Christmas.

✉ Gwen

Merry Christmas girls and Bobster (as I believe we're now calling you!). Just to let you know that me and Susie (from the agency) have just delivered the unit's first Christmas Day baby for this year, a boy. I know the local paper is going to want a picture, as usual, so I've just had a crafty spritz of the new mum's very expensive-looking hairspray and now I can give Claudia Schiffer a run for her money! Going to get

the new dad to snap a photo, but I'm waiting until Susie has gone.
There's no way I'm giving agency staff any credit!

Most people would have stuck to a short message with
contracted textspeak, but Gwen never even left out an apostro-
phe. There was a series of laughing emojis after her text, though,
but Toni couldn't even manage an upturn of her mouth, despite
being able to picture Gwen sneaking around the new mum's
ensuite only too clearly. All she could think about was Bobby.
Everything went back to him. The mention of a new baby was
suddenly enough to make her throat close. The excitement that
the press, not to mention this new baby's family, would feel at his
arrival should be what Toni was feeling and maybe, if Bobby had
followed up the kiss with any indication that things had changed,
there'd finally have been a chance of excitement overtaking fear
and guilt for her too.

After the kiss, when the small crowd watching them in Joyce
and Scott's lounge had finally drifted back to their own conversations, he'd looked at her for a long moment and she'd been sure
he was going to say something. Then Scott had bowled in
between them, offering to get more drinks and food, and Toni
had made her excuses to leave. Bobby didn't even try to stop her.
He'd just given her one of his heart-stopping smiles and it was
like he'd finally found peace. Closure, wasn't that what people
called it? The kiss had been enough for him, it seemed, the
perfect full stop to their relationship.

Staring at Gwen's message again, Toni shivered in the darkness of the room, wondering if Bobby would pick up on the none-
too-subtle suggestion that the agency staff would never be considered part of the Port Agnes team. Bobby would be giving up so
much by leaving the unit and the fact he wanted to get away from
her badly enough to do that was like another stab in the gut. He

wanted to draw a line under everything they'd been; the kiss and the plans to leave the team were all part of that. He probably wouldn't even think about her a few months down the line, at least not unless something jogged his memory. Hot tears coursed down her cheeks as she slumped back against the pillows. She'd never forget him, no matter how far she tried to run away from the memories, but he didn't want her any more and it was just one more reason why it wouldn't be fair to the baby, or to Bobby, to bring a child into the middle of that. It was over, she had to accept that, but she had no idea how. For now, even the prospect of being able to stop crying seemed like an insurmountable goal.

Toni arrived at Judy and Simon's house at ten-thirty on Christmas morning as agreed, pulling into their driveway behind them just as they arrived back from their visit to the church. Her face was raw from crying and even trying to layer on foundation in an attempt to cover it up had been excruciating. She wished she could have stayed curled up in a ball under her duvet, letting the tears come. Instead, she was going to have to hold it all in somehow.

The days when Aaron's absence was all the more poignant were incredibly tough at the best of times, but today was going to be unbearable. Judy had always taken on the role of chief mourner and Toni had never resented that. Aaron's mother had loved him in a way that Toni hadn't: wholeheartedly. She had loved him too of course, there was no doubt in her mind of that, but she knew now that it wasn't the same way she felt for Bobby. That was an almost chemical reaction and just as impossible for her to control.

Judy's status as the most broken-hearted meant that no one

expected her to hold it together and there was a guarantee that she'd dissolve into tears at several points during the day. All of them would get tearful at some stage too, but there was an unspoken rule between them that those tears could never upstage Judy's grief; she needed to wallow in it and they all indulged it without question. So if Toni were suddenly to burst into noisy tears – the sort that felt as if they were already brimming over at the back of her eyes, waiting to release a tsunami of emotion – it wouldn't go unnoticed or uncommented on.

Just a question about how her work was going could be enough to set her off and risk her letting slip that her tears weren't for Aaron – not this time – but for another man and the child she could never have with him. For so many reasons. Thankfully, her work, or anything else not related to Aaron's absence, was unlikely to be a topic of conversation with Judy. So Toni was just going to have to grit her teeth and get through it somehow.

'We've been to see Aaron and there were some escaped sheep on the road between here and Port Agnes.' Judy gave her an apologetic smile as she climbed out of the car, followed by Simon and Toni's parents. When Aaron had first died, Judy had insisted that they all go and visit his grave together on Christmas Day and every other big occasion throughout the year. It had been torture standing next to Judy as she wept so hard she could hardly stand up. The row Toni and Aaron had had the last time they spoke would be playing on a loop in her head too, making her question all over again if he was lying in St Jude's churchyard because of her. Knowing that she might have had a hand in Judy losing her beloved son made her feel sick to the stomach and, even hours later, she'd end up pushing the food Judy had cooked for them around her plate to make it look like she'd eaten when she could barely face swallowing a mouthful.

It had taken her almost three years to work up the courage to tell Judy she didn't want to accompany them to the grave and that she needed to have that time on her own with Aaron. Meeting Bobby was what had given her the strength, partly because the knowledge of their clandestine relationship had added an extra layer of guilt, but also because she'd wanted to reclaim a tiny part of her life for herself. Back then, she'd secretly hoped that it might be the first step towards being able to eventually tell Judy that she'd found someone she loved, but she'd missed her chance and now there was no point. Not when Bobby had already checked out.

'Did you have to get out of the car to round up the sheep?' Even as Toni tried to imagine the comical scene, she still couldn't muster a smile. She felt hollowed out.

'You should have seen your dad and Simon trying to make out they knew what they were doing, but it was me and your mum who managed to get them back in the field in the end.'

'Only because you were screaming like a couple of banshees and the sheep were even more terrified of you than you were of them!' Toni's dad, Steve, grinned. 'Oh Netty, you should have seen them. Happy Christmas by the way, darling.'

'Happy Christmas, Dad.' Toni could picture her parents, along with Simon and Judy, trying to herd the sheep back into the field and she tried to arrange her mouth into a smile, but it felt really weird, as if she was attempting to manipulate her facial muscles in an unnatural way. 'That must have been some sight.'

'I got some of it on film when your dad and Simon were jumping from side to side to stop the sheep running straight past them!' Her mother planted a kiss on Toni's cheek. 'I haven't laughed that much in ages.'

'I kept imagining what Aaron would say if he was there with us.' Judy shook her head. 'He'd have been crying with laughter when Simon was saying *"Come on ladies, all we're asking is for you to go back into your own field. It's all for your own good!"* I think I must finally have started to turn a corner now that I can think about what his response to something funny would be and laugh instead of cry.'

'Aaron would be so pleased to hear that.' Even a week before Toni would have been thrilled to hear Judy say what she just had, but now she had no idea how to feel. It was too late to change things for her and what Judy said next damped down any flicker of hope she might have had left.

'I hope he'd have been proud of me and I know he'd have been thrilled that you've done everything you can to fill some of the space he's left in our lives.' Judy linked an arm through hers. 'No one can ever replace him, but losing you too would have finished me off, because it would have been like losing another child. I thought we'd have had a gaggle of grandkids by now and, even though that's never going to happen, we just have to cele-brate the fact that we're all together for Christmas Day and that we get to raise a glass to Aaron, with all the people who loved him most in the same room and the daughter we never had still at the absolute centre of our lives. It makes everything bearable, other-wise I think I'd have just given up and let the MS take me so I could be with Aaron.'

All Toni could do was squeeze Judy's arm. She couldn't trust herself to speak. Aaron's mother had laid out the starkness of the situation in a way that left no room for any doubt. If Toni could be her daughter by proxy, maybe there could be a grandchild by proxy too, and for a few seconds hope had surged in Toni's heart. Maybe there really was a way to fit the jigsaw pieces of her life together, with a space for the baby at the heart of that. But then Judy had dropped the killer blow, almost as if she could read her mind. If Toni didn't stay right at the centre of their lives, making them her number one priority as she'd done for the past five years, pushing Bobby and even the baby lower down the list, then there was every chance that Judy would decide life wasn't worth living. Toni couldn't carry the responsibility for Simon losing a second member of his family. That was something she definitely couldn't live with.

'Let's get inside then, for the smoked salmon and scrambled eggs!' Simon was already heading for the front door.

'Not to mention the champagne.' Toni's dad gave her a double thumbs up. 'Aaron had a great idea when he introduced that particular tradition the Christmas after he turned eighteen.'

'I might just stick to the scrambled eggs today. A few too many Christmas Eve drinks for me!' Toni kept her tone light, the false brightness making her cheeks ache all over again. It was almost ridiculous to hold out on blurring the edges off the day from hell with alcohol when her decision was almost certainly made. She tried to tell herself that she just didn't want to risk alcohol lowering her defences and making her say something that would mean all the secrets came spilling out. But the truth was she was still holding on to the 'almost' aspect of her decision. While there was even the tiniest slither of hope that she could find a solution that wouldn't break anyone's heart, she was going to hold onto it until the last.

* * *

Bobby had volunteered to take his parents' dog, Barney, out for a walk, about an hour after they'd finished Christmas lunch, even though the dog had looked perfectly content curled up on the rug in front of the fireplace for most of the day. The old basset hound didn't even seem to notice when two of Bobby's nephews started firing Nerf guns at each other, using Barney as the dividing line between enemy territory, or when his youngest nephew had started rubbing Barney's velvety ears between his fingers like he was some sort of comfort blanket. He only opened his eyes and got up when someone started rustling sweet wrappers in the tub of Celebrations that was being passed around.

Bobby, on the other hand, had definitely noticed the presence of his three nephews and two nieces after they'd spent almost twenty-four hours together in his parent's cottage four roads back from the harbour in Port Agnes. It wasn't that he didn't like spending time with them; the problem was it reminded him of what he didn't have. At twenty-seven, he was quite young to be so desperate to be a father, but he'd always known he wanted to be one, long before he'd ever dreamed that he might end up working as a midwife. Maybe it was because his parents were such brilliant role models of family life and he wanted everything they had. A family that made the house feel like it was bursting at the seams every time they got together, with too much noise and chaos for anyone from outside the family to deal with. There were also so many pairs of shoes piled up in the hallway that it was impossible to navigate your way to the kitchen without feeling like you were in an episode of Total Wipeout. The coat rack on the wall above the shoe mountain was groaning under the pressure too. All the walls in his parents' house had scuff marks adorning them, or crayon drawings that someone had decided were a vast improvement on the existing decoration. It was messy and hectic, but it spelled home to Bobby.

He'd wanted all of that with Toni, and now they weren't together he had to try and picture having it with someone else. The problem wasn't that he *couldn't* picture it, he just didn't want to. Not yet. It would have been so easy to go back to the way things were with Toni after that kiss. It had started off as a way to silence his mum and niece, so the excruciating embarrassment of being commanded to kiss would at least be over. But as soon as their lips had met, his nerve endings had lit up in a way they only ever had with Toni. It was probably a good thing that there was a room full of people, so there wasn't the option to take things any further or tell her how he felt – that he still loved her and always would. The words had almost slipped out anyway, but then his father had barged in between them and Bobby had been able to stop himself, just in time.

The last few years had been the definition of bittersweet, but the realisation of just how much he wanted a family had only hardened his resolve. He would have loved Toni to be the person he built a life and family with, but she already had an allegiance to another family, one that he could never be a part of. It was the one thing that had stopped him texting her after his parents' party, despite picking up the phone and clicking on her name in his contacts at least three times. He'd even got as far as typing out the words, telling her that he loved her and that if she could find any way of being open about their relationship then he'd try anything to make it work. His finger had hovered over the send button and then Gwen's text had come through and he'd pictured the excitement of the new family welcoming their Christmas Day baby. He wanted to be able to tell the world that he loved Toni and, one day, if they were lucky enough to be parents, he wanted their baby's arrival to be greeted with the sort of excitement that warranted a photo on the front page of the local paper. He didn't want there to be anyone who was important to Toni who resented her happiness and made the guilt that already weighed her down any heavier. He couldn't be a part of that, so instead he deleted the text.

Fuzzy from lack of sleep, an escape to the beach with Barney and the hope that the biting December wind blowing off the sea would clear his head seemed like the best solution. He hadn't anticipated that his youngest nephew, Romeo, would insist on coming with him. But it turned out you needed the mediation skills of a hostage negotiator to try and persuade a four-year-old when he'd made up his mind.

'Come on Uncle Blobby!' Romeo's shout was loud enough to drown out the sound of the seagulls circling above the beach, and a couple walking their dog turned to look in his direction – probably expecting to see a four-hundred-pound man struggling across the sand. His eldest nephew, Monty, had mispronounced his name as a toddler, coming up with the moniker 'Blobby' which his sister had found hilarious, and it had stuck with the rest of his nieces and nephews ever since.

'I'm coming, Rom, but Barney isn't as fast as he used to be!' The old dog looked distinctly put out at having been forced to go for a walk and was literally dragging his feet as they crossed the sand. Romeo, in stark contrast, was like a bird that had been released from its cage, darting across the beach and flapping his arms like the seagulls above him.

'I can fly, Uncle Blobby, look I can fly!'

'I believe you, Romeo, I reckon you could do anything you put your mind to.' Bobby smiled as he watched the little boy's unadulterated joy. When did people stop running just for the sheer pleasure of it, or because simply to walk wasn't enough? When did everything you did – even a run-of-the-mill walk on the beach – stop being as exhilarating as Romeo was finding it? Maybe it was when reality started to grind you down and you realised you couldn't actually have everything you wanted. If that was true, it would explain why Bobby's feet were dragging across the sand at a pace more akin to Barney's than Romeo's. The tide was a long way out and there was three times as much beach for his nephew to explore as there would have been at high tide.

'I wanna go in the sea!' Romeo was already heading in the

direction of the water and Bobby suddenly had no choice but to pick up the pace, unclipping Barney's lead so the old boy wouldn't have to try and keep up.

'It's too cold, buddy.' Bobby broke into a run. 'Wait, Rom, don't do it!'

'Do you want us to head him off at the pass?' Brae called out from across the beach, with Dan at his shoulder, both of them breaking into a run as they tried to catch up with the four-year-old boy who suddenly appeared to have what it took to become the next Usain Bolt. Bobby hadn't noticed before now that his friends were walking along the beach too, but he'd never been happier to see them.

'Yes please!' Anna and Ella were further down the beach, too far off the pace to attempt to join in the mission to block Romeo's path to the sea, even if Anna hadn't been almost six months pregnant with twins.

Dan managed to overtake Romeo and get between him and the incoming waves, with Bobby catching up a couple of seconds later.

'Gotcha!' Picking the little boy up, Bobby swung him in the air, making Romeo squeal with delight. 'I'm sorry buddy, you can't go in, not today. It's too cold and you might get poorly, but I promise to take you to the swimming pool next week, the one with the wave machine.'

'And Monty?'

'Of course, and Benji, if he wants to come.' The idea of supervising all three of his sister's boys was already making Bobby's heart rate rise. It would be like herding cats.

'And Lily, and Poppy?' Romeo was obviously keen that his cousins, the daughters of Bobby's brother Jackson, could come swimming too, but there was no way he could cope with all five of them on his own.

'Why not? Mummy and Uncle Jackson can come with us too.'

'Yay!'

'You promise if I put you down on the sand again, you won't try to run into the sea?'

'Promise.' Romeo nodded sagely. 'Barney's coming now anyway.'

Bobby set his nephew down as the basset hound caught up with them and Romeo threw his arms around the dog's neck, not the least bit bothered about how much Barney was slobbering.

'Thanks so much for your help. My sister would have killed me if I'd taken him home wet and freezing.' Bobby turned to Dan and Brae just as Anna and Ella finally caught up with them too.

'Thank goodness for Dan, he was too quick for me!' Brae laughed. 'I take it he's your nephew?'

'One of them. I've got three, and two nieces, and he's just made me promise that I'll take all of them to the wave pool next week. So I might have to have a tag team there too, to stand any chance of keeping them all safe!'

'We might need a tag team of our own when these two come along!' Anna stroked her bump.

'That's why we've asked Dan and Ella to be godparents.' Brae winked.

'Hey, I didn't realise that was part of the deal!' Ella was looking anything but put out though. 'Happy Christmas by the way Bobby.'

'And to all of you.' He smiled at his friends, trying not to think how lucky they were just to all be out together instead of having to take secretive walks on the beach when no one else was likely to see them, like he and Toni had always done. Or at least walking far enough apart to keep up the 'just friends' pretence.

'Your sister must love you for taking the little guy out to burn off some energy.' Dan smiled as Romeo went back to spinning in circles, his arms outstretched like he was flying again.

'He's great, all the kids are. You'll find out how much fun it is being an uncle figure when your godchildren are here. It's part of the code to give mum and dad a break you know!'

'I can't wait.' Dan smiled. 'And it'll be good training for when me and Ella finally feel grown-up enough to have our own kids. Although my mum always said she never really felt grown-up until me and my sister Lissy came along. You'll be an expert by the time you have kids, though, Bobby.'

'I hope I get the chance one day.' He swallowed hard, surprised at how off-guard Dan's comment had caught him. 'I'd better go, otherwise there's a good chance Romeo will get the better of me again and I don't think Barney will survive another chase across the beach. Enjoy the rest of your Christmas all of you.'

'I'm on call with Izzy, so it's a teetotal celebration for me and Anna, but the boys are making up for us. Mum and Dad are knocking up cocktails as we speak.' Ella reached out and touched his arm. 'You have a good one, Bobby, and make the most of the time with your lovely family.'

'I will. See you next week.' Getting the Christmas holiday completely off from work – when it wasn't his turn to be on call – was a premium Bobby usually savoured, but this year it was just making him miss Toni all the more. Seeing her at work had always been a double-edged sword when he had to pretend they were only friends, but it had been even harder since they'd decided to make that true.

The problem was there was every chance that not seeing her at all was going to have to be the answer in the end, if he was going to stand any chance of getting over her and moving on. He didn't want to, but as much as he loved being Uncle Blobby, he really wanted to be a father one day too and that was never going to happen with Toni, even if they took up where they left off. That meant that the agency job, at least as a first step of moving on from the unit, was looking more and more likely. Last night that kiss had proved just how fine a line they were treading and there was too much risk he might not hold his nerve. He wasn't like Romeo; he'd stopped believing a long time ago that all your dreams could come true. But maybe it was time to start running again, to put enough distance between himself and Toni, so at least one of his dreams would stand a chance.

16

Jess snatched up the phone on the second ring. Dexter's name on the caller display always made her heart gallop so fast she was surprised she couldn't hear it. Staring out of the window as she hit the button to answer the call, the boats bobbing about in the harbour were still draped with Christmas lights which reflected back into the darkness of the water.

'Hello.'

'Hi Jess, is it a good time to talk?' Dexter's words were innocuous enough, but they did nothing to still the pace of her heart. She was always waiting for him to say that he was sorry, but he'd realised she wasn't cut out to be a foster carer after all. It meant, as much as she liked Dexter, that every visit and phone call came with an innate sense of unease lurking just around the corner.

'Yes, it's fine. I've just finished work.'

'Great. I wanted to call you because I've got some news. I know the whole assessment process ended up taking a lot longer than you were originally told it would because of the backlog with the statutory checks, but the panel administrator emailed to ask if you'd be happy to go to the next panel on the sixth of January? There was another assessment due to go in, but one of their references hasn't come back and they need some more time to chase it up. But seeing as yours is ready to go...'

'That soon?' Jess shivered despite the heating being cranked up in the flat. This was what she'd been working towards for months and some of the delays had been really frustrating, but the reality of facing panel so soon was terrifying.

'Yes. I know it's really short notice but she needs to know by tomorrow so she can get the paperwork out to the panel members in time for them to read it, especially as it's still the holidays for some people.' Dexter's voice was full of warmth, making goosebumps break out all over her skin. 'You're going to be absolutely fine and they'd be idiots not to recommend you.'

'Let's just hope they're not idiots then.'

'So you'll do it?'

'I might as well get it done.' Jess nodded, despite the fact that he couldn't see her, trying to convince herself she was ready to do this. It was all she'd been thinking about for months now, and she just had to hope she was up to the job. It would have been so much easier if she'd known that Dexter would be there to support her with the next stage of her journey, but she was just going to have to be brave and do this on her own. Just like she had with so much of her life.

There were only two days left of the year and just over a week until the foster panel. Jess was scrolling through the Foster Chat website for what must have been the tenth time that week, looking for advice on how to perform best at panel. @Mumtomany75 had plenty to say on the subject:

The one thing you need to be really clear about is your motivation to foster. What brought you to this point? The panel will definitely want to know that!

Jess tried to rehearse the answer to the question, but whatever she said, she ended up sounding like a contestant from a beauty contest throwing out platitudes on a level with wanting world peace. The fact she really did want to give kids a better childhood than they might otherwise have had, and certainly better than she'd had at times, sounded too idealistic, as though she didn't really understand what fostering was about. Clicking over to another thread on the forum, she started scrolling down, hoping she might finally come across the perfect thing to say.

@notamama had some advice that Jess needed to think about:

If you haven't had kids of your own, panel will want to know if you see having foster kids as a substitute. DO NOT SAY YES!!!

She'd spoken to Dexter about it during the assessment, but it was the one time Jess hadn't been entirely honest. She'd told him that she and Dom hadn't been ready for children and that she had no plans to have children of her own. Strictly speaking it wasn't a lie, her *relationship* with Dom hadn't been ready for children and, even if she'd managed to fall pregnant, in the long run she was pretty sure they wouldn't have lasted. Dom needed to grow up a bit more before he was ready for fatherhood. It wasn't a lie to say she wasn't planning on having children of her own either; it was more an omission of the truth, that she *couldn't* have children of her own. At least not without a lot of help, and even then there were fairly long odds of it working.

She could have explained it to panel. After all, the fact she had pelvic inflammatory disease that had damaged her fallopian tubes and made it impossible for her to get pregnant wasn't that unusual, but she hated the reason why. Spending her teenage years looking for affection in all the wrong places had meant a string of casual relationships and encounters, none of them resulting in the love she was so desperate to find. But one of them had left her with something else she'd never forget and she'd been left with scarring on the inside in more ways than one. Maybe it would be a good idea to bring that up at panel and show she understood what some of the foster children might be going through, but she still found it hard to say out loud and Dom's judgement, when he'd discovered the truth, hadn't helped either. If panel thought she had unresolved issues about her own fertility, they definitely wouldn't let her through. Sometimes keeping quiet was for the best.

* * *

Everything was happening so fast. Toni had known she was pregnant for a few days and the private scan she'd booked had said she was already eleven weeks pregnant. As a midwife she knew exactly what that meant in terms of foetal development and that the baby she was trying not to even think of as existing was already the size of a fig. Bobby still hadn't called and Judy had come down with a virus on Boxing Day that had knocked the stuffing out of her. Bouncing back from things like that was always complicated by her MS and it was another reminder, if Toni had needed it, of how vulnerable Aaron's mother was to the sort of knocks that other people could recover from much more easily. It was the worry that had been etched on Simon's face when Toni had dropped in to check on Judy, that had been the final decider. Toni had cried all the way home, but calling the clinic when she got there, she told herself she was doing it in everyone's best interests. She had no choice, no Plan B and even Plan Z was not going to work, but that didn't stop her sobbing again as soon as she'd put the phone down.

She'd been given only one choice of appointment if she wanted to have the termination before she got to twelve weeks pregnant and, in her head, that was the cut off. She'd never judge another woman for whatever decision she made about a pregnancy; the reasons why women did and didn't decide to go ahead with unplanned pregnancies, and sometimes even planned ones, were as diverse as the women themselves. But for Toni there was a line in the sand she felt she could stand a chance of living with afterwards. Even sticking to that line she wasn't sure if she'd ever really be okay again, but she couldn't see any other choice, no matter how hard she tried.

She'd never admitted the truth about how she'd argued with Aaron that day about the plans for their wedding. Or how stressed he'd said he felt trying to keep everyone happy and keep the peace. She'd tried to tell herself that his death wasn't her fault, but it was still there, that question she'd never be able to resolve. She'd never know with 100 per cent certainty if the stress of that last phone call had pushed him over the edge and caused the haemorrhage that had killed him before he could try and get the help he needed.

If this was her punishment – the ache inside her already more intense than almost anything she'd ever felt, apart from Aaron's death – then maybe she'd finally have redressed the balance. She was losing Bobby and the baby, just like Judy and Simon had lost their child. She deserved to go through hell, because there was every chance that it was her actions that had put Simon and Judy there. Her one hope was that the weight of guilt might lift a bit, but even if it did, she had a horrible feeling there'd be a whole other burden of guilt ready to land in its place. There was no good outcome to any of this and all she could pray was that the path she had chosen would cause the least pain to the fewest number of people and that the burden of taking it all on, without confiding in a single other person, wouldn't end up crushing her completely.

Her appointment at the clinic was straight after an early shift at work. Ella had put her on duty for deliveries with Gwen, and she was desperately hoping that she'd be busy so she wouldn't have too much time to think about what would come after. Okay, so she probably didn't have the best job in the world for taking her mind off everything that was about to happen, but being busy had to be better than sitting around and just thinking about it all.

As it was, she got her wish and then some. One of Gwen's patients, who'd already been in labour at home for several hours, arrived at the unit. Then Lucy Dench, Toni's patient and one of the original members of the infertility support group, called to say she thought she was in labour, too. Checking her over, Toni was surprised to discover that Lucy was already six centimetres dilated, which meant both she and Gwen were going to need support from other midwives. Izzy was called in to help Gwen out and Toni was expecting one of the agency midwives to join her at any moment, since there always had to be two midwives in the room for any delivery.

'Someone told me there's a baby about to be born in here?' Bobby had knocked on the door and Toni called him in without looking up from the notes she was consulting, still expecting to see the agency midwife until he spoke. Her head shot up at the sound of his voice, and he smiled at the sight of Lucy and Henry, both looking as round-eyed and anxious as a couple of bush babies.

'I really hope you're right.' Lucy grimaced. 'Although it's not hurting as much as it's supposed to.'

'I keep telling you, every woman is different.' If Toni's voice sounded blunter than it should have done, it was down to the surprise of seeing Bobby in the room, especially as they hadn't exchanged a single world since Christmas Eve. Watching a new life enter the world, with a man whose child he'd never know she was carrying, was absolutely the worst possible way she could imagine spending the run up to her appointment at the clinic.

'Sounds like you might be one of the lucky ones.' Bobby smiled, the killer dimples putting in an appearance and making Toni's skin tingle the way it did every time she looked at him lately. Would their baby have had his smile? Or maybe it would have had what Bobby had always called Toni's shy smile. He'd said it might be rarer than most, but it made it all the more beautiful. If anyone else had said that she'd have probably thought it was as cheesy as a comment could possibly get, but Bobby had actually managed to make her feel, for a moment at least, like she really did have a beautiful smile instead of the slightly thin-lipped look she'd always considered herself to have.

'Lucy's already one of the lucky ones, she's got me!' Henry winked, Bobby's presence immediately lifting some of the tension that had been in the room up until his arrival, at least for the couple who were about to become parents. Most of that had probably been down to Toni, though. She felt as if she radiated tension with every breath she released, watching the hands on the clock as they moved closer and closer to her appointment. Now Bobby was here and that internal voice was back again, but this time it had a new mantra: *just tell him!* Grinding her teeth together, she didn't trust herself to respond to Henry's joke in case something else entirely came out. Luckily Bobby seemed far more relaxed.

'Well, I won't argue with that.' Bobby picked up the iPad and checked Lucy's notes. 'Are you still planning to use the pool?'

'Uh-huh, but I was waiting until it got too bad to bear using the birthing ball.' Lucy gave another half-hearted bounce. 'Part of the reason I didn't want to find out the gender was because I thought being so desperate to know might help me get through the pain. And because, if it was a boy, I might worry even more, in case things ended like they did with Oscar.'

'We're getting our happy ending this time, Luce.' Henry grabbed his wife's hand. 'Just a few more hours and we'll be a family.'

'It might be a lot less than that. I think I should examine you to see where we're at.' Toni shook off her reverie, she had a job to do after all. This was Lucy and Henry's moment. 'We can see if you've made any more progress and then you can decide if you want to get into the water before you reach the second stage. I don't think you'll want to start moving locations at that point.'

'Okay let's do it.'

'I'll check the temperature of the water in the meantime.' Bobby moved towards the pool which had already been filled in anticipation.

'Shall I go and get my swimming trunks on?' Henry looked as if he was hoping Toni might say no.

'Let's just take a look at how Lucy is doing first. I'll try not to hurt you, Lucy, but like I said last time I examined you, you might find this a little bit uncomfortable.' Everything went quiet for a moment, as Toni carried out the examination, and it was Henry who broke the silence in the end.

'Have we got a verdict, then? Trunks or not?'

'You're at nine centimetres already.' Toni looked up at Lucy. 'So I think it's now or never.'

'Are you sure there isn't something wrong?' Lucy's eyes had taken on the wide-eyed anxious look they'd had before Bobby came in.

'Everything looks fine and, as Bobby said, you're just one of the lucky ones when it comes down to how severe your labour pains are. But the water should still help with the second stage when you're pushing.'

'I'd better get myself in the water then, whilst I still can, and you'd better get your trunks on Henry. But if you've packed your Speedos this could be the end!'

'Let's get you into the pool.' Toni helped Lucy, who was already wearing a red bikini top under her hospital gown in readiness, into the water.

'I think I might be having another contraction, but if my waters hadn't broken, I'd still have been at home waiting for them to get stronger.'

'Just try and relax and let yourself enjoy the process while the pain is as manageable as it is.' Toni's eyes met Lucy's and she could read what the other woman was thinking – that she didn't deserve to enjoy the process. She was still holding on to guilt about the termination she'd had, and the counsellor obviously hadn't been able to get to the core of the issue in time for Lucy to deliver her baby.

'Come on in then, Henry, the water's lovely.' Lucy smiled for the first time as her husband came out of the bathroom looking sheepish in his Bermuda shorts.

'When should I get in?'

'Whenever you're ready.' Bobby patted him on the shoulder. 'And if you decide you want to get out when things start to kick off, or Lucy wants you to get out, no one is going to judge you.'

'Here we go then.' No sooner had Henry got into the pool, than Lucy pulled a face.

'Ooh this one's a bit more like I expected them to be. My stomach muscles feel like I've suddenly done a hundred sit ups and they've gone into spasm. I feel like I need to push but I can't be ready to start yet, can I?'

'This is where thousands of years of evolution are going to kick in and your body will know what to do.' Toni moved towards the edge of the pool. 'Just trust your instincts and if you want to push, push.'

'You might find it easier to lean over the side of the pool. You know, gravity and all that.' Bobby made it sound like it was going to be the easiest thing ever and for Lucy it looked like that might actually be true.

'Should I lean over the side too, or just wait until something happens?' Henry was looking distinctly uncomfortable at the prospect.

'Maybe rub Lucy's back, if that's something she'd like?' Bobby smiled.

'That would be nice actually. Ow!' Lucy grimaced, dropping her head over the edge of the pool and groaning as a contraction visibly took hold.

'Are you sure you don't want some pain relief now? Maybe just a bit of gas and air?' Toni barely finished the sentence before Lucy shook her head.

'The baby's crowning already.' Bobby exchanged a look with Toni, his eyes a mixture of warmth and concern. If the baby was born too quickly, there was an increased risk of placental abruption and postpartum bleeding.

'Okay Lucy, this is it, just bear down with the next contraction.' Toni's eyes met hers again. 'You're nearly there and you'll have your baby in your arms really soon.'

'Do you promise?' Lucy's eyes filled with tears and as Toni nodded, another contraction took hold and Lucy gave a low growl.

'Well done, Luce, you're amazing. I can see the baby, it's here!'

Henry was sobbing as his child emerged into the world and Bobby lifted the baby out of the water as Lucy turned around. Rubbing the baby with a towel, he immediately laid it on its mother's chest for skin-to-skin contact.

'Have you seen what you've got?' As Bobby spoke, the baby gave its first cry and Henry's face flooded with relief.

'It's a girl.' Lucy looked at her husband. 'I'm so glad, it feels less disloyal to Oscar this way.'

'Having another baby isn't disloyal to Oscar, Luce. You were born to be a mother and now you finally get the chance and I'm the luckiest man in the world that I get to be your daughter's father. Although I'm going to be outnumbered now!'

'Congratulations guys.' Bobby looked close to tears himself and Toni was having to bite her lip to stop herself from crying too. She couldn't risk it because there was no way of knowing if she'd stop.

Bobby would have seen from Lucy's birth plan what she'd been through when she lost Oscar, and he might even have recognised her as the patient Toni had told him about that day she'd gone to his flat needing someone to talk to. All of which would explain why he was more emotional at a birth than usual. The trouble was, it was only part of the reason why Toni was at risk of bursting into tears at any moment, and he'd never believe that was all down to the delivery of Lucy's daughter. Not cool-hearted and closed-up Toni, and not when she'd delivered as many babies as she had over the last fifteen years. She'd spent a third of her life holding everything in, ever since Judy's diagnosis had changed everything. But it was harder than it had ever been, standing there watching a new family starting out and knowing it was something she could never have.

* * *

Bobby had checked baby Sasha over while Toni was overseeing the delivery of the placenta and checking that the baby's speedy arrival hadn't caused her mother any issues. Thankfully everything had been fine with both of them and the only worry was Lucy's almost robotic response to her daughter. She was doing all the right things, getting the baby to latch on with Toni's support, but it was the look in her eyes that worried Bobby. Henry was like a poster boy for new fatherhood, beaming at the baby and his wife, but Lucy kept repeating that she didn't deserve this, and that she wished she'd experienced more pain during Sasha's delivery so she could feel like she'd earned the right to have a healthy baby.

It didn't make any sense, but knowing Lucy's history, Bobby could understand where it was coming from. He just hoped that the therapist Lucy had mentioned she was seeing could keep working with her, so she'd be able to enjoy being with her daughter.

They'd have to keep an even closer eye on her than their other new mums, but if anyone could get her through the tough time ahead and come out the other side even stronger, it was Toni. She'd been through so much in her life and she was stronger than anyone Bobby knew – supporting everyone else around her and always putting herself last. That might have ended up coming at a cost to him, too, but it was also a part of why she was so amazing and why he was finding it impossible to stop loving her. He hadn't stopped thinking about her since Christmas Eve and being back in her company, the determination he'd had on his Christmas Day beach walk was already wavering. In the end, he'd needed to take himself out of the heightened emotion of the delivery room, so he'd left Toni talking to Henry and gone off to make tea for everyone.

'How's Lucy doing?' Bobby glanced up as Toni came into the

staffroom, looking suddenly totally exhausted. She was probably stressing like mad about Lucy. People who didn't know Toni like he did often thought she was standoffish, but she was always taking on other people's problems as if they were her own and there was so much going on underneath the surface that people didn't see. She kept her emotions hidden to protect herself from them.

Part of Bobby couldn't help hoping there was more to it and that, just maybe, Toni was struggling with the end of their relationship even half as much as he was. Anna, Ella and Jess had all mentioned that they were worried about Toni. Her cheeks looked hollowed out and apparently she'd even turned down all of Gwen's recent baking. Bobby hadn't felt much like eating, either; even his mum's Christmas banquet hadn't tempted him. The only thing he'd wanted was Marmite on toast in Toni's flat again, or anything really, as long as she was there. The tiny chance that Toni might be feeling the same way made him want to beg her all over again to give their relationship a proper chance, out in the open, where it could flourish. They were torturing themselves by being apart and everyone else could see it too.

'Sorry, did you say something?' Toni suddenly seemed as if she was miles away. She was much paler than usual and she'd definitely lost weight. He hated the thought she might have gone on some stupid diet, or that she felt she needed to change anything about herself. She was perfect to him exactly the way she was.

'I was just asking how Lucy was doing?'

'She's still in shock, I think, about how quickly it all went, and she's still processing her emotions after losing Oscar.'

'It must be really hard. Is she going to keep seeing her therapist, do you know?'

'She says so and I want to double up on home visits in the

short term, but I'm not feeling too great. So I've got a horrible feeling I might need to take some time off sick.'

'You seem exhausted. Is there anything I can do? You look a bit pale and clammy to be honest and the others have said they're worried about you.'

'Well the others can mind their own bloody business.' Toni was lashing out, the way she always did when she was on the defensive but knew the other person had a point. Knowing her, she'd probably made a commitment to someone else to help them out with something – probably Judy and Simon – and she was refusing to admit how unwell she really was. She needed a lot more than a couple of days off sick judging by the look of her; she needed a proper holiday, but it was almost unheard of for her to take sick leave.

'Have you got a temperature?' Bobby put a hand on her fore-head and for a second she put hers over his. It took everything he had not to pull her into his arms, but she dropped her hand and stepped away before he even had a chance.

'It's just a head cold or something, I'll be fine. I always am.'

'Are you really? Because I'm not.' It was more or less a repeat of the question he'd asked her on Christmas Eve, but he really wasn't fine. He'd missed her so much over Christmas and New Year, especially with no overlapping shifts, but seeing her now he somehow missed her even more, the talking to he'd given himself on the beach completely forgotten. 'My whole family were so happy to see you on Christmas Eve, but they kept asking why you hadn't come over in so long and when you were coming over again. I can't do this friends thing, it's just too hard.'

'So what *will* we be then?' Toni's face seemed to have drained of all colour now.

'I want us to be everything, Tee, you know that. I'd love to have what my brother and sister have got with their other halves.

It would be amazing to have kids, or at least one, who drives us crazy and never gives us a minute's peace, so that when we can grab a date night it feels like the most amazing couple of hours of the month. But the truth is, it doesn't matter if I don't have any of that, as long as I've got you. I kept telling myself I needed to move on and find someone who was free to start that journey with me, the whole package. But every time I tried to imagine it, I realised I didn't want to. I don't want *everything* with someone else, I just want you. Anything that might come after that would only be a bonus. I can't keep hiding how I feel, though, and the only thing I'll ever ask of you is to give our relationship a real chance, out in the open, instead of what ended up feeling like a dirty secret. If you can't do that, then I don't know if I can be around you any more. It's too painful. I can't be your friend when I want to be so much more and I know now that isn't going to change.'

'We've got to give it time.' She half reached out to him, pulling her hand back again as if she'd been burned. He couldn't work out what it meant; she seemed to blow hot and cold all the time – one minute acting as if all of this was torturing her too, and the next as if she didn't care less if she never saw him again. It was always going to be that way when she was fighting between what she wanted and what she thought was right, and she was never going to feel able to choose just him the way he'd happily choose her a thousand times over. He loved her, but he couldn't take any more.

'Why, what's the point? You're never going to put us first. You said it's because you can't, but I don't know if you even really want to.'

'You don't understand...'

'No, I don't! So make me understand.'

'I've told you a hundred times, but I don't think you'll ever understand because you weren't there when it all happened. It would kill Aaron's parents to see me move on and for us to do all the things you talk about; to have a child that isn't *their* grand-child. I couldn't do that to them, no matter how much I might want to. Even now, when—'

'When what?'

'I—' She didn't seem capable of finishing a sentence and as she held his gaze for a long moment, her mouth moved but no words came out. Eventually she spoke again. 'Even now, when you're saying you can't see me any more, which I know means you'll be leaving the unit. Even now, when I know that could happen, I *still* can't say the things you need to hear. But I don't want to lose you, Bobby, you do know that don't you?'

'Then don't lose me, Tee.'

'Please don't make this any harder than it already is.' Bobby took a step towards her, but she held up her hands this time. 'Look, I've got to go, I've got an appointment after work that I can't miss. I'm sorry Bobby, I really am, but if you feel like you've got to cut me off completely then you need to do what's best for you, because it isn't about me. It can never be about me, you know that.' Grabbing her car keys and mobile phone off the desk, she reached below it and picked up her handbag. She was leaving and this time he wasn't even going to try and stop her. She didn't love him enough to put him first, but what was far worse, was that she didn't love herself nearly enough to do what she wanted to do either. And nothing he said or did would ever change that.

17

Toni could barely see through the tears as she drove towards the clinic. The only sound in the car punctuating the half-hour journey was her own crying. She'd been so close to telling Bobby about the baby, but once he knew, she'd never have been able to go through with the appointment. She wanted something to stop her, anything. She could say no, of course, but she wasn't free to make her own decisions and she honestly couldn't remember the last time she had been. Unless somebody else stopped her, or something catastrophic happened – like a flash flood ravaging through the building where the clinic was located – the appointment would be going ahead. She had no other choice.

Pulling into the car park of the clinic, Toni wiped her eyes, fighting a losing battle as they immediately filled with tears again. She was going to have to get a grip, or everyone on the other side of the clinic doors would know that she didn't really want to do this and then what would happen? She couldn't hide this for much longer. She might have lost almost half a stone in the past week alone, barely being able to stomach anything because her insides felt as if they were twisted in knots, but her uniform was already starting to feel tighter across her abdomen.

All the good-natured questions she'd had lately from the other midwives about her health had almost pushed her to the edge. She'd wanted to scream that surely one of them had realised she was pregnant? They were midwives for God's sake. Maybe saying it out loud would have changed things and she could have made the decision she really wanted: to keep the baby. Instead, she was sacrificing what she'd always wanted for someone else, and the acid reflux – which seemed to be her latest pregnancy symptom – almost felt as if it was white-hot resentment boiling up inside her. But she still couldn't risk a doctor questioning what she really wanted, not when it would destroy Judy and Simon. Even if meant there was a risk of her resenting them, and hating herself, forever. The way she'd treated Aaron left her with no choice.

Opening the door of the car, Toni pulled her coat around her. The sky was grey, but there was a pink haze foreshadowing the snowstorm that had been predicted on the weather forecast the night before. Maybe she should just head home now before it started snowing and she got stuck twenty miles away. It didn't take much for the roads around Port Agnes to become banked up with snow and impassable to anything less than a four-wheel drive. Or maybe it was a sign that she should just get back in her car and drive away as fast as she could, anywhere but here. Yet there she was, still walking towards the building, all the while shaking with the sort of cold that no amount of wrapping her coat around her was going to change. It was like the cold had seeped down as far as her bones.

'I've got an appointment at four.' Toni's voice was shaking too, despite the fact that it was much warmer inside the building, but it had nothing to do with how cold she was anyway.

'What name is it?' The receptionist had a kindly tone and she could have given tips to one of the women who worked on the desk at the Port Agnes GPs' surgery, who always made Toni feel like she was wasting the doctor's time, no matter why she needed to see him. But it wasn't the sort of warmth she'd expected to get at an appointment like this and somehow that threw her all the more.

'It's Antoinette Samuels.'

'Okay, Antoinette. There's some information here that explains what's going to happen at your appointment and some forms for you to complete. Have you got your medication list and your referral letter from the GP?'

'Uh-huh and the scan report.' She hadn't been able to bear looking at the details of the scan since the appointment, but it was in the envelope in her bag, along with the referral letter from the GP.

'Great, if you just go into the waiting area, straight through the double doors, and complete the forms, one of the nurses will come out and go over your paperwork with you.'

'Okay, thank you.' Walking through the double doors Toni felt a blast of warmth, but she still couldn't stop shaking. This was it, there was no going back now.

* * *

'Oh no!' Cheryl, one of the agency midwives, who alongside Susie worked most frequently at the unit, had a horrified expression to match her words as she opened up the bag she'd pulled out from underneath her desk. 'This isn't mine! I knew this was going to happen when I bought this bag. It kept selling out on the Fossil website and I've been seeing it everywhere. One of the other midwives must have taken mine.'

'I'll see if I can see whose it is.' Bobby took the bag from her; there was nothing to immediately identify who it belonged to. A hairbrush, a lip balm and a can of deodorant filled one side, but there was a purse and a brown envelope on the other. Opening up the purse, there were debit and credit cards with Toni's name on, and her photo on the driver's license. 'It's Toni's.'

'Please can you try and get hold of her?' Cheryl was looking anxious. 'I've got everything in my bag, even my car keys, and I've got no way of getting home without them.'

'I'll give her a call now.' Bobby rang her mobile but it went straight to voicemail. There was every chance she was screening his calls so he tried again from the office phone, and when that went to voicemail too, he sent her a text.

'No luck I take it?' Cheryl had been watching him like a hawk all this time.

'Sorry, she's not picking up. I can drive round to her place and see if she's there?'

'I've got to get to the nursery by four-thirty to pick my son up; that gives me all of fifteen minutes. Otherwise they'll charge me a pound a minute for being late.' Cheryl rolled her eyes. 'I can call my husband, but he won't be able to get there before five at the earliest and as the nursery's in Port Kara, it'd take me even longer than that to walk there.'

'I'm finishing now. How about I take you to the nursery and we can keep calling Toni on the way?'

'Thank you so much! If I can borrow your phone, I'll call Darren and get him to meet me in Port Kara when he finishes work. I can take Casper for a piece of chocolate cake while we're waiting for his dad. He'll love it and thankfully I always keep a twenty pound note tucked behind the ID card in my lanyard. It comes from years of working at the hospital and wanting to have money on hand, if I desperately needed some chocolate when they brought the trolley round to the patients!'

'What about getting your bag back?'

'I'm working tomorrow, so I can get Darren to drop me at work in the morning before he takes Casper to nursery and swap the bags over then, if Toni's around? It might do me good to have a night's break from looking at my phone anyway, at least that's what Darren's always saying!'

'I'm not sure if she's working or not tomorrow.' Toni had told Bobby she might call in sick, but he had a feeling there was something going on that she didn't want to tell anyone about. Toni didn't call in sick, not unless she literally couldn't get out of bed, and she definitely didn't plan it in advance. 'But I'm working tomorrow, so I can go round to Toni's later, pick up your bag, give her the other one, and bring yours in tomorrow.'

'You're a lifesaver! But we're down to thirteen minutes to do a five-mile drive on country roads, so I hope you've got the skills of Lewis Hamilton too!'

In the end, Cheryl was three minutes late to pick up Casper, but she didn't seem to mind the three pounds surcharge and waived away Bobby's attempt to give her the money to cover the fine, along with chocolate cake she'd promised her son they'd go for.

Toni still wasn't picking up his calls and she hadn't answered his texts either. Driving around to her house was a dead-end too. She might have been hiding out and just not answering the door to him, but her car wasn't there either. It was dark and getting cold, the first flakes of snow slowly drifting from the night sky. Sometimes Toni walked to clear her head; she liked the coastal path best, and other times she'd walk up out of the village to St Jude's. He didn't like the idea of her walking in this weather, not when it was as dark and as cold as it was now, especially when she'd looked as unwell as she had. She'd said she had an appointment, maybe the letter in her bag could confirm where it was, then at least he'd know she was safe. It must have been something important for her to rush off so quickly after Lucy and Henry's delivery. The thought that she might have an urgent appointment at the hospital made him go cold, especially if she'd gone on her own.

Pulling the brown envelope out of the bag, he hesitated, but before he had a chance to debate the rights and wrongs of opening her private mail, something fluttered out, landing in the footwell of the car. Bending down to pick it up, the details written on the piece of paper hit him like a fist to the chest. There was only one service the clinic offered and so Toni's appointment there could only mean one thing.

Thumping the steering wheel so hard he was in danger of releasing the airbag, it was all Bobby could do not to wail like an animal. If there'd even been a single thread of hope left that Toni might ever choose a life with him, one day, over her sense of duty to Aaron and his family, this was proof that she never would. He had to get away from her flat, because at that moment he wasn't sure how the hell he'd react if he saw her. She had every right to choose, he knew that, and if this was what he thought she really wanted, he'd have been there to support her every step of the way. But she hadn't even trusted him enough to tell him and, even worse than that, she was putting a dead man before herself and before the baby he knew she'd always wanted deep down. Frustration and the injustice of it all were boiling up inside him. He had to drive away, for both their sakes it, but somehow he just couldn't do it. Not until he knew for sure that it was already too late.

* * *

It was crazy standing in the churchyard in the freezing cold as everything slowly got covered in a blanket of white, with tiny shards of ice crystalising on the snowfall and sparkling in the moonlight.

The night before her appointment at the clinic she'd spoken to Aaron again, in the stillness of their flat, and asked him one more time to show her a sign, any sign, so she'd know what the right thing to do was. She'd actually managed to dream of him, but when he'd tried to speak there'd been a hand over his mouth, though it hadn't been his. She couldn't work out if the hand was hers or Judy's, but she'd woken up wide-eyed and sat up bolt upright. Did it mean she didn't really want to know what Aaron thought, because the promise she'd made him should have been enough to tell her what he'd have wanted? Or did it mean that Judy was the one who'd never let her forget what she'd done? Either way, the message was clear: she couldn't break the promise, even if it ended up breaking her.

Looking down at her phone as she shivered in the biting cold of the church yard, Toni had twenty-six missed calls from Bobby. There were messages too, but she hadn't read any of them. Whatever it was he wanted to say, it couldn't fix anything, not now. It was too late.

She was saving her phone battery anyway, she needed the torch, otherwise she'd have been terrified in the darkness among the gravestones. It was stupid, she knew that. No one there could do anything to hurt her, it was the living who caused all the problems. But there'd been one too many horror movie marathons with Aaron when they'd been teenagers and first dating. He'd always said he loved them, but it was only later on that he'd admitted he put them on as an excuse to get Toni to cuddle up to him. Maybe even then she'd held her feelings back a bit, because she hadn't really needed an excuse to cuddle up to him at all, in those early days especially. Things had got a lot worse since then, though, and she'd forgotten how to even trust what *she* felt about anything any more.

'I knew you'd be here.'

'Jesus!' Toni literally jumped at the sound of Bobby's voice behind her, before turning to face him. 'You nearly gave me a heart attack. What on earth are you doing here?'

'I needed to find you and like I said, I knew you'd be here.' Bobby's tone was tight and she could see his jaw clenching, even in the low glow of the torch on her mobile. 'I know you come here all the time to talk to Aaron.' Bobby hardened his gaze. 'I suppose you told him you were pregnant as soon as you found out, but you didn't think I deserved to know.'

'How the hell do you know about the—'

He cut her off before she could finish, thrusting a bag into her arms. 'You took Cheryl's bag by mistake. You've got the same one and when I looked inside to check whose it was, I realised it was yours.'

'What, by opening a private letter?' Her voice was loud in the quiet of the snow-covered graveyard, but she didn't care. He had no right to open that letter.

'I never would have known, otherwise, would I? About the baby. Do you really think it was fair not to tell me something as big as this? It's not like we were some casual one-night stand.' He'd raised his tone to match hers. 'Is that where you've been? To the clinic?'

'That's none of your business.'

'None of my business?' Bobby was shaking his head, the

muscles in his jaw tightening with every second. 'Whatever you wanted I would have supported you, but you could at least have given me the chance to do that. But no, you came to Aaron. Just like you always have done. Even now, after going through all of that on your own, when I'd have done anything to be there for you, with you – whatever you decided – it's him that you turn to for comfort. I never stood a chance against Aaron.'

'It isn't like that, I've tried to explain, but you're never going to get it!' She was shouting again, lashing out, because she couldn't admit the truth, that he was right about all of it. She should have given him the chance and deep down she'd always known that he'd support her, whatever she decided. She should have trusted him to be the one person she confided in. He had every right to be hurt and angry, but there was nothing she could do about that now; he'd already found out in the worst possible way. There was no excuse for how she'd handled it, so she wasn't even going to try to explain. She'd already lost him for good – she could see that from the way he was looking at her, and if she lowered her guard even a tiny bit, she'd be in danger of falling apart in front of his eyes.

'No, I'm never going to get it, but I finally understand just how little I mean to you. I should have been the one to help you through all of this, either way, but instead I was the last one to find out.'

'I didn't tell anyone else and… I didn't go through with the appointment either.' Her breath made a cloud in the cold night air, her words hanging between them too, as she waited for Bobby's reaction. The shivers making her whole body shudder weren't about the cold any more.

'What, you couldn't go in without the stuff in the envelope?' She tried to read his expression as he spoke, the intensity of the way he was looking at her making her long to break eye contact. There was more anger bubbling under the surface with Bobby than she'd ever seen. He'd been frustrated before and hurt by the decisions she'd made, but this was different. He'd never looked at her the way he was now, like there wasn't a shred of what they'd had left. She owed him an explanation, but nothing she said was going to make a difference. Not now.

'I never got as far as looking for the letter. I didn't open my bag. I didn't even realise I had Cheryl's until two minutes ago. I just couldn't go through with the appointment, even though I know it's going to hurt so many people...'

'If I hadn't seen the letter, you wouldn't have told me about any of this, would you? Not even the decision to keep the baby. My baby! What were you doing, hoping that I'd do what we talked about and take another job? Leave a clear path for you to raise the baby in Port Tremellien, so your family and Aaron's can make up some weird little fantasy that it's somehow his?'

'Don't be ridiculous! I was going to tell you, but—'

'But you decided to talk to Aaron about your decision to keep the baby first too?' Bobby looked up towards the sky and let out a long sigh. 'I can't do this, Toni. Whatever you thought was going to happen when you told me about the baby, it's not. I can't be held on the edge of my child's life the way you've held me on the edge of yours for the past three years. I'm out.'

'What do you mean you're out?' He couldn't mean it. The Bobby she knew wouldn't walk away from his child no matter what, but his face was like a mask. It was like he hated her and it was all her fault. He wasn't just saying the things he'd said – that he'd support her, whatever she decided, regardless of how much he might want the baby. He meant them, because he'd always put her first, through every bit of their relationship. But she'd still shut him out and in his shoes, she honestly couldn't say she'd have reacted any differently. The truth was, she'd probably have reacted a lot worse and everything he was saying now made sense, no matter how much she might not want to hear it. She had crossed an uncrossable line, so there was no way of coming back. She didn't want to listen to him any more; she'd heard enough, but Bobby wasn't finished yet.

'I can't put a child through this. The confusion, the not knowing where they stand.' He was shaking his head again. 'You've got what you want Toni, go ahead and act out the fantasy that the baby is Aaron's, or that you found a sperm donor off the internet because no one has touched you since Aaron died. It might as well be his baby, seeing as he's still the one you share everything with, even five years after he died. I kept hoping that this wouldn't really turn out to be the end, that somehow you'd finally decide I was worth taking a chance on, but now I know this is it. It's finally over for good and I'm going to contact the agency tomorrow and see if they'll still take me, to make it easier on both of us. I can't be around you, Toni, not now.'

'Bobby!' Even as she called out his name, she knew he wasn't going to turn back to look at her. And she couldn't blame him. She'd shut him out too many times and even if he had turned around and walked back towards her, what would she have said? She couldn't promise him that they were suddenly going to be like Anna and Brae, or Ella and Dan.

She'd lost Bobby, it was too late to change that, it didn't matter that she'd give everything she had to go back and do things differently. There were some things that just couldn't be forgiven, but even so, something had to change. There was someone else now who was going to have to come before the promise she'd made Aaron, and before everything else, even Judy's illness. She had to let Aaron go. Nothing she did was going to bring him back or change those last months between them when she'd kept so much of how she felt from him, or that very last conversation they'd had. She was going to hurt some people who she'd done everything to avoid hurting for the past five years, but she'd already failed Bobby and lost him as a result. She wasn't going to fail their baby too, no matter what it took.

18

Bobby hadn't slept. As soon as he'd reached his car, he'd wanted to head straight back into the churchyard and tell Toni he hadn't meant it when he'd said he didn't want to be a part of the baby's life. What he'd really wanted to say was that he wanted to be in every part of the baby's life, not just a piece of it. But he didn't because he already knew that she could never offer him that. Even so, when he'd got home, he'd picked up his phone at least ten times to call her, but somehow he'd resisted all through the sleepless night that had stretched out ahead of him. It wasn't until he'd got into work the next morning that he realised he'd forgotten all about asking Toni for Cheryl's handbag.

'Did you drop this off last night? It was already here when I got in.' Cheryl smiled at Bobby as he came into the staffroom.

'I think Toni must have dropped it off after she got my message.' His voice sounded robotic, even to his own ears, like a bad actor playing a part he wasn't cut out for – which was exactly how he felt about his life right now.

'Oh great, did you manage to get her bag back to her too?'

'Yeah, I took it to her place and left it with her neighbour.' It was one of the things that Bobby had always hated about his relationship with Toni, that they had to tell so many lies to try and hide it just in case it got back to her parents or Aaron's. The last three years had been the best in so many ways, but they'd also contained the worst moments of his life too. And last night had been the peak of that.

'Morning everyone!' Izzy came into the staffroom. She had her long black hair in a high ponytail and her sparkly blue eyes always looked like they were smiling. She was beautiful and the same age as Bobby. It would have been so much easier to fall for someone like her, or Emily, who'd taken to buying him chocolate bars and packets of Starbursts, every time they worked together. She was sweet and Izzy was great, but whoever it was who said you couldn't choose who you fell in love with had been dead right. He'd never felt about anyone the way he felt about Toni and he couldn't just turn that off. What worried him most was that he might *never* be able to turn it off, but he'd just have to take it a day at a time. As for the baby, he couldn't even begin to think about that.

'Hi Izzy.' Cheryl gave her a little wave. 'Sorry I've got to dash off, but I need to go and check how Jess is getting on in the delivery room.'

'No problem, see you later.'

'Morning, Izzy.' Bobby tried to smile as she turned towards him, but even that felt exhausting. God knew how he was going to get through the day, let alone however long it took him to find another job. The agency had recruited all the staff they needed while he'd been putting off the decision, still hoping deep down that Toni would finally see sense and give things a proper go, even when the odds had been massively stacked against that possibility. He'd already put out some feelers via his alumni group at his university and a couple of his friends from the course had said they thought they might be able to recommend him for upcoming jobs. It wasn't the best time to be looking, though. No one had been advertising over Christmas and New Year, so it might be a while before he could avoid seeing Toni altogether. Attempting to shake off what felt like a black cloud looming directly overhead, he looked at Izzy again. 'I gather from the rota that you've got the dubious pleasure of accompanying me on home visits this morning. I can't say I'm looking forward to navigating the lanes after that heavy snowfall last night, but I'll do my best to get you back here in one piece! It said on Three Ports Radio this morning that the snowplough had been out from 6 a.m. making sure the roads are passable.'

'It's the last part of my induction before I'm let loose solo! So I'm determined to tick it off, even if it does mean navigating through the snow.' Izzy smiled again and Bobby willed himself to feel even a pang of attraction towards her, anything that would make him believe he might one day move on from Toni. But there was nothing. Izzy probably had a partner already, and she hadn't even given any indication she was interested in him. But it wasn't about that, it was about hope. Hope that he could get over Toni. He had to try and envisage a future without her, he had no choice. Maybe he'd just end up on his own forever, plenty of people were happy that way, but none of them had spent the last three years of their life with Toni. He needed to talk about something else, anything to stop his mind going back to her and hearing her call after him in the churchyard.

'How are you liking life in Port Agnes, Izzy?'

'I love it so far, but I'm commuting every day from Redruth.' She wrinkled her nose. 'I've put my name down with every estate agent that covers the Three Ports area, but no joy so far.'

'I've got a little studio flat in town, but now I'm qualified I might finally be able to start looking to buy a place. I'll ask my landlord to give you first refusal. It's probably not somewhere you'd want to stay long-term, but it might do for a while.'

'That would be brilliant, thanks. Will you be staying in Port Agnes? Trust me, a commute of any distance around these roads is a bit of a nightmare.'

'It depends where I'm working. If I want to progress with my career, I might need to apply for a job someone else.'

'Oh no! We'd all really miss you if that happened, it's great to have a male midwife on the team. It's still pretty unusual, but I think it's brilliant.'

'Sometimes you just have to know when it's the right time to move on, even if a big part of you doesn't want to.' The truth was that not even a tiny part of Bobby wanted to move on, but he had no choice. Loving Toni and not being allowed to put her at the centre of his world had been incredibly tough. That would be nothing compared to watching his child be taken over by a family he would never be allowed to be a part of either. Sure, he could push for access, assert his legal rights, but what would that do to the child? Toni had almost been broken by being pulled in two directions, knowing she'd never be able to please everyone, and it had killed him to watch her put herself through that. He wasn't going to make his child do the same and he couldn't envisage a scenario where he could be a part of the baby's life and that not end up being the result.

'Sometimes I suppose moving on is for the best.' Izzy frowned. 'But I still think it'd be such a shame.'

'We'd better get out on our rounds, otherwise Anna or Ella will give me the boot long before I even have the chance to go after another job.'

'I very much doubt that, but come on then, show me how it's done!'

Picking up his car keys, he followed Izzy out of the staffroom, still trying and failing to picture a future without Toni or the baby in it.

* * *

The back-to-back appointments that had kept Bobby and Izzy busy all morning were a welcome relief from the turmoil inside his head. Poor Izzy must have thought he was really rude, or at the very least boring, because the best he could manage was monosyllabic responses to her questions. Their last appointment of the morning was with Carly Phillips, who'd had her first baby five days before and it was her second check-up. Bobby had been her lead midwife during the latter stages of her pregnancy and he'd phoned ahead to let her know that Izzy would be with him this time.

'Hey guys, come on in.' Carly, who'd delivered her baby in the hospital after needing to be induced, welcomed them both at the door. She certainly looked as if she was doing well, even so soon after having the baby. 'Cassidy is asleep and I'm not sure she's going to take too kindly to being woken up for her heel prick test!'

'I always feel so guilty about doing it.' Bobby turned to Izzy. 'Which is why I'm going to let you do it.'

'I didn't have to do many as a hospital midwife. Unless mum and baby had to be in for more than five days for some reason.'

'Cassidy's got a great pair of lungs on her, so you might need a pair of ear defenders. She's in the lounge with Joel.'

Bobby and Izzy followed Carly into the room, where baby Cassidy looked every bit as contented as her mother had described, lying asleep on her father's chest. The old cottage's inglenook fireplace that they were sitting in front of was almost big enough for a nursery in itself.

'Izzy, this is Joel, Cassidy's dad.' Carly indicated towards the man sitting on the sofa.

'Lovely to meet you, and you've got a beautiful home.'

'Oh it's not my home, this is Carly's place. I live in Padstow, I've got an art gallery there. I'm taking two weeks paternity leave to be here full-time and then we'll be sharing Cassidy's care.'

'We're not a couple.' Carly shrugged. 'We're just friends, who desperately wanted a child and we both have demanding carers, so we decided to co-parent. That way we can both give Cassidy our full attention when we're not working.'

'I'm sorry, I must have missed that in your notes.' Izzy had flushed red, but Carly hadn't once mentioned this to Bobby during her pregnancy and he must have seen her at least six times.

'Oh, don't worry, you won't have done.' Carly raised her eyebrows. 'I just didn't feel like being judged all the way through, I've had enough of that from family and friends. So we just left out that we weren't together *in that way*.'

'You wouldn't have got any judgement from us.' Bobby smiled, but his mind was racing. His thoughts were never far from Toni anyway, but they were right back there now. It might be early days for Carly and Joel, but it seemed to be working so far and Cassidy would have two parents who both made her the centre of their world. There were plenty of children born in a traditional family set-up who sadly didn't have that. Suddenly there was a tiny glimmer of hope. Maybe something like this could work for them, even if it meant pretending to Aaron's family and Toni's that she and Bobby had a similar arrangement to Carly and Joel's. As much as he hated that idea, it had to be better than never knowing his own child.

'My mother still isn't speaking to me. First I got divorced from someone who was making me miserable three hundred and sixty-five days of the year and then I decide to have a baby with an old school friend before it's too late to be a mum myself.' Carly shook her head. 'All she could ask was what the hell she and my father were supposed to tell their friends at the golf club. Like it's any of their business! Most of them are on their second or third marriages anyway, and two of the couples swapped partners altogether last year. I'm not judging them, so what the hell gives them the right to judge me?'

'Nothing, the most important thing is that Cassidy is loved and there's no question that she is.' It was obvious to Bobby how raw her mother's reaction still was to Carly. Anyone who didn't speak to their daughter – and missed out on having a relationship with their granddaughter – for the reasons Carly had outlined, didn't deserve to be a grandparent anyway. From everything Toni had told Bobby about her own parents, and Aaron's, he couldn't believe they'd turn away from the chance to have a relationship with Toni's child. Maybe she just needed to give them the opportunity. The trouble was, he already knew she'd probably never take that chance.

'We're both infatuated with her.' Joel gently stroked the back of his daughter's head. 'But I almost took the excuse to pop out and get some shopping so that I wouldn't have to see her have the heel prick test and be in any pain. Until Carly said I was being a wimp.'

'And I told him he couldn't duck out of the tricky bits!' Carly grinned. 'We agreed that from the start.'

'That sounds like a fair deal to me. I know you felt happy with everything at your first visit, but do you still feel like you're recovering okay?' Bobby turned towards Carly. He couldn't let his professionalism slip just because there were a million thoughts racing through his mind. 'We need to check your blood pressure and temperature again and make sure your abdomen is still contracting the way we want it to.'

'I'm fine, but don't expect any pictures of me on social media with a flat stomach any time before the next decade. To be honest, it wasn't that flat before I fell pregnant with Cassidy.' Carly rolled her eyes. 'Would you mind if we got Cassidy's tests done before I have my blood pressure taken though, otherwise it's likely to be through the roof with me worrying about how she's going to react to the heel prick and whether everything's going to be okay with her hearing tests.'

'Everyone tells you what the worry is like, but you never really understand it until you've got your baby in your arms, do you?' Joel stroked his daughter's head again. 'It's just a good job you don't have to take my blood pressure.'

'She'll be fine, honestly.' Bobby looked at Izzy. 'Are you good to go?'

'Absolutely.' A couple of minutes later, the test was done and Cassidy's initial squawk of indignation had passed. Both her parents were comforting the little girl and they looked the epitome of new family bliss. If it could work for them then maybe, just maybe, it could work for Bobby and Toni, if only he could persuade her to take the risk. He could even put up with her telling the rest of the world whatever she wanted about how they'd come to the decision to co-parent. It was either that or get as far away from Port Agnes as he could, because the one thing he was certain of, was that he couldn't live with being anywhere near Toni and the baby and not somehow being allowed to make them his everything, when that's exactly what they already were in his head.

* * *

'Look at those two, the pair of them suddenly seem so grown up and not like my little girls any more.' Bobby's mother Joyce gestured outside to where his nieces, Lily and Poppy, were lying in the snow making snow angels. 'I measured them on the door frame last week and they'd both grown a couple of inches since the last time. Monty, Benji and Romeo are growing up so fast too; it's about time we had another baby in the family.'

'You'd better have a word with Chantelle or Jackson then, because I'm in no position to grant your wish.' Bobby kept his gaze fixed on his nieces and nephews playing in the snow in his parents' back garden. He was terrified that if he looked at his mother, she'd see something in his eyes and know that he was lying. If he didn't know better, he'd have sworn she could read his mind, bringing this up now, two days after he'd found out about the baby.

'What really happened between you and Toni?' Joyce touched his arm. 'I know you're in love with her.'

'I don't why you'd say that. We were never that serious and the last time I did so much as peck her on the lips was when you forced us to kiss on Christmas Eve.'

'That might be true, but the way you feel about her would still be obvious even if I wasn't your mother. Why don't you just admit to the girl how you feel? Don't tell me you're holding back on settling down until some mystical age when it's okay for a man to do that sort of thing – like thirty or something – because that's all just nonsense.' His mother wagged her finger at him. 'When you know, you know. Whether you're twenty-seven or seventy-seven.'

'What if I'm not the one holding back on settling down?'

'I've seen Toni with the kids; you can't tell me that girl doesn't want to be a mother. Don't get me wrong, I haven't got any problem with the age difference, but she hasn't got the time to just hang around and wait for all the stars to align, or whatever it is she's waiting for.'

'Maybe I'm just not what she wants.'

'Now you're really talking rubbish. I've seen it all over the years and I know two people in love when I see them. As your grandma always used to say: *the older the moon, the brighter it shines.* And this old moon has seen enough to know what I'm talking about!'

'Bloody hell!' Bobby jumped as Monty, his eldest nephew, threw a snowball straight at the kitchen window they'd been staring out of.

'I think your nephews and nieces want you to go outside and play with them.' Joyce wagged a finger in his direction again. 'But you mind that sort of language around those kids or you won't get the chance to tell Toni how you really feel. If Monty picks up any swear words from you, your sister will be after your blood.' Another snowball hit the window before he had a chance to answer.

'I think this is Monty's none too subtle way of reminding me that I promised to take them sledging on the hill that leads down from lookout point, and seeing as this is the first time we've had a decent covering of snow since you and Dad bought those sledges, I guess we shouldn't really miss the opportunity.'

'You're a good boy, Bobby, and a lovely uncle.' Joyce patted his arm again. 'And nothing makes me happier than seeing my family together, having fun. I just don't want to see you miss out on doing that with a family of your own. Don't leave it so long that me and your dad don't get the chance to know your kids. You're our baby, but we're not getting any younger.'

'I'd hate any child of mine to miss out on knowing its cousins or having you and Dad as grandparents. But I can't help thinking that maybe it would be easier for things just to stay as they are.'

'Easy is boring, Bobby. And I know you, if you want something enough you'll find a way to make it work. Look what you did with the midwifery when everyone said you'd never do it.' Joyce stood on her tiptoes to plant a kiss on her son's cheek. 'Now off you go and take those kids sledging before Monty ends up breaking a window! You've got to get out and have some fun while there's enough snow to do it.'

'I think I've kept them waiting long enough already and you're right, the snow could start melting any time. I'll see you later then.' Bobby squeezed his mum's shoulder before he headed out into the blanket of white beyond the kitchen window. The snow wouldn't be around forever and what his mother had said was true – you had to grab some opportunities when they came along, however unexpected they might be. He just wished he knew for sure whether his mother was right about Toni too, and that if he wanted something badly enough he could find a way of making it work. Because right now, it felt as if he was as far away from finding a solution as ever.

19

Jess had been awake since exactly eleven minutes past four and for once it had been her waking Luna up rather than the other way around. When she scooped the cat up for a cuddle on the sofa in an attempt to distract herself from watching the time on her watch move all too slowly, Luna had given her what could only be described as a dirty look. As payback, she'd hooked her claws into Jess's thighs, her tail thudding stroppily against the cushion next to them. It had taken Luna at least twenty minutes to forgive the interruption to her beauty sleep and start purring instead.

Maybe Jess should tell the panel that as a cat owner, she knew exactly what to expect from some of the foster children who came to stay with her. She was a dab hand at rejected affection and ingratitude for the roof she provided over Luna's head, not to mention the food she devotedly served up, but that didn't stop her loving the cat. Not that all the children would react in the same way, Jess knew that better than anyone. She'd been so desperate for attention and signs of love and affection, that she'd gone completely the other way – forcing down meals that disgusted her, like her foster carer's signature dish of liver and bacon, just in case rejecting it might result in her being rejected again too. All Jess could hope was that the panel, who were meeting to consider her application later that day, would see her first-hand experience as her key strength. She was relying on it.

By 6 a.m. Jess was trying to decide if she could possibly face the idea of breakfast. She was having enough problems stopping herself from hyperventilating every time she thought about how much was hanging on the outcome of the panel, but she didn't want her rumbling stomach to drown out her responses to the questions either. A bit of porridge was probably doable and she was just waiting for the microwave to ping when the first of the good luck texts came through.

📧 Message from Port Agnes midwifery unit
To our pocket rocket Jess. We're all rooting for you today and we know you're going to do brilliantly! Love you lots, Anna, Ella, Toni, Bobby, Frankie, Gwen and the rest of the gang xxxx

Less than a minute later there was another notification.

📧 Message from Lucy
I promised the girls from the infertility support group that I'd send a message from all of us, so you didn't keep getting harassed all morning! Good luck and we all think you'll be a great foster mum. Don't forget to come round for a cuddle with Sasha next week and you can tell me all about what the panel was like xx

Jess hadn't told that many people when the panel was. It felt like too much pressure having everyone else's expectations weighing her down when her own were already more than enough. She'd told all of team at the unit, of course, and the girls at the infertility group, because they understood better than anybody the weight of those expectations. When Dom had called to tell her that his Mum was being referred to the hospital for some tests, she'd found herself blurting out the date to him too. She might have come to terms with the fact that their relationship was never meant to be, but that didn't mean she could wipe out their shared history and act as if they were only acquaintances, just like that. She'd always been close to his parents and he'd sounded genuinely terrified that there might turn out to be something seriously wrong with his mum. She'd started babbling about everything she could think of to try and take his mind off things and that's how she'd ended up telling him about the panel. When the next text came through, just after she'd finally managed her first spoonful of porridge, it didn't take too many guesses to work out who it was going to be from.

✉ Message from Dom
JJ, UR gonna knock their socks off 2day! Still hope we can do this 2gether 1 day. Love you Dom xxx

She had no idea what he was trying to achieve by telling her he loved her or that he hoped they could both be foster parents. It had never been what he'd wanted and it had only taken him about five minutes to dismiss the idea of being adoptive parents when they'd first had to face up to the prospect of infertility. He'd only seemed to want her since she'd made it clear she was moving on, but at least he was being supportive. Dom wasn't all bad, she'd never have married him otherwise, and she hoped one day they could get back to a friendship – something their relationship should probably never have gone beyond in the first place. But right now she wasn't up to replying to any of the messages, least of all his.

Deciding what outfit to wear to panel was a welcome distraction. She'd already bought a nice dress from Zara a couple of months before, in anticipation of the occasion, but suddenly it had seemed like a ridiculously formal choice. Four outfit changes later, Luna was sitting on the pile of discarded clothes regarding Jess with something close to pity.

'It's all right for you. You've got one fur coat that's perfect for every occasion.' At that point, the cat actually turned away, stalking up the bed and settling down on the pillow. With half an hour to go until her slot with panel and a twenty-minute drive ahead of her to get there, Jess was back in the original dress from Zara. It didn't matter what she looked like on the outside anyway, it was the inside that counted. She just hoped she'd measure up.

* * *

'Do you think it went okay?' Jess's legs were still shaking as she came out of the panel room. She was more grateful than ever that she'd had Dexter's support throughout the process. Every time a panel member had asked a question and she'd wondered whether her response had come out right, she'd looked at him and he'd given an almost imperceptible nod of his head, letting her know he believed she could do it.

'I think you did great. There was nothing you said that made me think *"for God's sake keep your mouth shut, Jess."*' Dexter grinned.

'Well, that's something then!' She couldn't help laughing and her body seemed to flood with relief that it was over. Whatever happened now was out of her control. The panel were in the room behind them, discussing her responses to their questions, and it was too late to change the outcome.

'You did brilliantly, honestly and I think we deserve a cup of tea whilst we're waiting to be called back in. I'll grab us a cup and I'm sure you've got a million messages from people wanting to know how it went.'

'I'm not telling anyone anything until I've got a definitive decision. I don't want to jinx it.' The panel had been nothing like she'd expected, despite all the reassurances from Dexter beforehand. She'd thought it'd be like the Spanish Inquisition, or one of those police interviews on a Channel Four documentary – just waiting to catch her out when she said something she shouldn't, something that would prove she didn't have what it took. Unfortunately, she knew the stock answer given in those sort of police interviews of 'no comment' wasn't going to cut it either. But the panel members had been lovely, almost as if they wanted her to get approved as a foster carer every bit as much as she did.

She'd kept waiting for the killer question, the one she wouldn't be able to answer – even with Dexter there willing her to get through it – but it had never come. They'd only asked five questions in total in the end, telling her that Dexter's assessment had more than addressed most of their concerns and how impressed they were with the way she'd supported herself through university and made such a great success of her career as a midwife. She'd had to pinch her leg at one point to stop herself from bursting into tears, the compliments turning out to be far more difficult to deal with than any of the questions she'd anticipated.

* * *

Dexter had been right about something else too; there were messages on her phone from almost all of the team from the unit, not to mention Dom, asking how the panel had gone, but she didn't want to reply to any of them until she knew the outcome.

She didn't much feel like talking either, but after spending ten minutes reading all the messages, she needed to do something else to stop her wondering what the panel members were saying about her on the other side of the door.

'Do you ever sit in panel meetings with an applicant and wish you hadn't put them forward?'

'If I discovered something about them that made me think they wouldn't make a good foster parent, I'd stop it before it got to that point, even if it was on the day of panel itself.'

'How do you know I'll be good?'

'Because all you ever think about are the kids. Although that's also the only worry I've got about you being a foster parent.' Dexter held her gaze, even as she had to force herself not to look away. 'You're going to have make sure you look after yourself in all of this. At least with doing respite first, you'll have plenty of down time in between.'

'I wish you were going to be my supervising social worker.' The words had come out of her mouth before she'd had a chance to stop them. Whenever she thought about the things that scared her most about fostering, she thought about turning to Dexter for advice – but she couldn't do that if he wasn't her social worker. They had a professional relationship which would end as soon as panel was over, probably not even a friendship. It was sad, but this might be one of the last conversations she'd ever have with him.

'We're ready for you now.' The panel chair came out to get them before Dexter had a chance to respond, which was probably just as well. If he'd said he wished he was going to be her social worker too, it would have been even harder to learn to trust her new social worker the way she'd trusted him. Either way, she was about to hear the verdict that was going to dictate the next phase of her life.

* * *

'I still can't believe it.' Eventually Jess was going to stop shaking, but her legs were definitely still wobbly as she walked across the car park with Dexter.

'I told you they'd love you. I never had any doubt about that.'

'I'm glad one of us was confident!' Jess turned towards him as they reached his car, trying to decide if it would be appropriate to hug him, or whether she should stick to shaking hands. In the end, she leant in for a hug, breathing in the subtle scent of his aftershave. 'Thank you so much for everything.'

'It was my pleasure, but it was all down to you. This is your success and you need to enjoy it.' Dexter smiled as she forced herself to let him go. 'I hope you're going to do something to celebrate.'

'The other midwives have got something up their sleeves apparently, I think it's going to be at the wine bar in Port Agnes tomorrow night. We would have done it tonight, but my friend Toni has got a family birthday thing to go to and I really didn't want her to miss it.'

'It sounds like a party in the making!'

'You could come.' Jess hoped she didn't sound desperately unprofessional, but she really didn't want this to be the last time she saw him.

'Riley's with his dad tomorrow night. So, if you let me know where you're going to be and when, I'll definitely come for a celebratory drink.' Dexter unlocked his car. 'Just drop me a text.'

'Okay, see you tomorrow then.' Jess's attempt to act casual might have fooled Dexter, but sadly there was no fooling herself. She didn't want Dexter to disappear from her life altogether, but like so many of the people who'd done that over the years, she probably wasn't going to get a choice.

20

Toni hadn't ended up calling in sick the day after her confrontation with Bobby, but she'd asked Anna to put her in clinics for the
next couple of days so that she wouldn't have to speak to him
again. Everything he'd said about the way she'd treated him was
true and he had every right to walk away from her the way he
had. She just couldn't deal with seeing him again yet because she
didn't have anything new to say – and she couldn't bear to see that
look in his eyes for a second time either.

She was keeping the baby, that was the only thing she knew
for sure, but all the questions he had about what that was going
to look like were still as uncertain as they always had been. She
wasn't going to be able to avoid him forever, but she needed at
least one more day. So she'd asked Ella to put her on home visits
on the day of Jess's panel – anything to avoid being in a delivery
room with Bobby for hours on end, or trying to pretend to be
normal in front of the others in the staffroom.

Lucy was still receiving home visits every other day, although
she didn't seem to be showing any signs of the postnatal depres-

sion that Toni and Bobby had both been so worried about when baby Sasha was born. If things were still okay this time, then Toni would be handing Lucy's care over to the health visitor and she'd have no reason to go and see her any more. Something else that other people would probably find surprising about Toni was that she found it so hard to say goodbye to her patients, and that she missed the vast majority of them after they were no longer a part of her life. She wasn't an effusive person like Anna or Ella, and she didn't have Jess's bubbly personality, even though she'd bet a month's salary that there was a lot Jess was hiding behind that façade – sometimes the mask would slip and she'd go really quiet. Despite what everyone thought though, Toni liked being around people, even if – as Gwen had pointed out more than once – her face didn't always show it.

'Toni, great to see you again. Have you come to check how my two gorgeous girls are getting on?' Henry met her at the door of the cottage he shared with Lucy and Sasha. He had a ruddy complexion and he still seemed to be wearing the same broad grin he'd had on his face when Sasha had been delivered.

'I can't wait to see them both. And how are you doing? Is life as a new father what you expected?' Toni had always tried to include both parents on her home visits after the birth of their babies. Her first priority as a midwife was always to the mother of course, but the realities of parenthood could be a huge shock to fathers too, and the same system of support didn't exist for them. The truth was that Toni's interest in knowing how Henry was coping had been heightened by the fact that she was now pregnant herself, and she wasn't able to even talk to her unborn baby's father. At least not yet.

'No, it's far better than I expected.' Henry was still smiling. 'I mean I knew it was going to be exhausting and that sleep was going to become a thing of the past for a while, but I don't think anyone can explain the feeling of holding your own baby in your arms until you do it for yourself. We thought we might never get to be parents, but I'm already finding it impossible to imagine life without Sasha. I might be biased, but you'll see for yourself that she's getting more beautiful every day.'

'I don't doubt it for a moment.'

'Come on in then. You go through to the sitting room and I'll make you a cup of tea, if you've got time? Milk and no sugar isn't it?'

'You know us midwives, we've always got time for tea, which is pretty evident by the fact you know my order off by heart.' Toni followed Henry down the hallway of the cottage, heading into the sitting room as he went ahead to the kitchen. Lucy was in a chair by the bay window which overlooked the front garden, the winter sunshine bathing her and the baby in a pool of sunlight.

'You look like you should be on the front of a mother and baby magazine or something.' Toni spoke softly, so as not to wake Sasha who looked as if she'd fallen asleep in the middle of feeding. 'It seems like you've got the breastfeeding sorted, too.'

'The first week was literally toe-curling at times, but I'm glad I stuck with it.' Lucy dropped a kiss onto Sasha's downy head.

'It doesn't work for everyone, but judging by her chart, you've got gold top stuff and her weight gain has been pretty steady.'

'Do you need to weigh her now?'

'I'll do it before I go, but don't wake her up just yet, she looks so peaceful.'

'She's already going four hours between feeds at night.' Lucy looked towards Toni. 'And I keep asking myself what I've done to get so lucky, but I'm finally starting to believe I'll get to keep her and that I deserve to as well.'

'Of course you do.' Toni took the seat opposite Lucy. 'I wanted to do the Edinburgh test with you again today if you don't mind? It's a bit earlier than usual, but we can always run it a third time later on, if you've got any concerns. I just think it would be useful to compare with the results of your antenatal test.'

'Do you think I'm doing okay?'

'Absolutely and, like I said before, it's not about judging you, I just think it would be helpful for the health visitor to get an up-to-date picture.' The Edinburgh scale was a tool Toni and the rest of the team used to monitor new mums and mothers-to-be for indicators of depression. Usually the health visitor would do the postnatal test six weeks after the baby's delivery, but the midwifery team also ran the test during pregnancy to check for signs of antenatal depression. With Lucy, Toni wanted to do the first postnatal test too, just because of some of the things she'd said in the run-up to Sasha's birth, and so that she could arrange for Lucy to keep having extra support if there was any indication she needed it.

Mostly the midwifery team or health visitor would just ask the questions from the screener, without explaining its purpose to their patients, to make sure they got the most honest answers. But Toni felt it was important for Lucy to understand the purpose of the test and to be aware of the signs to look out for, after everything that had happened in her past, which was why Toni had explained it all to her the first time she'd carried out the test.

'Actually, I'd like to see the results too. I feel so much better and Henry's finally made me realise that loving Sasha doesn't mean I have to forget about Oscar. I've also surprised myself with how well I've coped with meeting Sasha's needs. What with that and Henry telling me what a great mum I am at least thirty times a day, I think I can finally believe it's not my fault that Oscar didn't make it.'

'That's great and I've got to agree with Henry about what a great job you're doing.'

'Life's too short to keep punishing myself for things in the past that I can't change. I suddenly realised, with Sasha looking as if she's changing every couple of days or so, that if I carried on spending all my time doing that I'd miss out on so much with her. And I don't want to miss a second of it. I'm so lucky to have her and Henry, I've got to stop beating myself up for something I couldn't control in the first place.'

'It sounds like you've got it all sorted.' Toni smiled, blinking away the tears that had unexpectedly filled her eyes. If Lucy could finally forgive herself and stop living in the past then there was a chance Toni could too. Maybe she should make an appointment to see the same therapist she'd referred Lucy to. Reaching into her bag to get a copy of the Edinburgh scale, Toni tried not to let the thoughts filling up her head take over. There might be a tiny chance that she could forgive herself, but the real question was whether the rest of the world would allow her to stop living in the past. Even if they did, there was every chance that it was already too late to ask Bobby to forgive her for doing that too.

Either way, there was no getting away from the fact that if she wanted to be the kind of mother Lucy was turning out to be, there couldn't be any more secrets. She was going to have to confront Aaron's parents, and her own, with the truth – not just about the baby, but about everything that had happened leading up to Aaron's death. If any of them couldn't cope with that she'd be sorry, but she was starting to realise that having been through hell twice over already, there wasn't much left that could scare her. Except the thought that her baby was going to grow up without the chance to have someone as great as Bobby as its father, all because of her.

* * *

Toni was running twenty minutes late for Judy's birthday celebrations. After finishing her home rounds, she'd had to stop off and pick up the birthday cake that Aaron had always bought his mother from Mehenick's bakery each year, from the time he was old enough to drive two villages along and pick it up. Judy had loved the coffee and walnut cake he'd bought her the first year he'd ordered one from Ella's father, Jago, and it had become another of their traditions; one more that Toni had taken over when Aaron died.

This time, she'd done the whole thing almost on autopilot, trying not to think about whether this might be the last time she'd ever be allowed to be a part of Judy's birthday celebrations. Just because she was going to put the baby first, it didn't mean she wanted to cut Aaron's parents out of her life, but she might not get the choice. The need to tell them the truth, now she'd decided she had to do it, was burning inside her. But she had to let Judy have this one last day. Telling her everything on her birthday would have been unnecessarily cruel.

There was one thing that couldn't wait, though; she had to reach out to Bobby. She had to know if there was any chance left. After she carried the cake to her car, she stared at her phone for a full three minutes before eventually summoning up the courage to text him.

I saw Lucy and Henry today. Baby Sasha is doing brilliantly, and they said to pass on their thanks again. Something else Lucy said really made me think and I wondered if we could meet? I really need to talk to you.

Setting off before Bobby would have had a chance to reply –

so she didn't waste another twenty minutes waiting for him to and worrying when he didn't – Toni drove along the winding country roads to Port Tremellien. It was still getting dark by just after four, but the sky was almost a navy blue rather than black, and it was lit up with millions of stars as she followed the route she must have driven thousands of times over the years. Thinking about the hugeness of the sky above her was strangely calming. She'd read somewhere once that there were supposedly more stars in the sky than grains of sand on every beach on earth. Surely that had to mean that her problems weren't as significant as she'd made them out to be. After all, how could anything she said to Judy and the others be the end of the world when they were such a tiny part of an infinite universe?

Pulling up on her parents' driveway, she could see the 'Happy Birthday' banner in the window of Judy and Simon's house next door, hanging above the windowsill which housed just a few of the hundreds of photographs that Simon and Judy had up of Aaron. There were photos on every available surface and wall space around the house – a reminder that they might all be a tiny part of the universe, but Aaron was still the centre of theirs, even five years after he'd gone.

The nausea that had been one of the first indications that Toni might be pregnant had finally begun to abate, but now she felt sick for an altogether different reason. At some point she was going to have to tell the people behind the door of the house, which was as familiar to her as her own family home, that she was having somebody else's baby. There was no response to her text message to Bobby either, so there was every chance she was going to be doing this alone and the only support system she'd even known could be taken away from her too. Her parents wouldn't choose Judy and Simon over her, deep down she knew that, but they'd end up changed forever and a little bit broken by the loss of their best friends, just like she'd been when she lost Aaron. For now, though, she just had to get through this one night and then she could try and work out when and how to tell them everything she had to say.

'Hello sweetheart, we were starting to worry that you might have got caught up at work.' Simon greeted her with a kiss on the cheek. 'And I was just about to lose the battle with Judy to start calling you to check that everything was okay. You know how she gets when anyone is late.'

'I'm sorry, I was out on home visits today and I got caught up on one and then ended up playing catch-up all day to try and get back on track.'

'It's not a problem at all, sweetheart, and you've got the cake, so it's all good.'

'I'll never miss a year, whatever happens.' Toni's voice was suddenly thick with emotion and Simon gave her a quizzical look.

'Oh love, what's the matter?'

'Nothing.' She shook her head, screwing up her eyes so there was no chance of any of the tears escaping. 'I just need you and Judy to know that I'll always want you in my life.'

'Just as well, because there's no getting rid of us, *whatever happens*. But we'd better go through and see the others or Judy really will send out a search party.'

The birthday party went much the way it always did. There was a pattern emerging in how all of their birthdays were spent these days, and at Judy's request, Simon got some photo albums out, although they were different to the ones they'd looked at on Toni's birthday of her shared childhood with Aaron. These albums documented Judy's previous birthdays and other celebrations, including the holidays Aaron's family and Toni's had shared to mark Judy's thirtieth and fortieth birthdays. There were no photographs of her sixtieth, but the day was etched in Toni's memory anyway. It was her third birthday after losing Aaron and her first big milestone without him. She'd cried all the way through and not even Simon, or Toni's mother Mandy, had been able to comfort her when she'd sobbed about the fact that she'd never be a grandmother now. She hadn't just lost Aaron when he'd died; the whole future she'd mapped out in her head had disappeared with him and Toni had known that feeling only too well.

'I'm really glad we've got so many photographs of you and Aaron together, because it means when I see you now, I can picture how he would have been too, standing by your side.' Judy reached out and squeezed Toni's hand, looking at her levelly. 'Having you here is like keeping a part of Aaron with us too and I'm sure it's why my MS has been so stable over the last three years. I don't know what I'd have done without you.' Toni could barely maintain eye contact with Judy as she spoke, wondering if the older woman could hear how loud her swallowing suddenly seemed to have become.

'That doesn't mean we expect you to be here for every birthday or big occasion for the rest of our lives.' Simon's tone was unusually forceful, but Toni didn't miss the look that Judy shot him as a result. She wouldn't have been surprised if her father had said something to Simon after her own birthday and she'd seen the look of exasperation the two men often exchanged. They'd be ready to hear Toni's news, she was almost sure of it, they might even welcome it. But judging by Judy's reaction to what Simon had just said, she was never going to be ready.

'We hope you will be a part of everything we do, though, sweetheart. It's what keeps me going.' Judy had widened her eyes almost pleadingly. Even after all this time, Toni couldn't tell if the emotional blackmail she wielded so expertly was accidental. It didn't really matter, because it was still just as effective either way and when the time came to cut some of the ties between them, Judy was really going to struggle with it.

'Right, I think it must be time for cake!' Toni's mother smiled, clearly deciding that a change of subject was called for. 'I'll do the honours with the candles.'

'You're not putting sixty-two on there are you?' Simon winked, defusing some of the tension that had filled the space between him and his wife. 'It'll burn the house down!'

'Cheeky.' Judy gave him a nudge, but she looked genuinely happy – despite having spent the last hour or so having pored over photographs of her beloved son – the downturn of her mouth at the possibility of Toni missing some future events disappearing.

'Shall I give you a hand, Mum?' The words were barely out of Toni's mouth before her phone started to ring. The name that flashed up on the screen was Betty. Usually, she'd just have ignored the call until after the get-together at Judy and Simon's was over and done with. But if she pushed Bobby away again, there was every possibility this might be the last time he'd reach out. As it was, there was a very strong chance it was already too late and that's what Bobby was calling to tell her, but she wasn't going to throw away even a tiny possibility that it might not be. It was finally time to start putting him first. 'I'm really sorry, but I'll have to take this, it's work. Just don't start the cake without me, okay?'

'We won't, Netty.' Her Dad touched her arm. 'But you're not on call, so if it needs dealing with, let someone else do it. We're all worried about how exhausted you've been looking lately and you need a break.'

'Uh-huh.' Toni pressed the phone icon to accept the call, giving Bobby an excuse for why she couldn't talk until she was out of earshot and praying that he'd understand why she still needed to. She wanted to tell him that she was ready to put everything out in the open with Judy, but that it just needed to wait a bit longer; she couldn't do it tonight. 'Hold on a sec, I'm just going to where the reception is a bit better.'

Heading down the hallway she went through the kitchen and out to the back garden as quickly as she could. She didn't want to keep Bobby waiting, but she had to get far enough away from her parents, and Judy and Simon, to not risk the conversation being overheard. It was cold outside, but she was already shivering anyway as she sat at the wrought-iron bistro table which was in a sheltered area of the garden, down the steps from the small decked area outside the back door.

'Sorry, I was in a room full of people.'

'The usual suspects?'

'It's Judy's birthday.'

'What time will you finish? Can we meet? I really want to talk to you too.' Bobby's tone was far friendlier than it had been last time she'd spoken to him and her body almost slumped with relief. He didn't sound like a man who hated her and he actually wanted to talk.

'I really want to see you, but I'm staying here tonight. Aaron's family have got this tradition where they have a special breakfast the day after birthdays, with one more present just to chase away the post-birthday blues.' Toni bit her lip, his sigh at the other end of the call all too audible. 'It's a whole thing and I don't want to spoil this for her. Not when I don't know how she's going to react to hearing about the baby. This might be the last time.'

'Can't you slip away for a bit, even twenty minutes? I don't want to do this over the phone.' Bobby's tone was tighter now and she was terrified that she was going to lose him if she didn't take this chance. She had to find a way.

'I'll get away at some point, even it means waiting until the others are asleep. Just let me know where you'll be. I love you, you do know that, don't you?'

'I love you too, but it's got to be all or nothing for me, Tee. I thought maybe I could do this, pick up whatever scraps I could get so I'd have some involvement in our baby's life, but I don't want to be a part-time dad fitted in around what Aaron's family need. I want to be the kind of dad my father has been. Always there and wanting to spend every minute he could with me, even when I found that annoying as hell when I was a teenager. If I can't have that, I need to take myself out of the equation because I can't stand seeing you being less of a mother than you want to be either, trying to fit our baby into a life where it can never be at the absolute centre. I just can't.'

'I wouldn't do that, I—'

'Oh God, someone help me!' Toni heard Judy's shout a split second before the noise of what sounded like the thwack of someone's palm against the decking outside the back door filled the air. Dropping her phone on the table, she raced up the steps to the decking, where the other woman was lying, only a faint moaning sound indicating she was still conscious.

'Can you hear me? What happened? Are you okay?' She was firing the questions at Judy, who slowly opened her eyes.

'I think so, it's knocked the wind out of me, but my legs just seemed to give way when I came out to find you.' Judy's gaze met hers. 'I just hope it's not a relapse of the MS.'

'I'm sure it isn't that.' Toni had never been more certain of anything in her life and she had a feeling that Judy had been standing on the decking for long enough to hear some of her conversation with Bobby. This wasn't the right moment for a confrontation though; all she wanted was to finish talking to Bobby so she could reassure him that she'd do whatever it took to get to him as soon as she could. Even if she was convinced the other woman was acting up a storm, she couldn't just leave Judy lying on the deck and she'd need help to move her. Shouting through the open French doors, she called out to the others. 'Mum, Dad, Simon! Quick, Judy's had a fall, we need to get her inside.'

Within seconds, there was a thundering of footsteps and Simon was the first to reach them. 'Oh Judy, what the heck have you done now?'

'I think it might be the MS.' Judy sounded very sorry for herself and normally Toni would have been filled with concern, but it was as if the veil had finally been lifted.

'I'm pretty sure it was just a slip. It could happen to anyone, the decking's lethal at this time of year.' Toni was itching to get back to her phone call and for once she didn't care what anyone thought of her. 'Are you okay to get Judy inside. I'll just finish sorting out this work thing and come in and check her over?'

'Can't the work call wait?' Judy furrowed her brow.

'I'll be two minutes. Just give me that, okay?' It might have been framed as a question, but Toni's tone brooked no argument.

'We'll be fine for two minutes and it won't take all four of us to get Judy into the house.' Simon's response was almost as unwavering as Toni's had been, but, as always, he found a way to break the tension too. 'She's not quite that heavy after all!'

'Thank you.' Shooting him a quick smile, Toni almost sprinted back down the steps to the table, despite the risk of going sprawling herself. Snatching up the phone, she spoke urgently into the mouthpiece. 'Sorry, Judy tripped and... Bobby, are you still there?'

The silence was deafening. He'd ended the call and every time she tried to call him back it went straight to voicemail, making it obvious that he was rejecting the calls on the first ring.

Ten attempts later, she finally gave up. Judy's acting might have been as hammy as a low-budget lunchtime soap opera, but she'd still achieved her aim. Toni's last chance to sort things out with Bobby had imploded and, just like he'd said, he was finally done.

* * *

'Netty, come on, your Mum said the candles are going to burn down to nothing if you don't hurry up!' Toni's father hooked his arm into hers, pulling her from the hallway into the lounge, where the candles had finally been lit after they'd established that Judy's only injury was a splinter of wood in her right hand. If Toni had been forced to guess, she'd have bet that Judy had already lain down on the decking before she called out, and had sustained the splinter whacking her hand against the wood to try and replicate the sound of a fall.

When her father had come out to find her in the hallway, Toni had been making what she told herself was one last attempt to call Bobby and explain everything. Now she was supposed to sing 'Happy Birthday' to the woman who'd made sure she never got the chance. Her face was aching from the effort of trying to smile as she let her father lead her into the room.

'*Happy birthday to you, happy birthday to you, happy birthday dear Judy, happy birthday to you!*' The chorus filled the room, but Toni couldn't prevent her tone from being anything other than flat and half-hearted.

'Make a wish!' Toni's mother called out the order as Judy extinguished the flames in a single breath. There were only two candles in the end, a big number six and an accompanying two.

'You can't say what the wish is, or it will never come true.' Toni's father tapped the side of his nose.

'She's already made sure her wish comes true. She didn't want to take any chances, did you Judy?' There was such an edge to Toni's voice she barely recognised it as her own. But she had no more control over that than she did the words that were coming out of her mouth. She'd been determined not to ruin Judy's big night, but that had been before Aaron's mother had been perfectly happy to run the risk of ruining the rest of Toni's life.

'What on earth are you talking about?' Mandy looked close to tears, clearly unable to understand why her daughter would talk to their oldest friend that way, especially at a time like this.

'I think I know.' Simon reached out and squeezed Toni's hand before turning back to his wife. 'You staged the fall, didn't you?'

'Of course not, why on earth would I do that?' Judy's voice had gone up at least two octaves in an attempt to emphasis the denial. But the game was finally up.

'Because of what I told you, after Steve and I spoke.' Simon exchanged a look with Toni's father. 'You've got to let Toni start living her own life again, she's put it on hold for our benefit for the last five years, a lot longer than that if we're honest, and it's time to stop. I don't know what happened tonight to make you want to take such drastic action, Judy, but you can't keep playing the MS card every time you think Toni might be pulling away.'

'That's not what I was doing!' Judy's voice was higher still and for a second or two, Toni almost felt sorry for her again. But then her hand instinctively moved to her abdomen. This wasn't just about her.

'I don't know how much you overheard when you were standing on the decking, but I know you heard something. It doesn't matter anyway, because you all need to know the truth.' Toni took a huge breath. 'I'm in love with someone I work with. His name is Bobby and we've been together three years, but I've never felt able to tell you because it felt like I'd broken the promise I made to Aaron. I've made Bobby keep it all a secret too, but now he's had enough.'

'You can't really believe we'd resent you for being happy again can you, darling?' Toni's mother was openly crying now.

'Of course she did, because none of us gave her any reason to think otherwise. We were all too busy trying to keep Judy happy; we're as much to blame as she is.' Simon shook his head, turning back towards Toni. 'I'm so sorry sweetheart.'

'Simon's right, we should have told you at every opportunity we had that all we wanted was for you to be happy. But what I don't understand is the promise you made to Aaron?' Toni's father slipped an arm around her shoulders and she leant into him, glad of the support he was offering, otherwise she wasn't sure she'd have had the strength to get through the next bit.

'On the day he died, I'd argued with Aaron about the wedding. I wasn't even sure if I wanted to go through with it, at least not straight away. Ever since, I've felt that his death was at least partly my fault because of all the stress I put him under. So I made him the promise that I'd do my best to fill his shoes for Judy and Simon, but I can't do it any more. I just can't.' Toni was crying now too, partly out of relief, but the guilt she'd hoped would be unburdened by her confession hadn't just disappeared. Even through her tears though, she could see how vigorously Simon was shaking his head.

'Oh my love, I wish you'd told us that you were blaming yourself and then I might have been able to make you see sense.' Simon took her hand again. 'Aaron's death had nothing to do with you, it was down to faulty blood vessels in his brain and it doesn't matter if you argued, or if Aaron knew you were having a few doubts, because he also knew how many sacrifices you'd made for him to try and keep Judy happy. He told me more times than I can count how amazing you were about it all, but I can't help wishing both of you had been more selfish.'

'Simon, please.' As Judy interjected, Toni was fully expecting her to launch into another denial, but not this time. Her voice was straining to almost breaking point. 'What you said about tonight is true, Toni. I pretended to have a fall because I heard you telling the man you've been seeing that you loved him. And what Simon has just said is true, too. If anyone contributed to Aaron's death, it was me. Constantly putting pressure on him to live his life the way I thought he should.'

Judy hesitated for a second, wiping her eyes with back of her hand, before going on. 'When you cancelled your plans to travel after my diagnosis, I started to see the MS as a gift, despite how much it terrified me. It meant I could keep my son close and have much more of a say in what he did than I would have otherwise. When he said you were thinking about travelling again, I was terrified you might visit somewhere like Australia and decide to settle there. So I pushed for the wedding, even though I knew there were other things you both wanted to concentrate on. When Aaron died I was even more terrified of losing you, because you're all we've got left. I kept telling myself how wrong it was to manipulate you, even as I was lying on that decking tonight, waiting to call out to you. But I just couldn't seem to stop myself. Now my only birthday wish is for you to be able to find a way to forgive me and to live your life the way you've always wanted to, but haven't because of me.'

The tension in the room was fizzing and Toni was desperate for someone to fill the silence, but then she realised they were all waiting for her to speak. She couldn't find the words, not yet. All she could do was make her own silent wish, the same one she'd made on her birthday – that she could find a way to be with Bobby and have the whole package, just like he'd always wanted.

There were things she still had to say to Judy too and she hadn't even mentioned the baby yet, but she needed to finish processing everything herself first. She had to hand it to Judy, she'd had the courage to admit everything in the end and Toni knew only too well how hard some things were to admit, even to yourself. The tragedy was that it had all come just a little too late for Toni's wish to ever come true.

21

Jess lifted the champagne out of the ice bucket and topped up five of the glasses, the sixth of which was already filled with pink lemonade. Anna was still having a rough time with the pregnancy and she wouldn't be staying long, but Jess was incredibly touched that she'd come out with the rest of the midwives to toast the news of her being approved as a foster carer. Toni, Ella, Emily and Izzy were also there, but Gwen and Bobby were on call and had gone out to a home delivery, which didn't stop them ringing the wine bar and paying in advance for a bottle of champagne before the others had even got there. Jess was so lucky to have her friends from the midwifery unit; they were the only people who'd never once let her down.

'Let's raise a toast then. To our Jess and all the lucky children who'll now get to have her as a part of their lives.' Ella held up one finger. 'But only on the condition that she doesn't stop being a midwife all together!'

'To Jess!' Everyone clinked their glasses together and Jess tried not to turn towards the door again to check if Dexter had arrived. She'd texted him to let him know what time they were meeting, but he hadn't replied. She must have looked at her messages twenty times, just in case she'd missed the notification, and now she was fighting the urge not to do it again.

'So what happens next?' Izzy's question brought Jess back to the moment and she forced herself to focus on the conversation.

'Once all the paperwork is complete and the panel's recommendation is officially signed off, I get assigned a social worker and wait to be matched with a child who needs respite care. They try to set it up as a regular arrangement with the main foster carers, so that the child gets to know me and feels comfortable whenever they come to stay. Technically speaking, I could start getting potential matches within a couple of weeks.'

'So Dexter won't be your social worker then?' Ella asked and Jess shook her head. She'd hoped he might at least end up being her friend, but the fact he hadn't even answered her texts, despite the promises he'd made to be there if she needed him, had really hurt. He'd been the last person she expected to reel off meaningless platitudes about staying in touch if he didn't mean them. He knew better than anyone how badly she'd been let down in the past.

'That's a shame. You two got on really well, didn't you?' Anna gave her a sympathetic look, but Jess refused to feel sorry for herself. She was used to being let down and she'd get over it. With any luck, before too long, she'd be so busy with fostering that she wouldn't even have the chance to give him a second thought.

'We did, but it was just for the assessment. That's the way it works and he's leaving the local authority anyway, so we won't even be working for the same organisation.'

'It's probably just as well.' Toni raised her eyebrows. 'Everyone knows that having a relationship with someone you work with never turns out well.'

'It wasn't like that, we were only ever friends, if that.' It was ironic that Toni was looking at Jess as if she didn't believe a word she said, when she and Bobby had attempted to disguise their relationship as a friendship for years, but then maybe that explained her reaction.

'Some of the happiest couples I know have met through work.' Anna exchanged a look with Jess as she spoke. There'd definitely been a development in Toni and Bobby's not-so-secret relationship, the air filling with tension every time they were in the same room together lately. All Jess and the others could do was carry on pretending they didn't even know there was a relationship to get into trouble, unless Toni decided she wanted to confide in them. She was obviously on edge and she hadn't even taken a sip of her drink. 'Sorry, I should have checked if everyone was okay with champagne. Do you want something else, Toni?'

'I love champagne normally, but I've had another ear infection and the doctor has put me back on antibiotics. It's quite painful, so I don't want to risk them not working, especially if the infection is going to keep recurring.'

'I'd better drink it for you then!' Emily whipped the champagne away from Toni before she even had the chance to answer, but Jess was more worried about whether her friend was okay. Toni really didn't look like her normal self and the last thing Jess wanted was for her to make herself really ill, just because she felt like she should come out to celebrate the panel's decision.

'It was really lovely of you to come out Toni, but I don't want you to feel like you've got to stay if you're not feeling up to it.'

'Don't worry about me, I'm fine. I might not be able to drink, but I'm happy just to be here and see you all. It's ages since we've managed a night out together.'

'It'll be even longer once the twins arrive and Jess is busy with fostering.' Anna looked the picture of bliss at the thought of her babies' arrival, despite anything else she might have to sacrifice, but there were butterflies dancing in Jess's stomach. Dexter had said it was a good sign that she was nervous about being up to the task, because it showed how much she cared. She just hoped she didn't end up letting him down, even if he wasn't around to see it.

'The next time we're out could be my hen night if we're not careful!' Ella rolled her eyes. 'Although don't let my mum over-hear, or she'll want to start planning that too and she'll end up booking a ballroom somewhere. I'm having to keep talking her plans down for the wedding itself. I want to keep it low-key this time. Being stood up on the steps of a London registry office first time around, not to mention the video of it going viral, is enough of a splash for anyone. I just want to keep it simple and to actually end up married!'

'I can't believe how much has changed since you started at the unit.' Anna rubbed her belly. 'You're getting married, Bobby's finished his midwifery qualification, I'm married and having twins, Gwen's had a new grandchild, Izzy and Emily have joined us, and now Jess has been approved as a foster carer.'

'And I've achieved precisely nothing.' Toni pulled a face.

'Actually, Anna and Ella are only not mentioning it because they wanted this to be about my fostering approval, but I'm more than happy to share the night.' Jess exchanged a look with Anna and Ella, who both nodded. 'Because we got a call when we were in the staffroom today, to say you'd been shortlisted for the mentor of the year award by the university where Bobby studied. Apparently he nominated you a few months ago, and after they interviewed him last week, you're now in the top three, which means you'll be getting a bronze award at the very least.'

'And that's not just for Bobby's university, it's mentor of the year for the whole South West region.' Anna raised her glass again. 'It's a great achievement and it means it'll be easier for us to get funding to support more trainee midwives and MCAs as part of the team. Congratulations!'

'To our mentor extraordinaire!' Jess clinked her glass against the others, but Toni still didn't have a drink and she called out to a passing waiter, 'Excuse me, could we have another pink lemonade here please. The very least we've got to do is get you a drink to toast your achievement.'

'Are you sure Bobby nominated me, and that they only interviewed him last week?' Toni looked like she'd be less surprised if an alien spaceship suddenly circled overhead.

'Absolutely certain.' Ella nodded. 'I took the call and they said he couldn't speak highly enough of you. Then they asked me, Anna and Jess if we could provide some supporting statements to help them make the decision between the top three.'

'Yes, and we couldn't speak highly enough of you either.' Jess smiled at the waiter who'd brought another pink lemonade over to the table. 'Thank you so much.'

'Another toast.' Anna raised her drink in the air. 'To my amazing team. I'm so proud of you Jess and Toni – and Brae sends his love to both of you too. I just wish he wasn't picking me up in five minutes, but the anaemia is making it impossible for me to stay up past about eight-thirty these days. So unless he wants to carry me home and up to bed, I'll have to be a one-drink wonder tonight.'

'I'm just so glad you came at all and thank you for the brilliant reference you gave me for my fostering application.' Jess stood up and hugged her friend.

'And thank you all for what you said to the university. I still can't believe that Bobby did that either.' Toni was gripping her glass so hard her knuckles had turned white and even if the ear infection story was just a cover so she could leave early, after whatever had gone on with Bobby lately, she really didn't look well. They'd all been worried about her for a few weeks now. Jess could see Ella watching her closely too, and hopefully she or Anna would be able to get her to open up about what it was that was really bothering her.

'I'm so sorry, but I'm going to have to shoot off too. My grand-mother's been really poorly and we've been taking it in turns to go and stay at hers until she's back on her feet.' Izzy gave Jess an apologetic smile.

'I think I'll have to head off as well then, seeing as Izzy is the only one going my way.' Emily shrugged. 'Next time we'll have to be more organised and make a proper night of it. With Bobby and the others too.'

'No problem at all. I'm really grateful you all came and we'll definitely have to get planning Ella's hen night soon, and a few other nights out between now and then.' Jess grinned and there was a flurry of goodbyes until it was just Jess, Ella and Toni left around the table.

'Do you fancy going on somewhere else and getting dinner, as it's just the three of us?' Ella's tone was determinedly upbeat and, to Jess's surprise, Toni nodded.

'We might as well, otherwise we'll be in danger of turning Jess's celebration into a proper let-down.' Toni shrugged. 'And it's not as if we've got to wait for anyone else, is it?'

'No, it isn't.' Jess drained her champagne, desperate to stop staring at the door of the wine bar every time someone new came in and feeling disappointed when they weren't Dexter. He obvi-ously wasn't any more likely to turn up than Bobby or Gwen were, so it was definitely time to move on.

* * *

Toni, Jess and Ella all lived within walking distance of The British Raj restaurant where they'd ended up going to eat. They walked Jess home to Puffin's Rest first and Ella only lived a few hundred yards away at the end of Mercer's Row, on the other side of the harbour. It didn't give Toni long to work up to what she wanted to say and in the end she just blurted it out.

'I'm pregnant.'

'I did wonder... the not drinking, the hot flushes you've had in the staff room and furtive munching on dry crackers. It wouldn't take Sherlock Holmes to work it out and you're surrounded by midwives.' Ella turned towards her, taking hold of both of her hands. 'Are you okay?'

'I don't know... I've messed it all up with Bobby, but the baby is his.' If she was expecting Ella to be agog at the news, she was in for a disappointment. Deep down she'd always known her friends at the midwifery unit knew about her and Bobby, but they'd played along for her sake. 'And now he doesn't even want to be a part of things.'

'I'm sure that's not true.' Ella squeezed her hands again. 'Look, do you want to come to mine and we can talk about it there?'

'Is Dan home?'

'Yes, but I can send him upstairs if he hasn't already gone to bed.'

'No, it's fine, I can tell you here and I just want to get it off my chest.' Toni gave another shuddering sigh, despite her bravado. She was determined not to cry again, but she was finding it hard to even speak.

'You don't have to tell me anything and I know you're really struggling. Are you sure you don't want to come back to mine, or we can walk to your place?'

'That's where it happened.' Toni's eyes met Ella's, her friend's face blurring through the tears that wouldn't stay away. 'It was just before I started at the unit. Aaron and I had been together since we were thirteen, but we'd known each other our whole lives. He was my best friend too.'

'You lost him?' Ella's tone was gentle and Toni managed a nod, pausing again before she could say any more.

'He died from a sudden, catastrophic brain haemorrhage, just after we got engaged. He was so full of life and always trying to make everyone else happy, and then, just like that, he was gone.' For a second, Toni could picture Aaron laughing and she caught her breath. It was so long since she'd thought of him like that.

'Oh God, Toni, I'm so sorry, I had no idea.'

'No one does, but when Aaron died I made him a promise to try and fill his place in his parents' lives. Until the other night, they had no idea about Bobby and neither did my parents because I thought it would break their hearts all over again to know I've moved on. It's why I've tried so hard to keep things between us a secret.' This time, Toni's sigh felt as if it went right down to her toes, draining her whole body. 'It's also why I didn't tell Bobby about the baby, but then he found out by chance and now he's saying he's done. I can't blame him, I've put him through hell, protecting everyone's feelings but his.'

'I can't believe how much you've been through, but I'm sure Bobby doesn't mean it. That's why Anna wouldn't accept his notice when he handed it in this afternoon, she told him to think it over for another few days and make sure that a job in London is what he really wants. It's not too late.'

'He's actually taken another job? He only told me he was thinking about it.' The cold night air suddenly seemed to envelop her whole body and even her teeth were chattering as she dropped Ella's hands. 'He's made up his mind, then. If he's prepared to leave his mum and dad and the rest of his family, he must be willing to do anything to get away from me.'

'He's probably just as confused as you were when you first found out about the baby; it's a lot for anyone to process.'

'But why would he want to be tied to someone like me? Bobby could have anyone he wants. He's way out of my league in every sense and you see the way girls like Emily look at him, why would be want me?'

'Even though you can't see it Toni, we all can. You're beautiful inside and out, and it's obvious in Bobby's face every time he looks at you. It's why the pair of you did such a crappy job of hiding things from the rest of us!' Ella touched her arm. 'Just talk to him again.'

'It's too late, he's never going to trust me after everything I've done and maybe he's right, maybe it'll be easier on all of us this way, because I can't trust my judgement any more. I've kept our whole relationship secret because I thought it would kill Aaron's parents to find out about me and Bobby.' Toni swallowed hard. 'But last night, they told me all they've ever wanted is for me to be happy, so I've wasted all that time lying to the people I love and hurting Bobby.'

'You were just trying to do your best by everybody, that's what you always do, but now you've got to learn to look after yourself and lean on the people who want to help you.'

'I don't know what to do. I've got my scan tomorrow afternoon in Truro at three after I've run the fertility group meeting with Jess, but I didn't tell my parents, or Aaron's, about the baby. I don't want to say anything until I'm as sure as I can be that it's going to be okay. They've been through enough already.'

'Have you told Bobby about the scan?'

'He's made it clear how he feels.' Toni's scalp prickled every time she thought about it. But she still couldn't completely give up on the idea of changing his mind about leaving, not when he'd been willing to meet her on the night of Judy's party. She was going to give it one last shot, bombard him with another hundred calls and messages if she had to, and hope he had the heart to listen to just one of them. She had to try, otherwise she'd never forgive herself. The chances of changing his mind at all were almost non-existent, so she didn't even dare to hope that she might be able to do it in time for the scan.

'I'm only working until lunchtime tomorrow. Do you want me to come with you?'

'Would you mind?' Toni was weak with gratitude. She really didn't want to do this alone. If something turned out to be wrong, she wasn't sure she could cope with it by herself – not when it already felt as if she was made of glass.

'I'd be honoured, but I'll probably have to meet you at the hospital.'

'That would be great and would you mind telling Anna too? I'll tell Jess once I know everything's okay. Although I probably won't tell any of the others until after Bobby leaves, to avoid making things awkward.'

'He's the baby's father and more than that, Bobby's a great guy. He won't just walk away, I'm certain of it.'

'You didn't hear the things he said; I've finally pushed him too far. Even nice guys like Bobby can only take so much.' Toni gave her friend an uncharacteristic hug, but the truth was it wasn't just to thank Ella, she needed it badly too. 'But you being there means so much to me, I'm not sure I could have gone to the scan alone. I'm terrified something's going to be wrong.'

'It's all going to be okay, Toni, I promise. I'll see you tomorrow.' Ella sounded so confident and Toni desperately wanted to believe her. But it was never going to be okay again, not if Bobby was leaving and, whatever Ella might think, it was probably too late to stop that from happening. It still didn't mean Toni was going to let him go without a fight and, even as Ella turned to head home, she was already dialling his number. Straight to voicemail. She wasn't going to leave a message until she'd worked out exactly what she wanted to say. It was the most important voicemail she was ever going to leave and she had absolutely no idea where to start.

22

Bobby and Gwen had been called out on a home delivery while the others had been out celebrating Jess' news, and they hadn't left until just before 1 a.m. A separate team of three midwives usually covered most of the late on-call shifts, but when they needed time off for holidays or sickness, the day team would take over the on-call cover. It meant Bobby wasn't working the following day and the empty hours seemed to stretch endlessly out in front of him. It didn't help that he'd been up since 3 a.m., after all of about sixty minutes sleep, trying to work out what the hell he was going to do.

Anna had refused to accept his notice when he'd told her he was planning to take the job in London, telling him to think over what it was he really wanted. The trouble was that what he really wanted was to be with Toni and the baby, properly, exactly the way he'd told her he wanted to be. Not hanging around on the periphery of their lives, the way he'd hung around on hers, but slap, bang in the centre of it. She couldn't give him that, but Anna was right, he didn't want to walk away either. It might hurt him to only be a small part of his child's life, but it would kill him not to be any part of it. He couldn't even think about Toni and what not being a part of her life either way was going to do to him.

He'd clung on to taking whatever time she could give him for three years because he'd known not being any part of her life would break him, and he'd always kept hoping that if he hung on for just long enough, things might change. Now they had, in a way he could never have foreseen. He was at the biggest impasse he could ever imagine facing in his life and there was no one he could talk to about it, no one who would understand or who was capable of staying neutral. Except maybe one.

The whole time he was walking up to St Jude's, Bobby told himself he was being crazy. He was on his way to talk to the gravestone of a man he'd never even met and yet who he'd felt irrationally jealous of ever since he'd met Toni. She turned to Aaron all the time, though, so he must have something. It was probably just the peace and quiet of the churchyard that allowed Toni to work through her own feelings and make sense of them. That would be a good start for Bobby too though, and right now anything was worth a shot.

The pathway from the front of the church to where Aaron's grave was located was covered in ice and very slippery, and the grass on either side of it was frosted and crackly underfoot too. It was one of those cold days that felt as if it got down to your core. It was why he wasn't expecting to see anyone else there, let alone the couple trying not to keep slipping and sliding as they struggled down the pathway with a bench.

'Can I give you a hand?' Bobby called out, as the couple set down the bench on the grass and the woman put her hands on the small of her back.

'That would be brilliant if you don't mind, my wife's sciatica is killing her.' The man, who must have been at least in his sixties, smiled at Bobby. 'I should have waited until our son came down at the weekend, but Dora really wanted to bring the bench over on our daughter's actual birthday.'

'It would have been her thirtieth.' Dora was still holding the small of her back. 'But we lost her when she was just eight, so this is the only way we can give her a present. Over the years we've planted trees, released balloons and, when she was twenty-one, I even did the thing I said I'd never do and had a tattoo of a mermaid put on my wrist where I can look at it every time I'm missing Maria. Alan thought I was mad, but she loved mermaids.'

'And this year it's a bench. The vicar has given us permission to put it under the tree over there, where all the more recent burial plots are.' Alan gestured to where Aaron's grave was. 'Maria loved going down to the beach, she always thought it might be the one time she'd see a mermaid. It's why we moved to Port Agnes when she was diagnosed, so that she could go to the beach every day. Having the bench where she'd be able to sit and see down to the water just feels so right. We're lucky, because we've still got Dean, our son. I can't imagine what it's like for someone who loses their only child. I'm not sure we'd have found a reason to go on, but now we've got grandchildren too and life finally feels truly worth living again.'

'You probably think we're being ridiculous.' Dora gave a hollow laugh. 'How can a girl who's been gone for almost twenty-two years sit and look at a view from a churchyard bench? But being able to do stuff for her, like this, and being able to buy something each year on her birthday and at Christmas, makes it feel like she's still with us.'

'I don't think it's ridiculous at all. It's a gesture of love and just because the person isn't here any more it doesn't mean that love goes away.' Bobby was fighting to keep his voice steady; this wasn't his pain after all, but what Dora and Alan had said had really struck a chord. Aaron's parents had lost their only child and all those little rituals and traditions, and making Toni a part of those, was what allowed them to keep getting up and breathing in and out every day. He could see that now. How could he ever have expected Toni to have withdrawn from that, even a little bit? 'My nana always used to say that grief is what happens to the love that has nowhere to go once someone is gone, but you're still finding a way to share your love for Maria and that's wonderful.'

'You've really made my day.' When Dora smiled it lit up her whole face. 'I'd like to ask if I could give you a hug, but I don't even know your name.'

'It's Bobby and I'm really glad I got to meet you both too, what you've said has helped me a lot.'

'Have you got someone here as well?' Dora's face was immediately pinched with pain again.

'I—' Bobby wasn't sure how to explain his relationship with Aaron, but suddenly he knew how he wanted to. 'It's a family friend, someone my girlfriend was really close to, and it's funny how we still come to talk to him, to ask for his advice. That's what I was planning to do today.'

'It's a good idea.' Dora touched his arm. 'I always come here and run every big decision past Maria. When Dean was getting married, I even consulted her about what colour I should wear for the wedding! And when he's down from Plymouth for the weekend, he brings his two little ones up here to see their auntie and they talk to her like she can still hear every word they're saying. The whole family is in on the madness, but it works for us and we'd never leave Port Agnes because of it.'

'Shall we get this bench moved then?' Alan winked at Bobby. 'Then we can let this poor lad get on with his day and have a chat with his friend like he was planning to? After you've subjected him to one of your hugs of course, Dora!'

Ten minutes later the bench was positioned beneath the tree

and Bobby had said goodbye to the couple who'd unknowingly had such a huge impact on him. The hug he'd shared with Dora was filled with warmth and, in that moment, he wished that he'd been able to meet Aaron's parents and to maybe stand a chance of building some sort of relationship with them. Maybe Toni was right and they'd never be able to welcome another person into their lives, even if that person loved Toni with all his heart. But if Dora and Alan were anything to go by, there was a chance that Aaron's parents would embrace the fact she could be happy with someone else, as long as Bobby never tried to shut them out.

'Hi Aaron, it's Bobby.' Standing in front of the grave, he suddenly felt self-conscious, like he was leaving a message on some sort of spiritual answerphone where he'd never get a call back. Dora and Alan hadn't thought it was a stupid idea, though, and they seemed to have found the best way possible through all of this. 'I hope you don't mind me coming here without Toni, and I'm sorry that you had to hear us arguing last time. You know Toni, though, she can be infuriatingly stubborn sometimes and determined to look after everyone apart from herself. It's one of the things that drives me crazy about her, but it's also one of the reasons why I love her so much. I bet it was the same for you, right?'

Aaron might not have been able to answer, but Bobby nodded in response to his own question anyway. How could anyone not love Toni for that?

'She thinks she's got to deal with this all on her own now, the whole baby thing, because she's trying to do the impossible and keep me in her life without causing your parents any pain. And do you know what, for the first time, I really understand why that's so important to her, more important than what *she* actually wants.'

Bobby cleared his throat, staring at the blades of grass beyond the grave, which were losing their frozen stiffness as the morning sun finally started to have an impact.

'I was talking to a couple this morning, Dora and Alan, and they made me realise something. They seem to want to spread more love because their daughter died, not hold it all back for someone who isn't here any more. They want to share it between Maria and the people who are still here. I can't help thinking that your mum and dad would be the same. If they could see how much I love Toni, surely that would add to their happiness and not take from it? They seem to love her like a daughter and I'd like to be a part of their lives, with the baby too of course, because I think that's something that could eventually lessen the pain of losing you a tiny bit. But the thing is, I'm not sure if it's what Toni really wants? Maybe she's used you as an excuse not to be with me properly this whole time, even if she doesn't actually realise it herself? It's pretty hard to live up to someone who was as loved as you and if there was anything about you that annoyed the hell out of Toni sometimes, I think that's all long forgotten. You're perfect and I am so very far away from being that. Maybe she doesn't love me enough because of that and I can't say I blame her for that either. I've been a bit of an idiot lately, if I'm honest. I don't want to rock the boat and cause your parents any unnecessary hurt if she doesn't love me enough, but how can I still function if I walk away from her and the baby? It's all I've ever wanted.'

A seagull suddenly screeched overhead making Bobby jump, its plaintive cry, as it searched out the much scarcer food supply in the winter months sounding almost desperate. Aaron might have had no choice but to stay silent, but there were no easy answers to any of this. One thing Bobby knew for sure was that he couldn't just walk away. He was a parent now, like Dora and Alan, and that never stopped. They couldn't be a part of their daughter's life in the way they so desperately wanted to be, but they'd found a way of making the most of the bits they could still get – however tiny. Bobby would have so much more than that, even if it was only weekend visitation rights, and he was determined to make that work. He owed it to all the people who'd give everything they owned to be even half as lucky.

* * *

Jess and Anna were running what would probably be the last fertility group meeting before Jess got her first fostering placement, at least she hoped so. Jess was on call for home deliveries, covering for Bobby so he could get some proper sleep, which meant there was a chance she might disappear without much warning. That, coupled with the fact that the others were due to arrive at any moment, meant that Jess and Anna were making the most of the chance to catch up and wolf down some pastries, whilst the going was good.

'I keep excusing the constant eating I seem to be indulging in by telling myself that the nausea only abates when I'm stuffing my face. Trust me to be one of those people where it doesn't wear off at the end of the first trimester, like almost every other mother-to-be.' Anna laughed. 'The trouble is, there are plenty of low-calorie things I could be snacking on – rice cakes for instance – but the babies just seem to insist on only the highest calorie foods I can find!'

'You look brilliant.' Jess meant every word. Poor Anna might be struggling with lots of the less-than-pleasant pregnancy symptoms as well as the anaemia that clearly wiped her out some days, but she really did have that elusive glow that was so often talked about – yet actually not all that commonly seen. The thing Jess had seen for herself, in the mirror, in the days after she'd been approved as a foster carer. The glow came from feeling like she'd finally found her purpose in life and maybe that's where Anna's came from too. Whatever it was, it was no lie to say that Anna looked brilliant.

'How are you feeling now that the assessment is over and you know that your first placement is only the right match away?' Anna poured them both a cup of tea from the pot.

'I still can't quite believe it's going to happen and I'm a bit worried about leaving you in the lurch, especially as you've been having such a tough time.'

'We'll manage just fine and it'll only be a week or so at a time at first, won't it? So we can carry on using the agency cover and we've got the interviews for someone to take over Ella's hours while she's doing my job when I'm on maternity leave. That way I can always start that a bit earlier if needs be.'

'It'll usually be a week's respite at a time, pre-arranged, but I think the very most I'd ever be asked to do is a month if it was emergency respite that then turned into the need to find the child another permanent placement. At least that's what Dexter told me.'

'Have you seen anything of him since the approval?' Anna's tone was gentle. She was nothing if not perceptive and she'd obviously picked up on how attached Jess had inadvertently become to Dexter, even though she'd been able to rationalise it since then. Yes, she'd been disappointed when he hadn't made the celebratory drinks she'd invited him to. But since the news of being approved had sunk in, she'd started to put her friendship with Dexter – if that's what it even was – into perspective. Their relationship had been temporary, a means to an end for both of them, and they'd never have met if she hadn't applied to foster. The older she got, the more she realised that there were people who came into your life for a purpose. What was the old saying? *A reason, a season or a lifetime*? Even Dom, with all the hurt he'd caused her, had served a purpose in making her life what it was now. Her relationship with him and his reaction to discovering her infertility was what had led her to foster. It was all meant to be and, if Dexter wasn't supposed to become the friend she'd hoped he would, then that was meant to be too.

'No, he did his job brilliantly though and I couldn't have asked for a better assessor.' Jess poured some more milk into her tea. 'The only thing I'm worried about is getting a placement around the time when Faith Baxter is due to deliver her baby, because I've promised I'll be there for her. So I want to try and keep the two weeks either side of her due date clear and hope that turning down any placements they feel would work for me during that time won't go against me.'

'I'm sure they'll understand if you explain, but if you need any support with Faith, you know you've got me, Ella, or Toni to work with you on that.'

'Talking of Toni, I'm still really worried about her, she just seems so sad.' Admittedly Toni wasn't the most outwardly sunny of people, but she had a dry sense of humour and the warmest of hearts, if you were lucky enough to get below the surface. Just lately, though, she'd seemed completely worn down.

'Me too, but I think Ella might finally have got her to open up a bit after you all went out for dinner. She texted me about it when you were putting our order in. She's going to call me later, so I might have to break off from the group for a bit to take the call, if that's okay?'

'Of course it is. I'd dance through the streets naked if I thought it could solve whatever is bothering Toni and put a smile on her face again.'

'That should do the trick!' Anna laughed. 'Although it might not do a lot for your fostering career. You know you've got all of us too, though, if there's anything that gets hard about that for you at any point. Gwen already thinks she's going to be an honorary grandmother all over again.'

'Thank you. I'm so glad I've got you guys and that's why I can't imagine ever leaving the unit altogether to foster full-time, but I guess I'll cross that bridge if the opportunity ever comes.'

'You've got us in your life for good, Jess, either way. With everything we've all been through together over the last few years, that's a given.'

'I think I could live with that. Cheers!' She clinked her teacup against Anna's, trying not to spill too much of the tea. The next few months really were going to be the start of a new chapter for everyone. She just hoped that whatever it was that was making Toni look so unhappy lately would only play a very temporary part in her friend's life too.

23

Toni's stomach was churning as she stood in the hospital foyer watching the sliding doors repeatedly open and close as patients and visitors filed in. Every time the doors opened and let in another blast of cold air, she desperately hoped it was going to be Ella. She wasn't sure she'd be able to go into the scan by herself if her friend didn't show up. If something was wrong with the baby, or the whole thing had somehow been a figment of her imagination, she was going to need a hand to hold.

She'd fallen in love with this baby long before she'd even discovered she was pregnant. The idea of having a child with Bobby had unwittingly popped into her head almost from the moment they'd shared their first kiss and her legs had turned to jelly. It was like in the romance books she'd read with her school friend, Kirsty, one summer when they'd been about thirteen. She'd been staying with Kirsty for a week, and her friend's mother had a well-thumbed stack of Mills and Boon paperbacks on a bookshelf in her bedroom. Each night, Kirsty and Toni had 'borrowed' one and sat up late into the night, reading by torchlight under the covers about handsome sheikhs or Regency dukes sweeping the heroines off their feet and, almost without fail, making them so weak with desire that they could barely stand up.

It was not long before Toni had shared her first kiss with Aaron and it had been *nothing* like what she'd read about in the books – their braces meshing together in an uncomfortable clash of metal that made her feel faint for all the wrong reasons. They'd soon got the hang of it and she'd loved Aaron so much, but she'd decided it had been their familiarity that meant it was never quite like what she'd read in the books. The same familiarity that had made her want to be certain that they weren't sleepwalking into marriage. After Aaron had died, the other brief relationships she'd had were nothing like she'd read about in Kirsty's mother's novels either. So in the end, she'd decided that those sort of moments didn't exist at all in real life – until she'd met Bobby.

She'd been on autopilot when she'd discovered she was pregnant, and making the appointment with the clinic had felt like watching herself from above. It had never felt real. The truth was she'd wanted the baby from the moment she'd realised she was pregnant, but she'd thought it was one more thing she just couldn't have. All the times when she'd pushed Bobby away, fighting every fibre in her body that had wanted to shout from the rooftops that someone like him actually wanted to be with someone like her. She'd done it all for Aaron and his parents. Except when it had all come out – at Judy's birthday – Simon had ended the night by holding on to both of her arms, forcing Toni to look into the eyes that were so like Aaron's, and he'd asked her what she thought his son would have wanted for the fiancée he'd left behind.

'He'd want me to be happy.' Toni had barely managed to whisper the words, but Simon had nodded hard.

'Of course he would, sweetheart, and that's all any of us want for you. Even Judy in her own crazy way.' Simon had held her gaze, his eyes filled with the same kindness that Aaron's had been too. 'I know it's a hell of a lot to ask after everything we've put you through, but we just want to be a part of your life, whatever form that takes. We'll take whatever you feel you can give us, just like we always should have done. But you don't owe us or Aaron anything and, from now on, it's all got to be on your terms.'

In the end it had been as simple as that, and Toni just kept thinking about all the missed opportunities there'd been to have that same conversation over the past five years. She'd almost given up her chance to have a baby because of it and she'd lost Bobby too. She'd rung him so many times and there'd never been an answer. She'd texted, and eventually she'd even worked out what she wanted to say in the voicemail, but she might as well have shouted into the wind.

That's why she needed Ella, with her resolute belief that things would somehow turn out okay – despite the huge odds – because right now Toni's legs had turned to jelly again for all the wrong reasons and she wasn't sure they'd get her to the ultrasound department without someone to lean on.

Looking down at her phone to check the time, she sighed. There were no messages, not even from Ella, and in two more minutes she was going to have to head down the corridor to her appointment whether her friend turned up or not.

'Tee.' Even if she hadn't recognised the voice, she knew it could only belong to one person and her legs finally decided to give way. Luckily Bobby was there to catch her.

* * *

'Are you sure you're okay? Do you want me to ask if they can rearrange the scan?' Bobby had all but carried Toni along the corridor to the ultrasound department at her insistence it should go ahead and now they were sitting waiting for her to be called in. She'd leant on him so heavily that she wouldn't have been surprised if he'd been the one to fall over. The shock of seeing him standing there, instead of Ella, probably wasn't a good thing when her bladder already felt as if it might explode at any moment because of the amount of water she'd had to drink in preparation for the scan. Thankfully she didn't wet herself. That would just about have finished her off, especially when this was the sort of moment that might finally have been worthy of one of Kirsty's mother's novels. If only she wasn't still terrified that Bobby might disappear at any moment, or that he was only here out of some sense of duty that Ella had impressed on him.

'I'm fine. It's just that you were the last person I was expecting to see.'

'*The last person*? I hope that wasn't from a very long list.' Bobby smiled, those killer dimples putting in an appearance.

'I didn't think you'd want to come and I didn't think Ella would go behind my back like that either.' Even as Toni tried to feel aggrieved about what her friend must have done, she couldn't quite manage it. Not when it had ended up with Bobby sitting beside her and being the one to hold her hand. She might have no idea where their relationship stood, or even if it existed at all any more beyond the fact that he was the father of her baby, but she was still glad he was there.

'She didn't force me to do anything and it was me who spoke to her, not the other way around.' Bobby turned his body, so he was facing towards her. 'I finally listened to your message and there was no way I was going to be anywhere else.'

'Oh.' It was all she could manage to say. She wished she was the sort of person who could repeat the message she'd left, now he was sitting in front of her, but there was still too much of the old Toni left to manage that just yet, even if they hadn't been surrounded by people. She remembered every word of it though.

It's me. I know you don't want to speak to me, but I need to tell you this. You're the love of my life and I've known that from day one, but I let what I thought everyone else wanted get in the way. If I'd gone with what I wanted, I'd have told the whole world. I couldn't believe my luck that someone like you wanted someone like me. If even a tiny part of you still does, or if you can learn not to hate me so much that you want to be a part of our baby's life, then I'll be at the hospital in Truro tomorrow for the first scan at three. Even if you aren't there, I'll always love you and I'll always be devastated that I threw everything we had away.

'With an invitation like that I wasn't going to miss this for the world, but I didn't want to risk telling you everything I wanted to say over the phone. There's been too many misunderstandings and I needed to do this face-to-face, but when I got to the flat you weren't there. I had no idea if you'd be here with your parents, or even Aaron's, and I definitely didn't want an audience for what I wanted to say. So I rang Anna and Ella to see if they'd heard anything from you and when Ella said she was going to the scan with you so you didn't have to go on your own, I promised her that I'd make sure you weren't on your own for any of it.' Bobby squeezed her hand, but as he opened his mouth to say something else, the sonographer called Toni's name.

'Antoinette Samuels please.'

'Here we go.' Bobby smiled again and even the frustration at the sonographer cutting off what he was about to say couldn't cut through Toni's overriding concern that she was about to wet herself at any moment. It must have been a man who'd invented ultrasounds and thought it was acceptable to fill a pregnant woman's bladder with litres of water. In a weird sort of way, it was a relief that Bobby couldn't say any more in the crowded waiting room. Because although Toni might have moved on lately, tears or declarations of love in front of a room full of strangers was still a step too far.

'It's all going to be okay, isn't it?' Toni whispered the words to Bobby as the sonographer showed them into the room. Suddenly the sight of the examination table and the scanner brought it all home – he was about to see their baby for the first time and all she wanted was for everything to be all right. She'd barely been able to glance at the screen when she'd had the private dating scan and she hadn't wanted the sonographer to tell her anything about the baby she hadn't thought she'd be able to keep. Now she desperately needed to know that nothing was wrong.

'I really think it's going to be more than okay.' Bobby squeezed her hand one more time before Toni got onto the examination table.

'Okay, brilliant. Let's have a look and see what's going on in there.' The gel might be a bit cold.' The sonographer, who did this countless times a day, gave them a breezy smile as she squirted the gel onto Toni's abdomen. She didn't seem to realise that Toni had forgotten how to even breathe in and out. 'I've looked at all your notes and this is your first baby, isn't it? Although I gather you're a midwife, so I'm sure all of this is pretty routine to you.'

'Much less so than you'd think!' Bobby was the one to answer when Toni still couldn't do anything other than just lie and wait, holding her breath. 'This baby's going to have two midwives as its mum and dad, but we're just as terrified as any other parents-to-be. Maybe even more so, given that we know what can happen.'

'Ooh, a male midwife, how fascinating!' The sonographer was in serious danger of getting distracted from the task in hand, but thankfully she managed to overcome her curiosity as she began to run the scanner over Toni's stomach. 'There we are, a lovely strong heartbeat. The baby is looking spot-on for your dates from the viability scan you had done privately, but I'll take all my measurements as we go through just to verify it. The placenta looks really healthy too and the baby's perfectly positioned in the uterus, so I think you can be confident about starting to tell people your news now.'

'I'm going to have a baby.' Tears were escaping from the corners of Toni's eyes as she spoke and rolling down the sides of her face, but Bobby was shaking his head.

'No, *we're* going to have a baby, Tee. Whatever that looks like for you and however you want to play it is fine with me, but I want to be part of this, for the baby and for you too. The truth is I want to be there for all of it, every day, for the good bits, the bad bits and all the everyday routine bits in between. But if you can't do that, for whatever reason, I'll take what I can get. I understand it all now, I met this amazing couple when I went to see Aaron and—'

'You went to see Aaron?' As Toni tried to process what Bobby was saying, the sonographer was doing her best to pretend she wasn't listening and to get on with taking the baby's measurements, but the poor woman was only human. Bobby had taken Toni's breath away and she still couldn't get her head around the fact that he was willing to do whatever it took to be a part of the baby's life – and hers – when she'd put him through so much.

'I did and I met these great people, Dora and Alan, and I've got so much to tell you when we get out of here.'

'Not as much as I've got to tell you.' Toni grabbed his hand. Ella obviously hadn't spilt the beans about Toni finally confronting Judy and telling all of them about Bobby. There was nothing standing in their way now, but she needed to tell him that even if there had been, she'd choose him and the baby – even if it meant losing everyone else. The best news in the world was that she didn't have to choose, she could finally have it all. And for the first time in years she wasn't fighting to hold in her emotions, so the tears kept coming and she didn't even give a damn that there was a stranger watching their every move. 'But for now, all I'm going to say is that I love you more than I've ever loved anyone and I want you to be there for all of it too, the good, the bad and even the bits we know could be coming. We've all heard Gwen's warnings about the haemorrhoids!'

'I love you so much, Tee.' Suddenly they were both laughing and crying, and the sonographer had finally stopped pretending that she wasn't listening and was passing tissues around, even taking one herself.

This was better than any of those endings in the novels Toni and Kirsty had stolen to read under the covers at night. She only needed one more thing to make it completely perfect... and as soon as she'd had a wee, she knew she was going to be the happiest she'd ever been.

24

Toni hadn't wanted to break the news of her pregnancy to Judy, Simon or her parents on the first occasion they met Bobby; it was too much to expect from everyone. Instead, she'd gone to see them by herself straight after the scan and predictably there'd been lots of tears, but thankfully they'd been the happy kind. Judy was obviously still fearful that she might lose her position in Toni's life after how she'd acted, despite the reassurances Toni had given her that they all just needed to move on and treat this as a fresh start, with new ground rules. She'd apologised a thousand times for how she'd behaved, but in the end it had been easy for Toni to forgive. She was just a mother who'd loved her son a little bit too much at times and had forgotten where the boundaries were, especially after his death. Talking to Bobby about his encounter with Alan and Dora had helped her to see how easily that could happen and his understanding had made it also much simpler to forgive.

All the same, Judy had promised to do whatever it took to put things right and she'd been more than willing to agree to any ground rules that Toni wanted to put in place. It was probably her ability to stick to those boundaries that was making Judy so nervous, though, and she was desperate to meet Bobby as a result. She'd begged Toni to bring him over for dinner and he'd seemed only too happy to agree. They'd been over to see his parents, too, who'd greeted the news with their usual enthusiasm, and Bobby's sister had already claimed the right to throw the baby shower.

Toni had drawn the line at having a gender reveal party, though. Left to her own devices, she wouldn't even have been a baby shower sort of person, let alone want to let off a giant party popper that showered them with either pink or blue confetti. But it was so lovely to be around people who were so thrilled about the news of their baby she would have agreed to almost anything. Or at least anything except a gender reveal, especially as there was a big part of Toni that wanted to wait to find out the news. She and Bobby had missed so much time together and they'd already missed sharing almost a third of the pregnancy. So if it was romanticising things to think that waiting somehow made it all the more special, then she'd just have to excuse herself for such an out-of-character show of sentimentality. Although she was blaming the pregnancy hormones for the fact that she was becoming increasingly mushy.

Scott and Joyce were already known to their other five grandchildren as Grammy and Pop-pop, rather than just plain old Grandma and Granddad. It left the field clear for Toni's parents to have their choice of all the more traditional names for grandparents and they'd decided to go for Nanny and Granddad, the same as Toni had called her own grandparents. She'd asked Bobby if maybe Judy and Simon could be Auntie and Uncle, but she'd told him to think it through first. If he decided he found it too uncomfortable after everything she'd put him through over the last three years, then she wasn't going to force that on him. As long as he didn't want to shut Judy and Simon out of their lives altogether, which he didn't seem to think was even an option after meeting Alan and Dora, then the rest could be on Bobby's terms. It was about time.

'That was, without doubt, the best lasagne I have ever tasted.' Bobby pushed his knife and fork together, after polishing off his second helping of Judy's pièce de résistance. It had been Aaron's favourite and Toni had been wary at first that his mother might not be able to refrain from mentioning that several times, but Judy was definitely on her best behaviour. 'Although whatever you do, don't tell my mum I said that when you meet her!'

'I just hope we get to meet her one day, I'd like to tell her what a great son she's raised.' Judy hadn't stopped smiling since Bobby had agreed to a second helping of lasagne. It was strange for Toni watching him and not having to be on high alert in case she gave any indication that they were in a relationship. She'd never seen him the way she was looking at him now – or realised how his easy charm infected everyone around him when he was truly allowed to be himself. It must have been hard for him being thrust into such an intense meeting with four total strangers, all of them desperately trying to hold back such a range of emotions. Yet somehow, within minutes of meeting them, he'd bonded with her dad and Simon over the English rugby team's form in readiness for the upcoming Six Nations and had made Judy and her mum laugh with a story about his youngest nephew throwing a tantrum because he couldn't get in the oven with the gingerbread men his sister was baking.

'It doesn't matter how much time I've spent around my nieces and nephews over the years, I've still got no clue how their minds work sometimes.' Bobby turned towards Judy and Mandy, throwing his hands up in the air. 'So we're going to have to rely on the four of you, and my mum and dad, for loads of parenting advice. I just hope you're ready for us coming round and calling you up all the time?'

'I've never been more ready.' As Judy beamed again, Toni recognised the look on her face. She was falling in love with Bobby, hook, line and sinker. Not in quite the same way Toni had of course, but Judy could see the amazing person he was and so could she. Bobby was probably the only person who could fit into their lives the way he already had and yet not make it feel like he was trying to take Aaron's place. Managing to eat a second helping of lasagne had just set the seal on Judy's feelings for him. As for Toni, she didn't think she could love him any more than she had done already, but somehow he was making that happen too.

'And you'll get to meet Mum and Dad, in fact Dad's desperate to arrange one of his famous barbeques for when we can all get together, but be warned, he's not adverse to firing up the grill as early as March and he doesn't even care if there's still frost on the ground.' Bobby pushed back his chair. 'Can I help you clear, Simon?'

'Thanks, Bobby, but you're a guest and Judy would have my guts for garters if I let you do that!'

'In that case, I just need to grab something from the car. I won't be a sec.' Bobby's gaze met Toni's as he stood up and she raised her eyebrows, trying to send him a silent question, but he just smiled and disappeared outside, coming back with a bag in his hand.

'I thought we'd have a bit of break before dessert.' Judy topped up the wine glasses for those who were drinking. 'Unless you want it now?'

'Actually, it's the perfect opportunity for me to give you all a little present I bought for you.' Bobby was up to something, but

Toni had no idea what it could be. Whatever it was, she just hoped it didn't do anything to change how brilliantly they'd all been getting on.

'You've already brought wine and chocolates, as well as flowers for Mandy and me, that's far too much already.' Judy was shaking her head and smiling.

'I didn't want to leave Simon and Steve out.' Bobby bent down and lifted four small boxes out of the bag, one after the other, sliding them across to Toni's parents, Simon, and Judy in turn. 'I hope this is okay, it's just a little something that I thought would be a nice way to start things off the way we plan to go on.'

'Can we open them?' Even as Toni's mother asked the question, she was already untucking the lid of her box. 'Oh Bobby, that's so lovely! Look, I've got a mug saying *Nanny-to-be* and a matching coaster that says *'the best Mums get promoted to Nanny'*. It's really great Bobby, thank you so much.'

'I've got the same.' Toni's dad laughed. 'Except mine says *Grandad-to-be* of course!'

'Shall I open mine now?' Judy looked almost as nervous as Toni felt. She had no idea why Bobby wouldn't have discussed this with her first, and she was already silently praying that the gift wouldn't do anything to upset Judy too much as she was obviously trying so hard and she'd been doing really well.

'I just hope you like it, but if it's too much, I can take it away and get you something else.' Bobby's tone was gentle and it was like the whole room was holding its breath as Judy opened the box.

'Oh my God! Do you really mean this?' Judy eyes had already filled with tears, as Bobby nodded.

'Only if it's okay with you.'

'Okay? I love it! Look what it says.' Turning the cup so the others could see it, Judy was smiling and crying all at the same time. 'Mine says *Nana-to-be*.'

'And mine says *Grandpa-to-be*.' Simon reached out to shake Bobby's hand. 'I don't think you'll ever understand how much this means to us and I know Mandy and Steve won't feel side-lined in any way, but are you sure your parents are okay with this; the baby having three sets of grandparents, I mean?'

'Mum always says it takes a village to raise a child and just think how lucky our baby will be to have three sets of grandparents who love it. But no pressure, it needs to be okay with all of you too.'

'Toni will you just hurry up and marry this boy please?' Judy wiped away her tears with the back of her hand. 'You're never going to find anyone more perfect.'

'He'd have to ask me first.' Toni's eyes met Bobby's again and she had to agree with Judy, she was never going to find anyone like him. There was no one whose heart was that big and who could forgive all the things she'd put him through so easily; she'd have married him in a heartbeat and considered herself the luckiest girl in the world when she did. 'But if he doesn't, I might just have to be the one to surprise him next time around.'

'Are you sure you want two mothers-in-law, Bobby?' Toni's dad gave a fake shudder, earning him a playful nudge from his wife before she replied.

'He'd be truly blessed if he did.'

'I already know how blessed I am.' Holding his hand out to Toni, she took it and all she could do was smile. There were no words to express how she felt in that moment, because nothing had ever been quite this perfect before. It might look like a strange family set-up to anyone else, but Bobby was right. Any baby who had this many people who loved them so wholeheartedly before they were even born, had all the riches in the world. Just like its mother.

* * *

The morning after dinner at Judy and Simon's, Bobby suggested to Toni that they go for a walk to help work off the excesses of the day before and she seemed happy to agree. It was still only early February, but it was one of the bright winter days when the promise of spring really did seem to be just around the corner.

'Is it my imagination, or are we heading up to St Jude's?' Toni had her hand in his and he still half-expected her to whip it away at any moment if they caught sight of someone they knew. It was going to take a while to get used to the fact that she'd never do that again. It was brilliant, being able to stop and kiss her just because he felt like it; even if Toni was probably never going to be the sort of person who was entirely comfortable with public displays of affection. He loved everything about her though, even the things she didn't always like about herself. He always had.

'You guessed right, St Jude's it is.'

'We don't have to go up there today if you don't want to.'

'I thought there was a chance we might bump into Dora and Alan again. I wanted to thank them for changing everything.' It was only half the truth of why they were going up to the graveyard, but the rest was between him and Aaron, if he got the chance to say what he wanted.

'I can't see any sign of Dora and Alan. That's their bench over there, isn't it?' Toni gestured towards the wooden seat engraved with a dedication to Maria.

'That's it. It's a shame they're not here, but I'm sure we'll bump into them at some point.'

'I don't think I'll be coming up here quite as often any more.'

Toni squeezed his hand as they drew level with Aaron's grave. 'And I wanted to explain to him that just because I'm moving on with life, it doesn't mean I'll ever forget him.'

'You can come up here as often as you want, don't ever think I'd stop you doing that.' Bobby turned her to face him. 'I just want you to be happy.'

'I am and that's why I don't need to come here so much any more. I'll still come to see Aaron from time to time, to cut the grass around his grave, and I'll even bring the baby up when it's born. But we're going to be busy with our new little family and work, not to mention three sets of grandparents, and I know he'll understand.' Toni laughed. 'He might even be relieved not to have to listen to me wittering on all the time any more.'

'He might.' Bobby laughed too, as Toni pretended to elbow him.

'Just for that, you can take me down to The Cookie Jar for breakfast. The baby has got a craving for one of their banana and maple syrup pancake stacks.'

'Oh, the baby has, has it?' Bobby grinned. 'You start walking, I just want to check that Maria's bench isn't sinking into the soft ground under the tree after all that rain last night. I'll move it forward a bit if it is.'

'Okay, it's not like you can't catch me up if you need to. I'm already starting to get a bit of waddle.'

'I love your waddle and I'll only be two minutes at most.' Waiting until Toni had headed down the path, Bobby kept his promise and quickly checked the bench, which was still on solid ground. But there was another reason he wanted a moment alone. He had something he needed to say to Aaron, too.

'I just want you to know something.' Bobby put one hand on the stone that marked Aaron's resting place. 'I promise I'll look after Toni and do everything I can to never let her down. I know that you'd have made her that same promise if you could, but I'm going to love her enough for both of us.'

When Bobby looked up again, Toni had almost reached the end of the path that led back out of the churchyard and he broke into a run to catch her up. He was never going to let her go again. This was finally their time and he didn't want to waste a second.

ACKNOWLEDGMENTS

The support for The Cornish Midwives series so far has been beyond my wildest dreams! I can't thank all the book bloggers and reviewers, and Rachel Gilbey, who organises the blog tours, enough for their support. To all the readers who choose to spend their time and money reading my books, and especially those who make the time to leave a review, it means more than you will ever know and I feel so privileged to be doing the job I love.

I hope you have enjoyed the third of The Cornish Midwives novels. Sadly, I am not a midwife, or a social worker, but I have done my best to ensure that the medical and fostering details are as accurate as possible. I am very lucky that one of my close friends, Beverley Hills, is a brilliant midwife and I have dedicated this book to her. I have also worked with foster carers and social workers for many years and so I have been able to draw upon this experience and their expertise in beginning to tell Jess's story. The most amazing social worker I have ever had the privilege to work with, Danni Starley, has also been an inspiration for Jess's story and there will be a lot more of that in the fourth book. However, if you are one of the UK's wonderful midwives providing such fantastic support for new and expectant mums, or indeed one of our amazingly dedicated social workers, I hope you'll forgive any details which draw on poetic licence to fit the plot.

My thanks as always go to the team at Boldwood Books for their help, especially my amazing editor, Emily Ruston, for lending me her wisdom to get this book into the best possible shape and set the scene for the next book in the series. Thanks too to my wonderful copy editor, Cari, and proofreader, Candida, for all their hard work.

As ever, I can't sign off without thanking my writing tribe, The Write Romantics, and all the other authors who I am lucky enough to call friends.

Finally, as they always will, my biggest thank you goes to my family – Lloyd, Anna and Harry – for their support, patience, love and belief.

MORE FROM JO BARTLETT

We hope you enjoyed reading *A Winter's Wish for the Cornish Midwife*. If you did, please leave a review.

If you'd like to gift a copy, this book is also available as an ebook, digital audio download and audiobook CD.

Sign up to Jo Bartlett's mailing list for news, competitions and updates on future books.

http://bit.ly/JoBartlettNewsletter

Why not explore the first in The Cornish Midwives series, *The Cornish Midwife*.

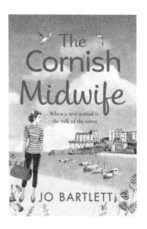

ABOUT THE AUTHOR

Jo Bartlett is the bestselling author of nineteen women's fiction titles. She fits her writing in between her two day jobs as an educational consultant and university lecturer and lives with her family and three dogs on the Kent coast.

Visit Jo's Website: www.jobartlettauthor.com

 twitter.com/J_B_Writer
 facebook.com/JoBartlettAuthor
 instagram.com/jo_bartlett123

ABOUT BOLDWOOD BOOKS

Boldwood Books is a fiction publishing company seeking out the best stories from around the world.

Find out more at www.boldwoodbooks.com

Sign up to the Book and Tonic newsletter for news, offers and competitions from Boldwood Books!

http://www.bit.ly/bookandtonic

We'd love to hear from you, follow us on social media:

facebook.com/BookandTonic

twitter.com/BoldwoodBooks

instagram.com/BookandTonic

Printed in Great Britain
by Amazon